*"SOLID AND
SATISFYING...
VIGOROUS ACTION,
CREDIBLE LOCAL COLOR
AND SOME TWISTS THAT
MAY SURPRISE YOU"*
—NEW YORK TIMES BOOK REVIEW

"An unusual, thrilling, plausible and well-written yarn. Mr. Black has a wonderful gift for dialogue and description which conveys to the reader a very real sense of being on the scene"
—F. van Wyck Mason

"Mr. Black, one of the better suspense-adventure writers, is in fine form"
—SPRINGFIELD NEWS

A WIND OF DEATH

BY GAVIN BLACK

POPULAR LIBRARY • NEW YORK

To Félix Marti-Ibáñez

GULF OF SIAM

THAILAND

ISTHMUS OF KRA

Kangar

Alor
Star

KEDAH

Penang
Island

George
Town

INDIAN
OCEAN

PERAK

Kampar

Linguin
Mine

Kuala Lumpur

Seremban

Strait of Malacca

SUMATRA
(INDONESIA)

Cape
Cambodia

Khota Baru

KELANTAN

Kuala
Kraï

MALAYA

Kuala Lipis

Kuantan

PAHANG

MALACCA

Malacca

JOHORE

Singapore

SOUTH

CHINA

SEA

N

Red guerrilla areas

0   50   100
Miles

H S

ONE

When I was recruited no one had told me that swollen feet were one of the occupational hazards of spying. I'd had a rough two weeks. The Isthmus of Kra, that thin, long strip of southern Thailand which separates the Indian Ocean from the South China Sea, is rough country on the whole, sizable portions of it still primary jungle. It had been my business to walk through this jungle in areas adjacent to the Malaysian frontier. The visit was highly unofficial and no one had rubber-stamped a passport with permission for me to be there. A long, hot snoop had proved totally unrewarding because I hadn't found a trace of what I was looking for or, rather, what other people were looking for.

The only things which seemed active in that area were the elephants. There were a lot of these, totally uninhibited by man, thrashing around on tracks they make for themselves which tend to run in great fifty-mile loops. We came on three herds of elephants, all minding their own business and expecting us to mind ours, which we did. Minding your own business is the law of survival in the jungle and if you stick to it you can move around in the daytime through the clutter almost as safely as you can in Westminster Abbey. That is, except for the snakes. Snakes have their own regulations and no one seems to have found out what they are. We were always watching for snakes.

I had traveled with two guides carrying sharp choppers. Sometimes we made as much as seven miles a day, but more often it was around five. I lost ten pounds in weight, became desalinated in spite of salt tablets, and at several points came near to the heat exhaustion which is a factor to contend with on this type of excursion. Also, I didn't trust my guides all that much, and they showed no signs of becoming fond of me, only liking my money, and wanting more of it than they were likely to get. It was a situation which made for slightly unhappy travel.

But I got out all right, into Kelantan, and very glad indeed to be there. Kelantan is the state up north where the Japanese first landed in their attack on Malaysia, but before and after this event it has existed in a condition of amiable and relaxed torpor. It has a pleasant climate, cool, beautiful mornings tending toward mist, and nights conditioned by sea breezes. There is a special breed of large gray monkeys trained to climb the palm trees as nut collectors, and these beasts sit chained at the edges of all villages looking more intelligent than the other locals, which they probably are. The humans, both male and female, are nearly all beautiful until they begin to get fat, which is early on. Nobody moves too much, and world crises, even Malaysian crises, don't get recorded in worry wrinkles on any face. The Sultan has a considerable number of wives but, in spite of this, and having no foreign commitments, manages to keep taxation down. The rich grow richer and the poor don't give a damn so long as their working monkeys stay in good health.

A state of this kind hasn't got a lot of need for its airfields. The one I was on had last seen scheduled use at the end of November, 1941. On December sixth of that year the Japanese came over and scored direct hits on three parked lend-lease Buffaloes, one Wildebeest, and one Blenheim, and that was the end of the RAF in northeastern Malaysia for some time. The strip was evacuated by road transport and the Nipponese came past it at such speed on their travels south that it never had any tactical use again until an American called Clement P. Winburgh took it over privately, very privately.

With feet still puffy even after twenty-four hours in bed, I stood by the ruins of what had probably been the officers' mess, but there wasn't much of the building left after a quarter of a century and steady overtime from white ants. The view, however, was splendid. To my left, looking north, was the spine of the main mountain ridge, bumpy in moonlight, formidable country into which a lot of people have ventured who have never come out again. It is tenanted by the hill people, the Sakai, as well as by another, even more primitive lot, who are rarely seen and reputed to travel through trees using their hands and arms just like their simian near relations. The area also contains a jungle fortress in that section which eases down into Thailand, this occupied by Lum Ping, the former Red leader during the Malaysia civil war, which was played down locally into an emergency.

Lum Ping is now apparently quiescent, but not in exile. So far as anyone knows, he has never been on a refresher course in Peking, just sits quietly in his hideout among monster anthills, listening to the radio or watching television. Every now and then someone like Clement P. Winburgh remembers about Lum Ping and can't believe that such an active man has mellowed in his maturer years and is now quite content with his pension. In Kota Bahru, Kelantan's one-street capital, I have heard it said that Lum comes down to the local race meeting disguised as a Chinese commercial traveler, but I've never met anyone who has had a tip on a horse from that retired butcher of helpless villagers.

I have always had a deep respect for those mountains. It has seemed to me nice country to stay out of, and for all my long residence in these parts, I've never allowed idle curiosity to prod me into mounting an exploratory expedition. The locals leave that to crackpots out from tame Europe, giving these characters hospitality and good advice before they go in and—on the rare occasions when they come out again—gently packing up what's left for a return to source. I once had quite a lot to do with a man who had spent two months alone in the Malaysia ridge jungles and I don't want ever to look anything like that myself.

The fact that I had begun to was one of the reasons why I couldn't warm to this impending meeting with Clem. I had agreed to serve him in a certain limited capacity suited to my role as a businessman in the country, but this would never again be stretched to taking on the job of border scout, which in no way fitted my years, position in society, and more than slightly sybaritic temperament. On that decayed airstrip I was keeping my anger over a hot flame.

I wasn't even curious about who had cleared grass and scrub growth sprouting through tarmac on a section of a runway, this for American interests and at the expense of the US taxpayer. That it had been done at all in a country which is touchy about outside interference was perhaps surprising, but I had seen stranger things. And someone had certainly been working here, quite hard, and within the last few days, and to pretty precise instructions.

I had the two-hour wait, with my feet continuing to ache, which is somehow nearly always closely associated with air travel. Then there was a drone of engines in the distance. I pushed down through long *lalang* to the cleared area and stood by it with my head up, watching for a light to blink.

9

Nothing blinked, even when the noise came close, international regulations smashed by no in-flight flicker. The sound wasn't from light engines, either; props of some kind, and big ones. Then moonlight hit a shape coming from northwest to avoid passing over Kota Bahru, at about three thousand, and certainly no small plane.

A landing here in anything larger than a tycoon's plaything was lunacy. The cleared strip ended in black jungle which seemed just waiting to claim another wreck. I could now make out a solid fuselage and dumpy wings, and hear a power cutback. I was going to send up a warning flash from a pocket torch when something about the bulk coming straight at me, matronly and fat-bellied, kept my finger from the button.

It was a twin-engine Prestwick Pioneer, built in Scotland, at least fifteen years old, and once the workhorse of these parts. The plane has a seventy-mile-an-hour landing speed and the kind of brakes they don't seem to fit anymore, these able to cut from touchdown to a dead stop in seconds. If it had to, that plane could drop down sideways like an old cow gone skittish, and the heavily built undercarriage was reinforced to take astonishing punishment from a landing surface.

With all the resources of American production behind him, it seemed ludicrous that Clem had to bump around Asia in an antique British model. And yet I could see that the thing might be an answer to his needs. It could land on a clay laterite road if there was wing clearance. Further, it didn't begin to suggest anything remotely military. A few jobs like this were still in use by local contractors and mining engineers, and their lumbering, deliberate flight made them highly suited to aerial surveys. For Clem that commercial-seeming innocence might be a big attraction; the last thing you would expect to see jumping out of a Pioneer's cabin door were men armed with tommy guns.

I got out of the way, and just in time. The pilot came in to land on what I thought was a runover, apparently having decided suddenly, putting down the nose sharply. She made contact, bounced, leveled out from this, settled, trundled, and then stopped. There was a distance of twenty yards to the first of the big trees.

I didn't hurry and the door was open by the time I reached the plane, a set of folding steps dropped. At the top of them, moonlight on his face, was my old friend from a little revolution.

"Hello," he said at the start of what I hoped wasn't going to be another. "Glad you could make it."

"So am I. After your assignment."

"Rough up there?"

"Only part of me got out. The rest belongs to Thai leeches."

I climbed gleaming aluminum stairs. The plane had originally been a twenty-five-seater, but was now a traveling office, with desk, filing cabinets, and a typewriter for reports which at once went into a top-secret folder. The chairs, four of them, were of the executive-suite type, which could rock you into the position most restful for your ulcer, and didn't appear to be bolted to the floor. Two of these were occupied by silent shapes wearing US Army uniform, but with rank tabs invisible. The back end of the cabin had been partitioned off, perhaps to accommodate a double brass bedstead. Light was poor, from a single gooseneck which stretched its neck out over the desk and had a cloth on the shade to create semi-blackout. From the smell of cigar smoke, no one had observed fire precautions during a landing.

I would have appreciated a warmer note of cordiality after all my sufferings for a dubious cause, but Clem did remember basic duties as a host.

"Like a drink?"

"Very much. Any ice?"

"Yes."

"Then bourbon on the rocks."

It was a shade surprising to find the plane not dry, in view of US official service temperance. Clem's area, of course, avoided the ostentation of insignia and could probably please itself about detail, but there were still a couple of what might be high-ranking officers sitting in their chairs as though they belonged, too.

I had an impression of being under surveillance from the military, almost close scrutiny, in fact, as much as the dim light permitted. There was some natural illumination coming through the door and in this I saw that one of the seated gentlemen had gray hair clipped tight to his head. Clem went beyond the partition without any introductions, which left me standing in something of a social vacuum, being observed by a couple of characters whose present roles had obviously rusted their skill in small talk. A door to the pilot's cabin opened just beyond me and two figures, these in civilian white

11

shirts, went wordless down the aluminum steps as though they had been told to do that.

"Had a nice flight from wherever your base is?" I asked.

Clipped gray hair cleared his throat but he didn't get beyond this before Clem came back with a glass, one glass. It wasn't going to be a party.

I drank standing up because no one had offered me a chair and there is still a lot of British diffidence in my makeup. Clem didn't sit down either, but stood waiting, as though a minimal politeness demanded he hold off the interrogation until I had quenched my thirst. I could see his face better now, remembering how a kind of durable boyishness had once pleased me, as had agate-colored eyes when they were warmed by laughter. My first impression of him, some time ago now, had been of a man whose head neatly declined to acknowledge the years which burdened mind and body, and in this light he still looked rather like a high school cheerleader who didn't make the first basketball team so went for the next best thing from the point of view of getting the girls.

"What have you to tell us about the Thailand frontier, Paul?"

His question was almost solemnly formal.

"It's still there, richly populated with natural fauna."

"Nothing else?"

"Not that I saw."

"You think your search was effective?"

That nettled.

"It's a big area and I may have missed a snake or two. But I did notice a population explosion of elephants."

One of the military moved in his chair, the other pulled up the cloth of trousers baggy at the knees. The puffing of cigars continued.

I tried to assess the plane's passenger list. There was Clem, the Brass, the two men who had got off, and there could be anything behind that partition. The lack of open candor in my reception was starting to irk just slightly. I felt I had earned the right to handshakes all round and some smiles.

"Our information," Clem said, "was practically positive."

"So your courier told me. Which all goes to show that a lot of positive information about these parts still has to be classified unreliable. You can take it from me there is no major supply route from Malaysia into Thailand through that jungle. Or even a minor one. If there had been, I'd have walked across it. I was going east-west. Which doesn't mean there isn't infiltration from time to time. There's no means of keeping tabs on that. But steady coming and going would mean a defined track, and there isn't one. I know."

"You say," Clem corrected. To make that slightly less bald he added, "We never take as gospel anything from one source."

"Fine. Are you going up there to look for yourself? You can have my route maps. They're in the car I've got parked up on the highway. And I should think my guides are still hanging around in Kota Bahru, if you'd like to use them?"

Clem was looking past me.

"Had you thought that those guides might have been a special issue to you?"

"I took fairly adequate precautions, I think." My voice was crisp. "I didn't chat about why or when I was leaving home. And I arrived in the village where I picked up my guides without any advance notice. They were neither of them lovable fellows. But then a man who knows his jungle rarely is. It's not a gracious life. I'd remind you that picking men for my junk crews is something I've been at now for a good many years. The right men, too."

Clem stayed the dogged interrogator.

"No chance you were steered around anything you weren't wanted to see?"

"Let me repeat, I traveled east-west across the whole peninsula. Any Red track would have to be north-south."

"They could be using water part of the way. You were down where the rivers are navigable in places, even stretches of a few miles where boats are practicable. Did you swim any rivers?"

"Two."

"Rapids?"

"No. Gentle water. If you think this is a possibility, why didn't your courier warn me about it?"

Clem didn't answer that. I wished I could see him better. There was enough light to show shape and features of a man I thought I knew fairly well, but in that semiblackout he stayed totally remote. The hiding could have been deliberate, a planned screen, because there was change in him he didn't want me to see. I was liking less and less those two seated figures representing another authority, related to Clem's but still not his.

"What the hell's happened to you?" I asked.

13

It wasn't a particularly discreet question. Discretion isn't one of my portable virtues, and what I do carry about wears very thin under any kind of stress. The stress was real enough now. I had come onto this plane meaning to protest vigorously about an assignment I thought both unnecessary and unsuited to my talents. I had expected a heated interchange as a result of my candor, but nothing like this, nothing like a court of inquiry in a cabin under doused lights.

"How about taking the cloth off that shade?" I suggested. "Or are you expecting attack at any moment?"

"You never know, do you?"

"I'd like some introductions."

"This is Colonel Hackett, here. And that is General Winsdale."

I had been right in my guess about seniority. Brass had come to see me, and gone to considerable trouble and perhaps some risk in an old plane to do so, which isn't something Brass does without good reason. From the two seats I got the kind of grunts you might expect from an Englishman in his club who wants to be allowed to get on with his *Times* in peace. If I'd been in a position to buy them a drink they wouldn't have accepted. And they wouldn't have lunched with me, either.

Quite a number of Americans in high places beyond their own borders are these days tending to take on the airs and graces of Britannia's old proconsuls. They are obliged to run sizable areas of the world, and it's a total headache, and the least you can get out of it is a little personal dignity. The British haven't a scrap of dignity left and are having fun for the first time in at least a century, going about like imminent bankrupts who have got everything tucked away in their wives' names, which leaves them astonishingly light on responsibility. And positively gay.

We haul down the flag at midnight, with a band playing, and the Queen's representative talking about a secure future for democracy in a former colony, knowing damn well that the next morning—and a good thing, too—the Americans will be jetting into the place with a great deal of money to bolster up the shaky economy we've left behind, against Red infiltration. At times I feel very sorry for Americans in this half of the century, but those minutes in the plane weren't one of the times.

I took a long, deep breath.

"Clem, I rather gather you don't think a lot of my powers

of observation. In view of this I hereby offer my resignation. And it gives me a great deal of pleasure to do it. Primarily I'm a businessman. And for the last two weeks I have been the world's most uncomfortable businessman."

It seemed a long time before Clem got around to words.

"We don't accept resignations."

"All right then, let me claim my pension. Even though six months isn't exactly long service."

He should have smiled, but didn't, even with all those good teeth. And quite suddenly I got a feeling of his hurt, of betrayal and damage done, of which I was totally innocent. I was now certain that his traveling companions weren't the ones he would have chosen for this excursion, and that in some manner he was on the mat himself before these two men.

"How about sitting down, Paul?"

"Thanks, but I'm on my way back to Kota Bahru. It doesn't look as though a detailed report is going to get us anywhere."

"Just sit down," he said.

I went to the cabin door. At the bottom of steep steps were the two crewmen in white shirts. One of them looked up, then the other. Both gave a sharp impression of having received their orders and being quite ready to act on them. I was still staring down when Clem moved after me, quickly flipping my Luger from its hip holster. He had made a football pass to the Colonel with the gun even before I could swing around.

"What the hell is going on?"

Clem answered right away.

"We were interested in what you had to say about picking your crews. How you always got the right man . . ."

"Give me back my gun!"

"Later. Maybe you ought to meet someone."

Clem went through the door at the back of the cabin. It was the General who reached out for the gooseneck, pulling the cloth off it, and spinning the lamp around as a spot on the door. Clem appeared again, acting as escort to a Chinese who kept his head bent low on a squat neck. Then, while I stared, the man's chin came up.

I found myself looking into the eyes of Kim Sung, my oldest and favorite junk captain. He is practically the commodore of my fleet, a man with all the instincts of a pirate, who has gone through life with a shaky set of moral values. But I would have backed his loyalty to me against all comers.

15

Now he looked sick. He had the complexion of a Javanese wood carving from which the deep brown dye has been bleached by sun exposure. The core of his personality, an unassailable impudence, seemed to have been drained away, too.

I didn't say anything, neither did Kim. I was conscious of the Colonel holding my gun and of his fingers probing it gently, as though the Luger had an unfamiliar feel which demanded this professional exploration. The muzzle was also more or less pointing at me.

"Is this the captain of your junk, the *Anwei?*" Clem asked finally.

"You know damn well it is."

"When did you last see this man?"

"About two months ago. And what's it to you? Why the hell is Kim Sung here and not in my ship doing his job?"

"I'm asking the questions, Paul."

"On what authority?"

Officially he didn't have any, not on Malaysian soil, but this was a quibble over which he didn't waste time. Clem's authority was uniquely portable, and took small notice of national frontiers.

"Tell us your last orders to Kim Sung as captain of one of your junks."

I glared. The light was now bright enough to show Clem's face, his eyes. I didn't like his eyes. They had been cold quartz like that once before in our contacts, and it hadn't been a particularly nice moment.

"Paul, what were your last orders to this man?"

"I don't remember. I don't think there were any last orders."

"And yet he made a special trip to Kuala Lumpur to see you?"

"It was a routine trip. My base is in Kuala Lumpur."

"Not many of your other captains seem to visit you there."

A few people have opened files on my activities, but Clem's dossier would appear to offer pretty comprehensive and detailed coverage. I had suspected this before, and it had been something of an irritation that in spite of very positive efforts to identify Clem's man in Kuala Lumpur, I hadn't been able to do so. Probably he had half a dozen contacts in this increasingly important Asian capital, all laying trip wires for each other on separate orders from on high. And, of course,

16

I had been one of these wire-layers myself, on an unpaid, honorary basis.

Clem wasn't enjoying my pauses. He knew perfectly well that pauses on the part of the man you are interrogating, if permitted, allow him space in which to organize his own defense.

"Why didn't your other captains come to your Kuala Lumpur office? Why just Kim Sung?"

"It wasn't just Kim Sung. Only him more often than the others. He was really my fleet admiral."

I used the past tense for my captain, and a realization of this made me look at him again. He wasn't trying to send me any message, just standing there in the extraordinary passivity of Chinese defeat, which seems like a total acceptance of what has happened. All the fires of resistance were out, doused, without even an ember sparking. Kim looked now like a wax effigy of the ruffian to whom all the piratical genes in my own blood had once responded.

"As your fleet admiral, Kim Sung had a position of special trust and responsibility?"

"You could say that."

"So that any orders issued to him would really be orders to the rest of Harris and Company's junk fleet?"

"No, they would not. My junks don't operate under orders from head office, except initially. They're tramps. They go where they can pick up cargoes. You could say they freelance. There are no specific signals sent from Kuala Lumpur saying 'Move from A to B.' I don't give that kind of order."

"Kim Sung says you did, in this case."

"What case?"

General Winsdale coughed. It might have been something he was holding until the movement of a symphony was over, a small spasm eruptive into a sudden silence. In a way it was seniority making its presence felt and we all waited, though in my case not from any deference. In those seconds I was still trying to make myself believe that Kim Sung had merely got himself into another of the recurring awkward situations which had starred his living, this time in some way tangling with American authority in Southeast Asia. It could happen so easily. American authority fans out now over these parts and in one way or another touches nearly all my trading areas. If Kim had broken somebody's new rules he had a right to my support, provided, that is, that he hadn't succumbed to any temptation to get in on a quick profits venture like the slave trade in indentured labor. This goes on quietly still, and I dislike it very much, something Kim knows well.

More than once in the past my commodore's zeal for increased turnover—from which he got his cut—had caused me considerable trouble and put the man on the mat in my office. But even at these times of real stress between us, Kim had never lost his grinning impudence or the self-confidence behind it. His face now frightened me. It said fear, stark fear, and I had never believed he could feel this.

"Shall we stop playing cat and mouse?" I suggested. "You know something and you intend to hit me with it hard. Supposing we have the blow right now?"

There was silence in the cabin. No one moved. The Colonel had even stopped that finger inventory of a piece of my property.

"All right, Paul, here it is." Quartz eyes held mine. "A US destroyer picked up your junk the *Anwei* in the Amphitrite Group. It was trying to use cover in the atoll of Lin Tao. You know where the Amphitrite Group is?"

I nodded. The Amphitrite Group is southeast of the huge Red Chinese island of Hainan. It is also about on a parallel with the southern portion of North Vietnam. At no time have any of my junks ever had any business in the area, which is at least eight hundred miles from our nearest point of regular trading. There are no cargoes to be had in those atolls and there is the very sharp danger of running afoul of portions of the US fleet patrolling the Gulf of Tonkin, the last thing I wanted to happen to one of my ships.

"You're astonished?" Clem's voice was gentle.

"Yes."

"I expected you to be. The *Anwei*'s cargo will astonish you even more."

"I'm sure."

"It was copra. But we dug down through that to what I suppose you could call the ballast. This was arms."

I didn't say anything. It was my hope that my face showed nothing. Clem watched me for a moment, then went on with that verbal gentleness.

"Forty British brens with thirty thousand rounds of ammo. Eighty-four Czechoslovak repeater rifles, with forty thousand rounds of ammo. There were a dozen French mortars as well, for which presumably they have the shells. Or these could be

18

coming on another junk. It all seemed rather like your old business, but to a new market."

There was a large ice clot moving toward my heart.

"Where is this stuff supposed to have come from?"

"We know it came from Malaysia."

I tried to smile. It didn't feel as though it were sitting on my face too well.

"You think I was getting rid of old stock?"

"No. The Czech rifles were made last year. We think the *Anwei* was being paid to do the transport job. Highly paid."

"No one was paying my firm. All I know about this is that the *Anwei* was supposed to sail from Kuantan some twelve hours or so after I saw Kim Sung in my office. It was bound for Bintulu in Sarawak for normal trading."

Clem broke his stare at me. He gave my captain the treatment I had been getting, using the same cool voice.

"What do *you* say, Kim Sung?"

The sailor looked at the floor. He swallowed. Then he used English, damningly simple English.

"Mr. Harris tell me to go to Kuala Marang in Trengganu when I sail from Kuantan. This one hour sail. I must anchor five mile south of the town, near small river. Not show light. In night time there are two boats coming. We all working to lift guns into *Anwei*. I am to take to Dong Hoi in North Vietnam. There is much money for me, Mr. Harris say. Also for crew."

TWO

I had asked for Clem's blow. It destroyed a major illusion. I had believed that in a violent part of the world, where brother's hand is too often against brother, Harris and Company was a sound business with a steadily increasing turnover because internally we had achieved a partnership in sharing. I had bought loyalty at first, offering a big cash return for it, but was sure that I had seen this loyalty confirmed into something real through increasing common interest.

Kim Sung's defection meant that I had been a damn fool. This man had for ten years been getting a swelling cut of trading profits. By local standards, and even Western ones, he was moderately rich. Money couldn't be the motivation behind what he had just done, which meant that, like so many others who owed their original motherland nothing, he had gone over to Mao's China because he had come to believe that she held all the cards for the future.

It is, of course, a perfectly reasonable point of view. I shouldn't have been so winded, and I don't think I would have been with any of my other junk captains. I watch them. And Kim Sung had been one of my means of doing this. He knew more about the way my company operated than anyone else outside of head office. And if Kim had been playing his own game behind my back, it meant almost certainly that other captains had been doing it, too, probably under the fleet commodore's orders. Instead of presiding over a nicely oiled trading concern stretching south from the Philippines, I was only the front man for a dirty shambles. And a big laugh for the crews nominally in my employ, who took in Harris and Company's bonuses along with payola from old mother China. At that moment I could have knocked in all of Kim Sung's beautifully white front teeth.

"Mind if I take over the interrogation?" I asked.

After a minute Clem said:

"OK."

The General cleared his throat again, as though he were about to intervene with a protest against irregularity in court-martial proceedings, but thought better of it, and didn't say a word. I stepped closer to Kim Sung.

"Look at me."

He didn't want to. But slowly that ugly mug came up. I had shared a lot of laughter with this man, on his ship and off it, and quite a few bottles as well. His sins, which I had thought redeemed by a large area of surprising honesty, had put deep seams in a sea-burnished face. What was visible of his eyes now seemed rigidly focused on my Adam's apple.

I used Cantonese. I told Kim that his mother had been the whore of his native village of Ch'in-k'an and his father an itinerant peddler of unspeakables, but that even their coffined bones were now twitching at what their by-blow had been up to.

"Say, what's all this?" the Colonel asked loudly.

"It's all right," Clem said. "I can follow."

The CIA give their top boys quite a good grounding in the Oriental classics when that is the sphere of their operations, not to mention the local dialects. But my southern Chinese was acquired during a somewhat unconventional boyhood in Singapore, with about 40 percent of it idiomatically pressing close to the gutter. I was using all of that percentage, and if Clem was staying with me, it says a lot for contemporary intensive-study methods.

When I stopped, the only sound in that plane cabin was Kim Sung's breathing. I have never thought of him as ever wanting to see me dead, but that was now his wish. And not quickly dead, either. His chin came up just a little further and he widened those concealing slits, letting me have a real look into his eyes. I knew then that wild anger had served me badly, that a little deliberate, controlled stirring up of shame just might have strengthened my position.

"Who paid you to take these arms to North Vietnam?"

"You," he said.

"When were you to get payment?"

"I got it in advance. Over your desk in Kuala Lumpur."

"How much?"

"Five thousand dollars to me. Each of the crew got a thousand."

"You've thirteen men. That means I handed over eighteen thousand dollars risk money. Together with another twenty

21

thousand for normal cash trading, for which you had to account to me?"

"Yes."

"You went back to your junk and paid out your men?"

"Yes."

I turned to Clem.

"What sort of money did you find on the *Anwei* when you took her?"

"Around forty-two thousand dollars."

"Each man carrying a fat roll?"

"There'd been a lot of gambling. I wouldn't say it was evenly distributed. But your twenty thousand trading money was in the safe untouched. There hadn't been any time for normal business."

A little breeze came in the open door of the plane, bringing with it a smell of jungle, a movement of air that wasn't really refreshing because it was vitiated by all that vegetable use of oxygen. I was sweating. There was a fan on the desk but no one had switched the thing on, perhaps to conserve batteries. I turned back to my captain, to an impression of a man waiting, ready to return strike for strike.

"Did I tell you where the arms had come from, Kim Sung?"

"No."

"But you got precise sailing instructions from me?"

"Yes."

"What were they?"

"I was to sail in darkness for the Anabas Islands, where I was to pick up a cover load of copra. It was left over from our voyage home to Kuantan. After that I was to go to Great Natuna. At night. You told me to anchor during the day. We were to work north through the Luconia Group, keeping in reefs so we didn't run into other shipping. You were nervous about the open passage between Thitu and the Amphitrites. You suggested we wait for bad weather before crossing this. And that's what I did."

The statement was beautifully groomed. It could have been a direct product of Clem's Saigon office.

"Kim, you know perfectly well I never give you detailed sailing orders, which isn't surprising since you know the seas around here ten times better than I do."

"This time you were worried about me running risks."

"You're a rotten liar."

"You say that now, *Tuan*. When I'm caught."

22

The respect in that *Tuan* was sardonic.

"Did we talk about what you were to do if you did get caught?"

"No. But then I never have been before. Not like this."

The implication behind that was naked. And Clem could have picked it up even if his Cantonese hadn't won him all A's at the training college. Kim Sung had never been caught on any of the other jobs, like this one, which he had done for me. I had the feeling that at his interrogation in some US base up in Vietnam, Kim had driven this home, deliberately, to destroy me because he had been brought down himself. There might have been strong inducements to do this, possibly a promise of leniency if he would dig a pit deep enough to trap and hold his boss. Clem had been thorough.

And yet the military were along in this plane, which could mean that some knives had been sharpened up for Clem, too. It looked very much as though he had put a foot badly wrong somewhere, perhaps by recruiting me. There was a somewhat complex multiple trial going on in the belly of an old airplane, with the proper authority not too clearly defined.

I looked at Clem.

"So you planned that trip across Kra as a check on me? Litmus test. You *know* there is Commie traffic up there. If I came back and said there was no sign of it, that shows me up bright Red?"

He shook his head.

"Not bright Red. Just working for your own interests. As you were when you sold those diesel engines to China."

My voice went loud.

"I might have known those diesels would be coming into it. Look, Clem, I sold my engines in competition with the Japanese, the Germans, the Czechs, and one Italian firm manufacturing under license from a company in Jersey City. If you don't call that open competition, I don't know what the hell it is. Just because you have a trade embargo on China doesn't mean that the rest of us who don't go along with you here are criminals. We're capitalists trying to survive in a market area which has to include selling to Communism. I'd sell more diesels to China tomorrow if I got the chance, but I won't, and never have, done secret deals with them. Any sales I've made in that area have taken gold away from the Reds because I was paid in outside currency. With the diesels they got an engine that couldn't conceivably have anything but a commercial use."

This wasn't strictly true, and I wished, the moment it was out, that I hadn't said it. Clem's eyebrows lifted.

"I'd say your diesels have an interesting variety of uses. They give an average junk five knots an hour more speed than any engine they're mass-producing themselves."

"All right, granted. But they're still a power plant for junks. They can't be developed to get anything like the thrust needed for a patrol boat, and you know it."

"A fast junk is a useful supply medium in war."

"If you're going to produce that kind of argument, you could say that plastic toothbrushes are war potential because soldiers use them."

Clem's expression checked me. It hadn't changed much—it rarely did—but the little was enough. I was being maneuvered onto the defensive and once there, faced the hard task of producing a credible apologia for fairly normal business ethics. It's not something that the sensible executive attempts, and in my case—possibly slightly more than in most cases—commercial morals mightn't always launder snow white. You need a stable order for a pristine effect and that kind of society was totally unavailable where I lived.

Clem folded his brown hands together in front of his hips and looked down at them. He was wearing trousers and shirt of military drab, both in a slightly shiny material which looked like service issue. His hands somehow drew attention to an older body functioning under orders from that boy's head. There was a slight thickening at the waist, not really any suggestion of too much weight, just a hint of a general slackening in youth's muscles, of sags here and there which would only come tight as a result of conscious effort. He asked a question, still looking at his hands.

"So Kim Sung here is a flat liar?"

"From a long line, all with unique talent at the job. He's fooled me for ten years, and with a happy grin on his face."

"You didn't give him eighteen thousand dollars as a down payment to carry out a special assignment?"

"I gave him his trading money, that's all."

"You knew nothing about the arms he was taking from Malaya?"

"I did not."

"And now you have no second thoughts about what you saw up there in the border jungle?"

He looked up at me. And as certainly as though I could see into Clem's mind, I knew he was checking down the list of other things he could throw at me if he wanted to. There were quite a few. Behind us the still neutrality of the military Brass was somehow positively officious. No chairs creaked and there was no wheeze of breathing, but they were there, and as big brothers with almost ultimate power.

"I've told you what I saw in the border jungle. Elephants, gibbons, and the sweating backs of my guides. Those guides could have been a clever plant, I suppose. Though I still don't see how. And it's possible, too, that I was deliberately steered past what I wasn't meant to see. If the Reds are using navigable water, then maybe I slipped up. But a water route would put them out in the open. Air reconnaissance ought to have picked up any movement of men in boats."

"Air reconnaissance has," Clem said softly

While I was absorbing this I noticed a smile sketched on Kim Sung's lips. Anger at me had completely eliminated an earlier apathy of defeat. The stretched skin of fear had gone. The man seemed suddenly to be almost enjoying himself. Because of Kim I was going to have to call in the wreckers for the job of smashing down my entire organization and then start it all again from scratch. The sooner I got moving on this the better. The first move was to escape from Clem.

Once clear of the plane I would be running free. The jungle was near, ready with all the prodigal hospitality it offers to fugitives until they get lost in it. I wouldn't get lost. I believed, too, that back in Kuala Lumpur I would be fairly safe from the long arm of the CIA. As a British subject I probably wouldn't have been safe at all, but as a Malaysian, and carrying a new nation's passport, I came under the umbrella of that nation's sensitivity about any rough stuff meted out to its citizens from foreign agencies. Friends in high places in the capital could be alerted on my behalf and Clem would have to walk softly, even though he continued to watch every move I made.

The general outlook for the escaper, however, wasn't too bright. It is just not good for a businessman in tropic Asia these days to fall out with the United States of America. And the trader who does this is liable to find himself up against the kind of economic quarantine which can play hell with company dividends. Also, that freezing order on my junk movements would at once cut off two-thirds of my operations, something to send a cold trickle down a managing director's spine even without any threat to his personal freedom.

The alternative to making a sudden bolt for it was to go on

25

proclaiming my innocence. This hadn't done me much good and I didn't feel that it was likely to do more at my trial, or court of inquiry, or whatever was scheduled. It was obvious that I was now under some kind of arrest, however illegal this might be. Clem had flown over here, accompanied by his unwanted guests, with the sole object of picking me up. Round one had been a preliminary questioning in which I had scored badly. Round two would now almost certainly be over in Saigon, to which I would be flown in this plane, these decidedly formal proceedings, but still with no one in the least worried about having to explain away my sudden appearance in custody in Vietnam. In time of war little points like this don't have to be explained, even when they involve civilians. And possibly, as a registered subagent, I wasn't technically a civilian any longer.

I hadn't seen guns in the hands of those two young men in white shirts at the bottom of the aluminum steps. Clem wasn't armed. The Colonel had the Luger, but it is a heavy weapon if you haven't fired one before, with a trigger kick upsetting to aim.

Even Clem, usually watching for everything, wasn't ready for that right to his jaw. He had been standing between me and the exit, but the blow spun him back to the curved cabin wall, with both hands out against it. He snapped forward again to grab my shirt, blocking the Colonel's line of fire. I went through a moonlit opening like a man whose back hairs have been singed by huge flame, hands clutching for a low rail, but feet not bothering overmuch about steps. There was a lot of shouting, none of it too coherent. I hit the ground. One of the white-shirted boys went into a routine subsidiary to his basic training in flying machines and landed a chop at the base of my skull. I went flat onto cracked tarmac.

When machine-gun clatter started I wondered why anyone was bothering with such heavy armament against a prone escaper. There was a scream. The man who had hit me pitched forward. The other scrambled up metal steps. I caught this movement without really turning my head, a visual message that came dully, along with another saying that the firing wasn't from anywhere in the plane, but directed at it, passing over me. Bullets struck metal struts to whine away again in ricochets, but most of them were getting into the cabin. Human noise said they were finding targets.

The man on the steps folded in two. He came down to a crumpled heap two feet from one of my outstretched hands,

26

his head jerked back. I could see his face in moonlight. His mouth was open as though he had something to say that would now never be pushed into words.

The cut sword grass ended on a line ten feet ahead of me. I started to crawl toward the cover of tall *lalang,* very slowly, pushing fingers into fissures in asphalt, pulling weight forward that way, scarcely moving my legs at all, expecting at any second to be caught by a lowered trajectory of bullets.

The plane stayed the target. I thought there was return fire from it, but couldn't be sure. I heard a loud cry from somewhere ahead of me, in the open.

My hands touched the uncut *lalang,* fingers at once sliced by its sharp blades. I edged in, trying to avoid making a betraying ripple up above, suddenly feeling screened, almost sheltered from a killing. I lay still, head down.

The attackers weren't being careful about expenditure of ammunition. They might have had a special issue for this job, to make certain it was thorough. It was thorough, all right. I was sure now that the attack had been from both sides of the plane, a sweeping cross fire carelessly dangerous to the attackers themselves.

The din eased, becoming a series of explosive postscripts before silence. Echoes were absorbed by a padding of thick jungle and into a tight stillness came the sudden squawking of frightened monkeys.

I couldn't seem to organize a coherent reaction to what had happened, or find my place in it. I was alive when a lot of others were dead, and from this came only ego-controlled relief. I had started along a line of escape and might make the rest of the distance, and had no real concern for anything else.

Human voices took over from the monkeys—first an order shouted, then a reaction to it, an excited jabbering followed by the crackle of trampled grass. A tide of men came sweeping through the *lalang,* and my ear against the ground picked up a vibration of their feet.

"Surround the plane!" That was in Cantonese. "But watch that door! They may not all be dead yet."

Grass rustled. A man coughed. Another called out something and there was a laugh. They passed by on either side, leaving me in my nest, safe in it. They made a row which provided cover for my movement. No one would see grass moving now. It was the plane they were all watching.

I sat up and looked at it, too, through my screen. A bright

27

glare from flashlights hit the open cabin door, glittering on the steps, a hard supplement to moonlight. A man came forward into the whiteness, left arm lifted. His trousers were tucked into heavy boots and his shirt was splashed with camoutflage. He wore a tin hat with netting over it.

The man's arm swung back, something heavy left his fingers. He spun about and ran, shouting. The darkened cabin erupted, explosive light briefly contained by smashed windows, but suddenly expanding through these, shattering the suspended frame of the plane, severing its heavy belly, and bringing this to the ground in a rending of torn metal. For seconds the pilot's cockpit and the heavy wings continued to be supported by the landing gear, then the nose swung upward as though for a frantic climb clear, like a disemboweled bird jerked into the reflex action of flight. The wing nearest me crumpled, ripped from the fuselage, and smacked down on tarmac. A collapsing undercarriage sent the cockpit sagging back onto the main wreckage. There was a shower of sparks. I waited for fire, but this didn't come; the fuel tanks somehow had not ruptured. Only the tail portion of the plane had hit the ground almost intact, sliced from the main cabin and slightly spaced away from it, with rudder fin still firmly erect and a window of unbroken glass continuing to reflect moonlight.

The entire disintegration of that plane had perhaps taken half a minute, but it seemed to have been run before my eyes in a kind of deliberate slow motion, a half-speed playback to get detail, starting with an arm lifted for a throw, then a pause while the unseen grenade traveled into a close darkness, and a wait again before the hideous flowering of the explosion. I was still remote from the reality of the moment, as though held in a mental breathlessness by the sheer miracle of my own escape. And somehow the dead in that wreckage meant nothing—the men who had been watching a ladder, the Colonel and the General in chairs watching me, Clem staring at his hands, and Kim Sung with just the hint of a smirk on his face.

Smell reached me, the thin, acrid air taint from discharged firecrackers immediately overpowered by the strong, half-sweet odor of barbecued meat. I found myself again, behind staring eyeballs. I wanted to be sick.

In a war there isn't often time for the elation of total triumph; action runs on to the next phase. But a successful ambush is something isolated, remote from that continuing action, allowing time for an almost orgiastic celebration of sudden relief from tension. In a total and complete victory, the men out there shook off discipline. They shouted and leaped about, not listening to a voice warning them back from wreckage; they surged toward the plane, flashing light on it. And then someone began to sing, a bellow triumphing over a leader's screeched orders, the song taken up by other voices, amplified, the men prodding at debris with automatic rifles as they sang. It was like the chorale finish to some repulsive Red propaganda documentary, the tune a war march imported from China. I knew then that the three hundred miles of sea between Vietnam and Malaysia buys no immunity from the thing which is seeping down through the whole of Southeast Asia.

But it was a moment for survival, nothing more. Din offered cover. I went up on hands and knees to crawl, and had been at it for minutes, sweating nearer that jungle wall, when noise died. Sword grass crackles under assault and I wasn't at once aware of that dribbling away of sound beyond me, just suddenly of total stillness again in possession of a forgotten airstrip. There were no voices and no orders. I had the hideous feeling that my movement through *lalang* had been spotted, reviving battle tension, putting men back into discipline. I could imagine them turned now in my direction, rifles lifted, all waiting for the command which would send out a blast of lead hail.

I had one chance in ten of making the jungle even under concentrated fire, but I'd have to run to do it. I stood, then had a look over my shoulder.

No one was turned toward me. Out on the cleared runway, men were as motionless as in a frozen still when the projecting machine has broken down. It took me a minute to see why. A man had come out from the tail portion of the plane. He was leaning back against a torn edge of fabric, sagging against it, as though near to collapse. His head was bent. Moonlight fell over him. He held his right arm in his left hand. One arm had been shattered. It was Clem.

He moved slightly. The projector started again. Stillness broke. A croaking voice gave an order. Rifles lifted. Others swung to target. I yelled in Cantonese:

"Don't shoot! He's important!"

One gun did go off, but the aim was wild. The noise of it jerked Clem's head up, as though to look at death. Then he was looking at me.

So were half a hundred others, swinging around to do it, an order totally forgotten, but automatic guns still at the ready in their hands. I had seconds in which to exploit total surprise, with a fractional tide in my favor, a new tension for action not quite achieved. And frenzy had been spent.

"We surrender! We're your prisoners!"

I blundered through long grass, throwing words at them in the thin hope I was throwing confusion, too.

The battle itself doesn't have room for the taking of prisoners, just sometimes the lull after it. No actor has ever held his audience more completely than I did in those seconds. I was inspired by a stark fear of the kind of death which smashes down a total, abject helplessness. My shouts were a kind of commentary on that death.

They listened. I even gained a certain confidence from this, conscious of the demands made by my role and at the same time submerged in it. I was putting on a display of anti-heroics which came near to the whimpering terror of complete defeat. The men with guns were watching what they could never believe would strike at them, a moral death in cowardice. And there was a pleasure in allowing the performance to go on which kept their fingers from triggers. The single enemy frenziedly begging for life was basically comic. If I got a laugh the scene was totally mine.

The laugh came. It was loud and a cue for massed support. Laughter dispelled residual fear and replaced it with contempt. Sound roared out, relief, delight even. When I reached cleared ground it was seconds before anyone touched me and my arms were then seized without any real roughness. Only their leader had to remind his men that there was a war on. He came up to hit me in the face with a closed fist.

That ended laughter. I was propped up from behind for the beating. It was administered slowly, an Oriental correction, something the occasion demanded automatically. There was no running commentary. The only really loud sounds were my grunts from blows and more than a grunt when I got a knee in the groin. Then I was thrown down and the leader used his boots, heavy boots. He was the man who had tossed a grenade into the cabin.

They rolled me over onto my back. A distant-seeming face peered down. The interrogation began, in Cantonese.

"Did you come on that plane?"

"No."

"Then you were the man waiting?"

"Yes."

"You're Harris from Kula Lumpur?"

"Yes."

Broad lips separated. I saw teeth.

"Good. We're pleased to meet you."

Someone tittered. The leader snapped that into silence.

There had been no gun fired. Clem was still alive. I couldn't turn my head to see him and anyway there was sweat stinging in my eyes. I answered questions fast to keep that boot from my mouth.

Those questions went on for a long time. It was an interrogation to confirm what they already knew, a cross-checking of the kind Clem went in for. The man above me had been informed about my excursion into Thailand and its probable purpose. That purpose had been foiled from the outset by my guides, just as Clem had suggested. It gave the leader pleasure to tell me this. In fact the whole scene was giving him pleasure.

An actor's moment of triumph was over. I was a bit player with a new lead at the stage's center. And the bit player was down for a bullet when his lines had been said. So was Clem. In the circumstances I should have tried to save one man, not two. We all take on more than we can cope with.

"Who's that man over there?" the leader asked.

"American."

"I know that, you fool. But what does he do?"

"Intelligence."

I got a kick, but not in the head.

"How big?"

"Very. Top."

"Getting your orders from him here?"

"Yes."

"Why here?"

"I don't know. I was told to come. After Thailand."

"Answer me, you!"

"I have. I just don't know."

"But you were working for them?"

"Yes."

"How long?"

"Only months."

The boot came in, to my ribs. I didn't seem to have any broken bones as yet, but couldn't expect my luck to hold. When I curled my body at all it just tempted him. I kept it straight.

"Liar. We know all about you. You've been at it for years. You were caught in Sumatra once. Only you got away then. You won't this time."

"I've only worked a few months for the Americans."

"Why? Your own country too feeble these days to make it worth your while?"

"I'm a Malaysian."

He laughed.

"You won't be for long, Harris. We're going to cremate you in the plane, along with the rest."

"You ought to take the American and me to Lum Ping."

He reached down then and pulled me up by the front of my shirt, which ripped, but left me sitting.

"Who told you anything about Lum Ping?"

"We all know he's in those mountains."

"Do you? How?"

"There's been no news of his leaving."

"Get up, Harris. Get on your feet."

This was to give him the pleasure of knocking me down again. I got up.

"Well, come on. What do you know about Lum Ping?"

"He's been seen in Kota Bahru."

"Who by?"

"I don't know. It could have been bazaar talk."

The blow came and I went with it, down again onto one-inch stubble spikes which would have made a nice fakir's mattress.

"Who saw Lum Ping in Kota Bahru?"

"I don't know," I said, spitting out blood.

The boot came in to my collarbone, which was a new area for it. But I had a small satisfaction. The Gauleiter was worried. And hope stirred that his worry would expand to the point where a rushed decision to cremate Clem and me might seem unwise.

My interrogator took time to light a cigarette, but without offering the pack to his men. He had removed the tin hat earlier to get comfortable for question time, and I saw his face clearly in the match flame. It was almost a pleasant face, the broad lips part of a bony, outsize cast of features which, together with a special issue in large fleshy ears, made their owner look un-Oriental. But he was Chinese, all right, born to good feeding and those imported sports which tend to alter physique wherever they are practiced. He went up to at least five feet eleven and I made him about thirty. A slight turn of

32

the chance wheel in another direction could have had us as partners at one of those all-male *towkays'* Singapore parties, both with sore palms from applauding imported Hong Kong striptease.

It is a comfort in war to be offered a clearly defined viciousness in your adversary—the simian Nip, the Mongolian wog, the slant-eyed Slav—but this was a man I'd have happily bought a drink at the bar of the Swimming Club and gone to dine with later up on the roof under the tropic stars while he told me all about the trouble he was having with women. As a friend he would be a comforting reserve for those occasions which do crop up fairly frequently out East, when you need ...lid support for the rough stuff.   ... . is the

                      ooking down at me as though on their assaults
                    ad popped into his mind... Mao Tse-tung and
                   t interludes i
               urprised perfectly well that no latent
             his ming to save my life or Clem's.
           of t ould be the direct result of in-
          v alm a situation which, for all the
         hing ust about maximum danger. I
        eir l ed. Round one was perhaps
       er standing up in the grass I
      her i re more rounds to come. It
     t Clem fighting with blood in my eyes
    eyes unk, resistance neutralized by
   captors Under stress you can reach the
   the le d for as the ultimate escape.
   plane t have a terror of deliberate
   act, e this scares me right down to
   the assa use I have had the course.
   ...de. It happens the circle round me, and
   ...e expendable, and happe... so...

...... think that the word would get about and lesse opera...w tors become difficult to recruit. But the mystique of mother China is powerful. It has a potent, emotional appeal which even pulls in the emigrant children to that great bosom, and quite often to their deaths. It is the hardest of all mystiques to fight because its demands are totally beyond reason. Converts to Communism in our time are rarely landed by the dialectic, but much more often because what is offered fills a vacuum, an emptiness of no faith. God is dispensed with under Marxism, but not the chanted prayers, not the sermons, and not the vast relief from any personal need to cerebrate which is the direct result of a total subjection to a disciplined conformism.

The man who had been kicking me was educated, this was plain from his voice, and very probably a younger son from a rich Singapore family, his loss to capitalism never mentioned at clan reunions, but not forgotten, either. It was possible that this eccentric was being discreetly pensioned as a kind of quiet insurance against coming days of change. The idealist crops up now and then even in the best-regulated families and it is unrealistic to attempt to keep him from his cause. This leader's cause, the only major one available in his environment, had turned him into a killer, and a killer for a truth which seemed to him as totally whole and complete a̲
one the Moslems once took with them
against Southern Europe. For Allah read
you have it.

I lay on the ground, knowing
humanity in my captors was g
If we were able to survive it w
telligence brought to bear on
temporary lull, still indicated j
rated our chances as thin ind
mine, in that thirty minutes aft
was still alive, but there we
mightn't be long before I was
and more than half punch dr
sheer fatigue more than fear. U
point where the bullet is longe
Also, I can take a beating, b
planned torture. Anticipation o
the soles of my feet, perhaps beca

I heard boots coming back to t
opened my eyes. The leader stared down.

"Your friend is dying, Harris," he said in English acquired at university level. "He may have been worth keeping. You're not."

There was a revolver in his hand, a Smith & Wesson. It is remarkable how they manage to get ammunition for all the assorted makes they pick up.

"Let me go to him."

"What for?"

"He could have fainted. Loss of blood."

"All right." That was almost mild.

My legs were stiff. The guerrillas moved with us, in a

shuffling mob just behind. Over in the jungle the monkeys had gone back to sleep. The full moon, carefully chosen by Clem, put almost harsh light over his defeat and the tumbled wreckage of his transport. He lay just beyond where I had seen him standing, clear of the plane, one arm flung out, the other, which had stopped the bullets, folded under his body. The dark tarmac showed a darker stain of blood. His face was in shadow.

I bent down and turned him over, carefully, watched by a silent and almost quiescent audience. Clem's mouth was open and his eyes shut. In the moonlight his face looked drained beneath tan, like the victim of a car accident who may in moments be dead. His breathing was audible in a way I didn't like.

"There ought to be a first-aid box in the plane."

No one was interested. A guerrilla cleared his throat and spat.

"Can I go for it?"

"All right."

The leader came with me, flashlight in one hand, revolver in the other. We crunched over wreckage into the tail of the plane, where it was dark, into a passage along one side of the fuselage, this flanking the stern compartment. Sudden light fell on a body in the corridor, folded down into a natural-seeming position, buttocks on the floor, back against one wall, legs propped against the other. The Colonel was dead, though his head somehow looked still supported by living muscle.

"Get over him," the leader said.

I stepped across the body, sickened into one of those moments of sharp awareness which are the most unbearable detail of any war. You forget the actual violence quickly enough, but not its punctuation.

A door was half-wrenched from its hinges by bullets but the cabin beyond showed little damage. Two bunks had neatly folded blankets on them. Under the lower one was a large box marked with a red cross.

I was shaking by the time I got that box out onto the tarmac near Clem. I didn't at once lift the lid but when I did, flashlights probed the contents. The container for morphia had phials and the syringe intact in cotton wool. I broke an ampul and managed to put a measured amount in the cylinder, guessing at what I was doing, wondering if a much larger dose mightn't be the humane thing. Someone noticed the trembling of my fingers and said in Cantonese:

"He's scared."

The leader asked a question.

"You know medicine?"

"This much."

It hadn't seemed to occur to him yet that medical supplies were valuable. I put a needle in Clem's good arm, taking time to find a vein, then pushed the plunger. I got scissors and cut blood-sodden cloth away from that other arm. There seemed to be three centers to a viscid coagulation, three drilled wells into flesh and bone between wrist and elbow. There was no way to wash the wounds and a sponging with alcohol and lint would have taken too long. I turned the arm gently to see if there were egress holes and made out one. Two bullets were still in there.

Clem had nearly bled to death, but not quite. And if I said he couldn't be moved they would finish him and me.

"Is he dying?"

"No. Just arm hits. His legs are all right."

"He can walk?"

"In a while, yes."

I put on emergency dressing pads and bandaged, using two rolls which dampened under my hands as I worked. I made a sling from the broadest roll and eased the shattered arm into this while all the time that accelerated breathing went on, now possibly from the drug taking effect. It was pain which had knocked Clem out and he would have partial relief from this, for a time.

My enemies were now engaged in what was happening, an involved audience which had no other distraction from that involvement. When I asked that Clem be carried away from the plane to the long *lalang*, the leader detailed men for this, and without comment. My idea was to dissociate the two survivors from the wreckage which contained the dead. If they were going to make a pyre of the aircraft there would still be the strong temptation to add us to it, especially if we were obvious during the excitement.

In the grass there was a four-foot anthill against which to prop Clem. I arranged the body, trying to make it seem not too near death, then sat down alongside. When I groped for cigarettes a couple of guns came up, but dropped again. I took out a cigarette and held up the pack to the nearest man. This was taken, but I wasn't offered a light. I had matches of my own.

It may have been the heat which stirred Clem from coma, or the strong red light of twenty-foot flames. Oil-black smoke went straight up, blurring a complacent moon. Investigators might eventually find traces of bullet holes in melted metal fragments on an old airfield, but I didn't think they would. What was left would only suggest a night crash and instant, enveloping fire. Even identification of the plane was improbable. They had used four more grenades to make certain of this and to start the blaze.

The fact that Clem and I hadn't yet been added to the fire didn't mean much. The leader might experiment with prisoners, starting off with us, but he could change his mind at almost any point on the trek. The Malayan jungle is probably the best place in the world in which to leave bodies you don't want traced. Wild-life scavengers get to work almost at once, even scattering the bones. And there is absolutely no danger that weeks later someone is going to stumble on something nasty at a picnic and yell for the police.

We had only one guard now, but his job had been made easy in that my hands were strapped back and held at the wrist by adhesive tape. I could still move legs and head.

Clem's lids lifted. His eyes were extremely bloodshot, suggesting a massive hangover, and the red light even spoiled blue irises. His mouth was open a little wider than he had been keeping it and his tongue pushed at the corners of his lips. He didn't seem to notice me at all; his stare focused on the big attraction. Then he looked down, lashes dropping, inspecting his own condition and taking some time over this assessment.

My reaction was a kind of joy at no longer being alone. I knew then how lonely I had been. Under acute stress a sentient friend permits an easing of terror in a sharing, and this was something I suddenly wanted very much.

"Hello," I said softly, and it sounded remarkably stupid.

He didn't move his head, only his eyes. The new focus stayed fixed, assessing me, too.

He was intelligently conscious, noting my strapped wrists, and the fact that I wasn't too comfortable. Again his tongue made an excursion out over cracked lips.

Our guard shifted his position and his rifle. Clem ignored the man. His voice, when it came, was almost normal.

"Your friends . . . didn't start firing until you were out of the plane."

37

THREE

What I wanted to do then was curse Clem, loud and long. But I had to conserve energy, so I looked back at the fire. For the whole of this contact with the man I'd had the feeling that he was functioning as some kind of projection from a computer, a technician absolved from humanity in the mathematics of logic. And to look for a friend here was like expecting a reaction to "How are you doing?" from a metal box with flashing electronic eyes.

Everything he knew about me had gone on strips of tape with punched hole symbols, these then fed into a machine which always came up with the infallible answer so long as a fuse hadn't blown somewhere. Certainly he had a lot of information for his computer, was able to give it a really balanced meal which it could swallow without any burps of technological indigestion. I could fill in all the courses on that menu myself, starting with the hors d'oeuvre of a somewhat unconventional youth in the Orient, through the entrée of what I had been up to in the last decade, a solitary trying to build his own little durable empire with ships and trade while the national empires in the area crumbled all around. There was very little indication of any specific allegiance on my part to loyalties beyond my own interest. I had shaken off any earlier slight attachments to Britain. As the European determined to survive in the new East, I had openly traded with the Reds from time to time. I had been in Peking on a selling mission. My engines pushed Red junks over the South China seas. One of my businesses involved working with Chinese codirectors who almost certainly paid regular tributes to the big boss up north. Many of my friends could be labeled political unreliables and my trading fleet was now just about as suspect as anyone's trading fleet could be. Finally, I had agreed to assist American intelligence simply to find out the extent of their penetration into the areas of my interest.

That excretion from the box's intestines didn't require any

detailed analysis at all. I played along with the Reds when it suited my bank accounts. And on this premise I had to be dealt with. The machine said so. The fact that in this case the machine was wrong was my little problem, one which inevitably faces the slight eccentric in an age when such eccentricity can only be interpreted in terms of mechanized psychological formulas.

I looked down at my knees. Those two knees covered by dirty trousers were a little oasis of the personal in the relentless desert of surrounding hostility. I stared at them.

The fire had turned to black smoke, its work done, a tall column tainting a purple night sky, the residue of a purge. Up near the wreckage a man went into a paroxysm of coughing, the sound, so violently beyond control, suggesting limits set on his mortality by lungs weakened from jungle damp. The leader's voice barked out again, producing a rustle of action through the grass. I looked up to see them carrying out their own casualty of battle. The scream I had heard must have come from this boy's throat. He was hit below the waist by a bullet which could have been a final shot from the plane or just a wild stray from an ill-sited cross ambush. The boy lay there unable to get up, but lifting the top half of his body, writhing to do this, propping himself on elbows as though to demonstrate that he had areas which were still functioning normally. He was talking, too, babbling with a desperate urgency to the leader, who stood looking down, very much as he had looked down at me. But this boy wasn't going to be able to walk. He presented an even more acute problem than we did.

The solution to it was swift. The leader took his revolver from a holster and without even leaning down, shot a babbling youth in the head. One bullet, one sharp sound, that was all. They then carried away the body, adding it, a bit late, to the pyre, where only half-charred remains would possibly complicate the task of investigators, adding a new inexplicable factor. A cloud of sparks went up, a little tribute.

I turned to Clem.

"I just hope you're going to be mobile," I said.

His eyes were shut again, perhaps from the pain he had to endure.

The Malaysian Communist party oath of allegiance apparently doesn't contain a clause binding recruits to total abstinence. I hadn't seen a looting of the plane before it was set on fire but this could have been carried out during one of my times of politic quiescence when I wasn't moving my head to watch anything because there was a boot too near it. But salvage there certainly was, all of it food and drink.

The food stocks went quickly, with a well-maintained discipline in the way these were portioned out. Someone who might have had sergeant's rank took pains in that dying red light to keep things approximately fair, one cooked chicken torn into as near equal portions as could be managed, with a ham for the rest, this chopped up into precise squares. Crackers and biscuits went out one each all around. There wasn't a hint of squabbling though it was clear everyone was hungry. Clem and I witnessed a fine demonstration of egalitarian sharing which might have been staged for our benefit but was probably normal practice. They shot a comrade who was no longer mobile, then neatly carved up a ham for the more fortunate survivors, and with no two-minute silence between one job and the other.

I didn't want anything to eat, but my throat was parched, and when they broached two cases of Coca-Cola I called out for a drink. No one appeared to hear. I sat watching those bottles emptied and then the hard liquor being passed from hand to hand, some of the labels recognizable—Booth's London dry gin, Old Granddad bourbon, a vermouth, a Bell's "afore ye go." There seemed to be some wines, too, probably Californian.

Things began to have the feel of a party, the kind of party which would call for cabaret later, and I felt pretty sure that Clem and I would be it. I wished then, and perhaps he did, too, that Clem hadn't done himself quite so well in his mobile headquarters.

I had quite a clear picture of what might lie just ahead for us, fun and games inspired by mixed drinks. The prisoners would be given a sporting chance to run for it, Clem first, with me handicapped because more mobile. The performance couldn't ge too long delayed, either, if, after it, we were to be added to a fire that still retained effective heat.

It was totally clear to me in those moments that my wild bid to save Clem was easily the most stupid thing I have ever done, impulsive lunacy which was going to produce the net result of two dead instead of one, and with no survivor to creep away to give an eyewitness account of the night's happenings. Further, my heroics hadn't even earned me minimal gratitude from the character they had been meant to rescue. Clem was going to take that computer verdict on me all the way, retaining to the last his deep faith in the reliability of machines as against the infinite potential perfidy of man. I was a no-good Joe, just as he had intuitively felt from round one over there in Borneo, a byproduct of collapsed empire who would sell out anything to keep intact a personal salvage from general wreckage. For me he had only burning red eyes. He was an impossible man to die with, let alone for.

I watched the last of the Old Granddad go into the leader, moving into a state that was vaguely euphoric, something suspended between a terror which has exhausted itself and a new one about to arrive. This lull was the eye in the hurricane and unfortunately you can't stay in its shelter for long, though it's restful while it lasts, almost permitting a return to personal norm. I even had time to wonder about how my Japanese assistant and new codirector, Ohashi, would run the business without me. Probably better than I had. And screened from the knowledge that most of our crews were undercover Reds, he might go on using them for years, with a steady annual increase in Harris and Company's business the end result.

I think I was the first to hear the sound which came from somewhere over the jungle. Certainly none of the guerrillas reacted to it quickly, which was perhaps not surprising in the middle of a party, even though the roaring soon became definite enough, suggesting a small tornado moving on a line that was going to include us. The air took on an unnerving localized turbulence, with great trees lashing their top branches. I saw the leader swing around, his mouth opening for a shout that didn't come, or if it did was inaudible. The din was clearly mechanical now, a steady beat of engines, though the sky stayed an empty deep purple and no star constellations were shadowed.

I realized what it was just before I saw it. The huge helicopter blundered at us from only feet above the jungle wall, pushing down a whirlwind from rotors which flattened grass and the guerrillas, too. Men dropped into *lalang* for cover that suddenly wasn't available, fifty of them falling flat like worshipers before a sudden, terrifying revelation. The leader was down, as well, part of a ceremony of agonized respect.

A first run over was made at no more than fifty feet. It was a personnel carrier, with one of the big side doors wide back and men visible in the opening. They seemed to have guns. The machine gave an impression of being quite ready to convert itself into a low-flying bomber and probably grenades were ready for this role.

Forward movement ceased over the wreckage and a suspended cabin almost as big as Clem's shattered plane dropped down like a jerky lift. It hung shivering for seconds over still rising heat before the pilot gunned motors into a banked sweep around the field before an even slower return over us.

The guerrillas recovered from stunned shock. The leader was first on his knees, bellowing. He never even looked in our direction and the guard over us, but took off with the rest, toward jungle and cover.

Fifty guerrillas were running as the helicopter came lumbering back in an ungainly sideways maneuver. The pilot gave chase, at twenty feet. Grass around the fleeing men turned into a flat carpet. Some of the Reds stumbled and fell, but got up again to run on. I saw white faces looking up at that thundering vengeance overhead but not one of our late captors raised a rifle to offer the resistance which would have brought down a hail of return fire. They just wanted away from that airstrip.

"The British Navy," I shouted. "A long way from base. Rule, Britannia."

I looked at Clem. He had pushed himself up from his anthill and was shakily on his feet.

"We move," he told me.

"Don't you want to be rescued?"

"Not by them. You got a car somewhere?"

He was trying to control a sway.

"It's about a mile away. And you ought to be in a hospital. That thing will get you there in an hour."

"No! Come on! Before they turn back."

The helicopter was now going into a startling bank almost at the jungle wall and the last of the guerrillas seemed to be stumbling into safety.

"We could run into the Reds again."

"Risk it," Clem said, getting command of that sway.

I didn't have to stick with American intelligence. I could sit right where I was and be shortly surrounded by countrymen who offer such charming charity to the afflicted. On the other hand, they would soon begin to ask questions, some of them not too easy to answer even if I did get my wits back.

I stood, too.

"Free my hands," I said.

"Not now. Where's the way out of this place?"

The overgrown track I had used in was beyond the

42

burned-out plane. We started to circle the wreckage as the 'copter headed for us, and with a little spurt of speed.

"Don't look up," Clem shouted, starting a shambling trot toward secondary growth which seemed a long way off. "You lead."

I got out in front. We must have made an interesting sight from above, one man with an arm in a sling, the other with his hands twisted behind his back, both taking an obstacle course around anthills while being pursued by one of man's most ingenious contraptions.

The shock of the blast wave from those rotors almost put me on my knees. What it did to Clem I couldn't see and I didn't risk a glance back. I was clinging now to a pious hope that the Navy, operating over land, would remain hesitant about using lethal weapons, for as targets we were quite perfect. I became horribly conscious of that hunk of metal suspended only feet above my head and sudden light down in a great white beam was almost totally demoralizing. I had the feeling that but for those mercifully towering anthills, arranged like anti-landing devices all about, the 'copter would have pulled on a little ahead to set itself down across our escape route. But the pilot remained conscious of the expensive piece of equipment he was handling. Further, he kept just a little behind us, which reduced the rotor thrust on his quarry. Probably the air was crackling with a radio request for instructions and I hoped that some duty brass back at HQ was sleepy and slow to react.

At any moment that machine could come low enough for some of its crew to risk a jump. And the damn maneuverability of these things meant that an anthill could probably be used as a landing platform. When it came to getting away from armed men on the ground our chances would be greatly reduced. In my mind there was a bleat about the folly of thus running from your own side, even when your own side meant uniformed servicemen. It wasn't quite Clem's side, of course, which gave him a better reason for flight than me, but he was a long way from home and was going to have to use someone's charity to get himself back to base.

I reached cover first, not very effective cover, the new growth through the tarmac only going up to fifteen feet or so, but enough to force that 'copter into a rise. I looked back. Clem had fallen by another anthill, and the vast machine hung right over him, flooding down light into which he reso-

43

lutely refused to look. He began to crawl. And as he did it a rope ladder dropped from the vibrating craft, a length of it which wobbled down into grass. Boots appeared on a swinging first rung.

Clem got up again. I saw his face if no one else did. It was the face of a man who isn't going to give up, even from staggering agony. His bad arm had fallen out of the sling and hung at his side. He ran toward me with a shoulder forward, an odd, crab-like movement, with a drag on one leg. Trussed myself, I could do nothing to help, and if I went out to offer a shoulder, it meant the man behind cockpit glass would have a very good look at me indeed. All this was Clem's exercise anyway. I was acting under a kind of moral duress and against my own instincts. I would have much preferred a plastic cup of lukewarm Thermos tea and young British faces all around as against a continued blundering about in a tropic night which would only be memorable for sheer horror.

Clem reached me when the man on the ladder was still only halfway down. He was swaying on those ropes as though he hadn't received much basic training in this particular act, or perhaps he was used to having water under him when he did it. At any rate his caution was our asset, and it gave me time to see that we would be up against hunters equipped with walkie-talkies. This actually struck no terror to my heart at all, for these gadgets are totally useless in jungle tracking, even when that jungle is secondary. Certainly you can keep in touch with your mobile HQ up above, but while you are doing that your quarry gets away.

Before I turned into deep cover I saw a second pair of boots on the ladder, but the 'copter appeared to be slightly upset by some fluke thermal, for it wobbled suddenly and the engines began to sound as though they were suffering from strangulation of the feed lines. Clem and I made fair speed, with me leading, but suddenly my head had taken all it could stand as a trail-breaker. I stopped.

"Get my arms free. You ought to be able to do that with your good hand."

"Don't yell!"

"Who the hell's going to hear with that row? Get me loose."

It seemed to take a long time. I felt him picking away at the tape. We had lost light, both from moon and from helicopter spot. In spite of that clanking din behind us, I could hear Clem's breathing near my ear. The pace of this made me

44

wonder how long he was going to keep on his feet. He sounded like an old man with asthma.

"I've got a hold," he panted. "Pull forward."

Someone shouted from the edge of our cover. I moved as a kind of involuntary jump for safety and the tape peeled. Clem followed me up and completed the job. Free hands and a moderating pulse rate seemed to restore me back into normal sentimentality.

"Get you good arm round my shoulder."

"Damn that," he said. "Just break trail fast. They're following."

But I did have to help him a few times. The most spectacular was when we struck a swampy stream and stayed by it for moonlight even though I wasn't too happy about the direction indications. Clem fell in. He did it slowly and with considerable grace for an injured man, giving a little yelp of pain first, then slithering through reeds down into a slime which had been waiting there quite undisturbed for a few thousand years and had built up a considerable stench. It had also acquired a huge population of leeches and Clem lurched out from near waist deep, accepting my hand, with the little worms already feeding on his blood and with an ecstatic wriggling over its beef-nourished quality.

"I've got matches. I'll strike one. Don't try to yank 'em off."

"We can't wait."

"Look, the 'copter is two hundred yards to the left of us. Which means the boys are right underneath. We're clear."

He didn't believe me but was glad of the rest. I used a match to sizzle off the first of those unappealing parasites and then went on to nearly finish the box. The leeches only had a short breakfast.

"Any in your boots?" I asked.

"I don't know. Let them stay."

But about two minutes later he eased himself down on a log and permitted me to take off his boots. We got a count of seven from behind leather. Clem's expression suggested that what was wrong with Southeast Asia was basically things like leeches. He also didn't like his own smell.

It took us an hour to reach the north-south highway. This was mainly due to my navigation, which had to be intuitive, and intuition has often let me down. But the hard metaling underfoot felt good, particularly in the stillness which had developed over the previous twenty minutes, the helicopter apparently having given up, taken on its wandering boys, and gone home. That was fine with me; the machine had served us well but any deepening of the contact was highly undesirable.

"How far is it to the car?" Clem asked.

"About half a mile."

"Back toward the airfield?"

"Yes."

We walked in shadow from verging trees just in case there might be anyone watching that road, though I was fairly certain that the guerrillas were in fast transit toward their safe mountains. We got to the trail leading in to the airstrip, and passed this, making for the wood where I had left my transport.

There is no rent-a-car service as yet available in the capital of Kelantan and the Fiat I was finally able to track down had first left the showrooms in 1937. It was an open tourer with a moldering canvas top as sun protection. It had a bulb horn fitted once as a classy accessory and now highly necessary because the brakes were erratic. There was a self-starter, too, but in case this let you down, the handle hung permanently under the radiator grille.

I approached this wreck with the feeling that we would probably find four flat tires; but that wasn't the trouble, it was night damp depressing the plugs. I didn't put any strain on the shaky battery but went straight for the handle like one of those characters of 1903 when motoring was almost as exciting as a blood sport. Usually when turning a handle you can feel the point of an engine's bid to come to life, but the old car was flaccid and defeated.

"Is there a morning bus?" Clem asked from his seat beside the driver's, where he had been holding out the choke with his good hand.

"I don't think so. Have you any money? The Reds left my matches, but took everything else. I saw them searching you."

"I haven't my wallet, either. What about those Reds? Where do you think they are?"

"A long way from here by now. They're not our problem anymore."

"Have you got a gun in the car?"

"No. You took my armament."

I yanked again and something happened under the hood, a faint burp. I tickled the carburetor and then went forward for another turn-over. There were two sharp cracks like cannon fire, followed by a roar.

"Keep that choke out!" I yelled.

The engine went on firing and even allowed itself to be revved back. I tried first gear and we jerked into movement, this almost vigorous, as though the Fiat had suddenly decided to approve of an early-morning rise. We pulled up a gradient and out onto the road. I eased her up to eighteen mph and waited for vibration, but this didn't come. The needle started to climb toward the speed records of the car's youth, reaching twenty-three, then twenty-six, finally twenty-eight, still without the hint of a knock from her big end. I took time off for a quick glance at Clem, risky with that loose steering. He had his eyes shut and was slumped down on sagging seat springs.

"You all right?"

"If you mean am I still alive, yes."

The potential male nurse in me surfaced again, a character rich in sympathy of an easy sort for physical suffering.

"The pain must have been pretty hellish."

"Oh, shut up," Clem said.

So I just drove. There was now, beyond tiredness, a hint of exhilaration, elation at an escape from a situation with the odds at least a hundred to one against. I am always grateful when I'm allowed a miracle, particularly when one of these lets me have a little longer on this planet. My luck, on the whole, had been indifferent, but I've had more than any man's reasonable ration of miracles, and they make luck superfluous, to say nothing of superficial. I have a secret conviction that if I ever start winning at cards or the races, it will be a sign that the miracle issue is over. So I never gamble. I don't want to know for certain.

"There was absolutely no reason," I said, "for a Navy helicopter to be five hundred miles from base tonight and over the Kelantan jungle."

"What?" Clem asked from the depths of a returned consciousness of three bullet holes.

"They don't patrol over Malaysia these days."

"I could do without your speculations just now," he said. "Is this wobbling about the car or your driving?"

"The car."

"Then give it all your attention."

The Fiat's engine had never been quiet even when it was

factory new and now, after a thirty-year run-in, the thing bellowed, taking us through a predawn tropic morning with all the discretion of a three-trailer articulated truck. We heard nothing beyond ourselves and couldn't be expected to. The first indication that we were no longer alone was a sudden, violent flapping from the canvas hood, then the sharp noise of this ripping.

"What the hell is that?" Clem shouted.

I knew. The rotor thrust down again. The Navy hadn't gone home.

We were on a gently winding road, a downstretch. The Kelantan River had joined us and was glinting through a thin row of trees. On the right was rubber, but set well back from the highway, which gave the 'copter adequate room for maneuver just over our heads. I couldn't see how near over our heads, but from the sound added to our own, it was pretty near. The sudden artificial hurricane upset the Fiat, which began to respond in a highly erratic manner to the wild sweeps I was giving the wheel.

The canvas top loosened from its windshield fastenings and dropped on us, a stinking, ancient shroud. I had to take one hand from steering to clear my face. This might have been what the car was waiting for. We went straight at a bank. I fought that with a triple wheel revolution and we moved left toward the Kelantan River. The top rose behind us like a sail and then detached itself completely as a piece of standard equipment, leaving Clem and me in a very open tourer indeed.

"Don't look up!" he yelled.

It was a message I'd had before. And anyway, I couldn't look up. No pilot ever fought a plane caught in turbulence harder than I was fighting that decrepit vehicle. From overhead we must have looked like a vintage movie comedy, one of those shots of an old car jerking back and forth over a road, filled with arm-waving passengers, and with the projector speed accelerated to stimulate laughter. The only thing we weren't doing was waving our arms.

The helicopter stopped tailing to move right over its quarry, the snout of the thing about level with our boiling radiator and blocking out a good part of my moonlight ration. The full downthrust of rotors let me share the experience of a new boy in a centrifuge seat being subjected to Mach One or whatever it is that starts to pull your face out of shape and loosen your teeth. The Fiat under my hands now had the feel

48

of a large plastic duck being propelled through bath water at well below buoyancy level, liable at any moment to pop free and shoot out of the tub onto tiling. The cyclone encircling began to make us go a great deal faster than our engine revs or the gradient would have permitted and it was frightening to see the speedometer needle reaching forty-two miles an hour. It was like getting toward the end of a runway in an overloaded plane which isn't going to become airborne and is just at the point of going out of control. The seconds then became stretched in a horrible, suspended elasticity when a man's cerebration for once races ahead of time and it doesn't do him a damn bit of good. The only possible hope lay half a mile ahead, where jungle trees again bent lovingly over the road, coming very near to a natural arch which would certainly force the beast above to rise again.

There was no doubt whatever that we had been identified as among those present at the airfield. The others had got away, leaving only two candidates for interrogation, and some very important people wanted us brought in for just that. I would have been moderately willing to oblige, but had got myself totally involved in keeping a piece of American security intact, this against all my sharp instincts of self-preservation and likely to be highly prejudicial to my personal interests. There was, of course, the fact that I was no longer technically a British subject, but I had a feeling that the battered old lion—still with a lair of sorts down there in the Singapore naval base—might be capable of reaching out a bandaged paw to give me a nasty cuff in the area of my vital business affairs. And if this happened I could scarcely expect much help from Washington. Or from Kuala Lumpur, either, for that matter. I could even find myself deprived of a new citizenship with no chance at all to recover the old, left one of those sad, stateless characters who try to keep a foothold on this planet with nothing to assist them beyond a UN ticket, which is a poor credit card.

The din had mounted above tolerance level. Any engine failure up aloft would see us a quickly squashed beetle. It was my feeling that if we had been able to hold anything like a steady course in the Fiat that pilot would have come lower than fifteen feet in an intimidation bid, but with our heaving about he couldn't risk it. Another possibility for him was to move his craft slightly to one side, which would allow a grenade to be dropped into the car, an explosive finale, but one eliminating any possibility of bringing us back alive.

49

In fact, the pilot's indecision lasted to the point where he had to allow our escape into the tunnel under trees, zooming up himself to get clear of them. The final kickback from his rotors was very nearly a last driving straw, and I couldn't quite believe it when we were running almost easily under shelter, our slalom progress ended. The racket ended, too. I said:

"The trouble with these little wars is that you never know really who the enemy is."

Clem didn't say anything. I suspected he had his eyes shut again.

The Fiat's screeching brakes brought us back to some kind of motoring norm, though I now had to peer ahead into a gloom only vaguely penetrated by glowworm headlights. I tried to remember what lay beyond this stretch of jungle, but couldn't. The 'copter's clanking was now inaudible beyond our own engine noise, but I could picture the thing hovering out there above the next open stretch of road like a horsefly waiting for a swimmer's head to surface. There was no doubt about it, they were taking their assignment to bring us in very seriously indeed.

I risked not being able to start again, switching off the ignition to coast down the gradient, though our lights didn't like no feed to the battery and almost packed in. The clatter from rotors penetrated again, but distantly. We moved toward that sound at a pace largely controlled by a held hand brake and what I was half expecting happened: the roaring noise zoomed up, there was a coughing of exhausts, then a total deep silence.

"They've landed," I said unnecessarily, yanking the car to a stop.

"What now then?" Clem asked, handing over all strategic planning to me. "If you're counting on my being able to walk, don't."

"They're laying a quick ambush for us down there. We don't run into it."

"You mean to go back up this hill?"

"After a little. Give them time to get well clear of their machine so they can't just take off at speed."

"Where do we get to—back up this hill?"

"Kuala Krai. Where there's a phone booth."

"How about cash for a call?"

"I'll reverse charges."

"Who to?"

"A friend of mine at the Linguin mine. He's the manager. He has a Piper to get him to the nearest bar quickly. He'll fly over the mountains and pick us up."

"Just like that, eh? No questions asked. Why should he?"

"For the money I'll offer."

"What do you do with the car when we get to this town?"

"Leave it."

"The owner will make a noise about that. I'll bet this is a family heirloom."

"I'll fix all that through the head boy at the Kota Bahru rest-house. He knows me."

"You really own this country, don't you?" He brooded about that, then said:

"What's going to be your personal alibi for this particular tropic night?"

"I was visiting a girlfriend."

"I see. It's well known that you keep one in every state of the Federation? For occasional use?"

I had no comment.

"None of this is going to work," Clem said. "It's a feeling I've got. And there's something else. Pretty soon, if I don't want to have this arm chopped off, it's got to be seen to. And in a hospital. It wouldn't surprise me to be put in bed after surgery with a transfusion bottle hanging over my head."

"Your arm will be seen to, but not in a hospital."

"Where?"

"In my house in Kuala Lumpur."

"You've got another friend who's a horse doctor spare time?"

"I've got a friend who is the best surgeon in town."

"Operates anyplace and no questions asked about the patient? Maybe you know he's sleeping with his pretty receptionist and his wife would shoot him if she found out?"

"You'll get the full works and no publicity," I promised.

"It's against medical ethics."

"Ethics can be stretched."

"I hope so. It's quite important for me to get out of this country without ever having been in it, if you know what I mean?"

"I gathered that was the position."

I switched out the car lights. We sat in a total, hot darkness. After a moment Clem said softly:

51

"It's quiet down there at the foot of the hill. But they're probably boiling up tea water on a primus. You people always stop your wars for the brew that cheers."

He was beginning to sound more like himself. After a moment he whispered:

"This masterly inactivity is getting on my nerves. Just what exactly are we waiting for?"

"Boots on the road."

"And what's your plan when you hear them?"

"We leave. I don't think that helicopter will take off again without its full complement on board. It wouldn't want to have armed men wandering around without transport in a country that is now sovereign and sensitive about this. Even if they have walkie-talkies, the boys will be called back to the mother ship. Which ought to give us at least half an hour of clear road."

"In which to do what?"

"Get back to that rubber estate we passed and hide somewhere in the middle of it. While the 'copter patrols the road looking for us and uses up its juice. It'll have to go back to base long before dawn. Then we drive to Krai."

"Terribly neat, Paul. But it all hangs on one thing. That this engine is going to start when you want it to. You're confident about that?"

"No."

"So it doesn't start—what then?"

"I run for it. You get caught."

Clem went silent. I was very conscious of the risk of trying to lure those men well up this road, but I had to buy time somehow. It also occurred to me that they mightn't just be airborne sailors, but active personnel from the late Sarawak-Borneo frontier fighting who knew all about night patrols on which boot clinking wasn't permitted. A really trained man could come right up to us and stick a cold gun muzzle against my cheek before I heard him. But fortunately someone boobed, a tactical accident of the kind which don't get in official dispatches, a flashlight came on a hundred yards down from us, a patch of brightness out into the roadway from just beyond a bend. A voice yapped and the light went out.

"Get working on that handle," Clem said. "And why the hell didn't you turn this thing?"

"Doing it would have made noise."

I switched on, using the self-starter floor button, and at once got a willing grumble. I put the Fiat in reverse and, rather as I had been expecting, she went better than in the two first forward speeds, probably because this gear was less worn. The driving was slightly chancy, reversing with no rear spot, but my eyes had got a partial feel for the dark and we worked up a fair speed.

"This makes me feel really at home," Clem said. "Running from the enemy. But I prefer doing it in a jeep the right way round."

FOUR

Mickey Davenport was a period character, an Englishman who had lived abroad all his adult life and hadn't got word that the right school background is now a positive social and economic liability. No one had told him that these days, if you're wise, you never hint at the terrible handicap of Eton or Harrow in your past, claiming instead a heritage studded with horny-handed proletariats. Mickey, in a curious isolation from the realities of his time, still brooded over the fact that his parents had sensibly saved their money and sent him to Clapham Secondary. And to surmount a totally imaginary disadvantage, he assumed a strained bid at the accent of long-dead empire builders, throwing an "old boy" in nearly every sentence. His talk was weirdly reminiscent of those cricket-playing-English Hollywood actors whose survivors are still hard at very highly paid work creating an eighteen-ninety image of the British for Midwestern Americans.

Dawn would have seemed a cruel time to get Mickey out of bed if he hadn't once told me that he always made a point of seeing the first shift down his mine. Here he had got his tin-mining traditions a bit mixed with those established for rubber planters, but no one could say he wasn't keen, and it was the keen chaps who rose to be managers, as he had proved.

The phone bell only rang three times and then there was the operator's voice asking him if he would accept the charges.

"Eh? What's that? Where from?"

"Kuala Krai, the call," sang the Malay girl, trying out her English, a remarkable effort for that hour.

"Oh, well," Mickey said. "I suppose so."

"I'm glad you agreed. Paul Harris here."

"Paul, old boy!"

"Eating breakfast?"

"Oh, no, I don't have that until after muster. Just a spot of tea now. And the old *papaya*. Up actually."

"I thought you would be. I'm in a jam, Mickey."

"Really? Good Lord!"

"I've been sweating here in this phone booth in case last night was one of your K.L. evenings and you hadn't come home."

"Oh, heavens no, I never go to the big city on a Wednesday. Have to ration me gay life. Especially with the old girl off in Majorca, what?"

He called it My-yor-ka, just like the natives.

"What I need," I said, "is your airplane. Now."

"Oh? You mean up in Krai?"

"Could you, Mickey? Just come for us?"

"Us?"

"Me and a friend."

"Some frightful Harris mystery, is this?"

"Well . . . sort of. Miss that first muster for my sake."

There was silence at the other end. It was time to talk money.

"Of course I mean this is a hire. Commercial rates; I must insist on that."

"Oh, my dear chap, don't be ridiculous." His tone was warm.

"A hire, Mickey, nothing else."

"Well . . . we'll talk about that later. And of course I'll come. Whereabouts in Krai?"

"We're not in the town. Betong rubber estate just north, about a mile and a half. There's a laterite road with plenty of clearance for the Piper. I could mark it if you like."

"Don't bother, will find."

"The road leads from the entrance to the estate; you can't really miss it."

"Be with you in about an hour and a half, maybe."

"I'm sorry to bring you over the mountains, but the mist ought to be clearing soon."

"Absolutely. Not to worry, old boy. Cheerio."

I blessed Mickey, then looked out of the booth for a strolling policeman. There wasn't one. I dialed for the operator again and told her I wanted another collect number. She was quite cheerful about it.

This time the bell went for much longer. The voice which finally answered was sleepy and irritated. It was also rather mean about being asked to pay for the call.

"Betty?"

"Oh, it's you? Just a minute. I'll take this downstairs. Tom needs his beauty sleep."

There was quite a long pause.

"Well, Paul?"

"I'm going to ask you to do something you ought to refuse."

"Like going to bed with you, dear?"

"More so. Ethics."

"I see. I'm not at home."

"I need your help."

"Of course you do. That doesn't mean you'll get it."

"A friend of mine has been pretty badly knocked up."

"That is not an adequate clinical description. Do you mean bullets?"

"Yes."

"How did I guess? Ought you to be chatting about this?"

"No. But I've got to risk it. Betty, I know I shouldn't ask you to do this, but I have to."

"And you do it with quiet confidence, knowing that I'll take any risks in the name of a beautiful relationship."

"That's about it."

"No, it's not! Bring your friend to the hospital. He'll have my personal attention."

"I can't do that."

"Then go to hell. I was called out last night. For surgery. I got to bed at three."

"I'm sorry."

"There's no need to go on saying that. You're not at all. You want something and you think the Harris charm is going to work over a wire. Well, it doesn't. Not at this hour."

"Tom . . . could be listening to this."

"So he could. And so could your operator. I suppose you want me to turn a bedroom in your house into an aseptic theater in twenty-five minutes?"

"You'd have three hours. And Ohashi would see to everything. You have his number."

"No! I mean, I have his number but I'm not going to use it."

There was a pause, then Betty said:

"Where are you?"

"Up north. Quite far."

"You told me you were going to Singapore."

"A change of plans."

"A flat lie, you mean. How can you get down here in three hours?"

"By plane. That's arranged. The wounds are hemorrhaging again. There is no question of a hospital."

"Damn you! Do you know what you're asking for?"

"Private medical attention."

"No! I'm to go out on a case of which there will be no record at all. I can't do it, Paul. I'm not even in general practice. You know perfectly well I have no private work. Bring your patient to the hospital and I'll keep things as discreet as I can. Use a false name if you want. That's not my worry."

"It would worry the police. In a matter of bullet wounds."

"So would a dead patient I'd treated privately and kept quiet about!"

"He's not going to die."

"Then your worries are reduced."

"He could still lose the use of an arm."

"I'm not doing this!"

"Betty, it's not so long since I answered a call for help from you."

"What? Why, damn you! You draw a parallel with that? You're a—"

There was a click as the line went dead.

I pushed open the door of the booth. The street looked oddly dusty for Malaysia, which gets frequent rain washdowns. The two-story shops were all still shuttered, except for an eating place with a cart outside it on which were tubs of night soil for the paddies. The big harnessed ox was quietly chewing its cud while the owner breakfasted beyond strips of shelter curtain. You could smell the cart. The air was dead still and the morning mist hung low. I had cover walking away, total protection from helicopters.

Kuala Krai didn't have the feel of a place which had been put on a police alert for two escapees in a Fiat. The Navy hunt for us had been handicapped by a lack of liaison with the official forces for the maintenance of law and order in Malaysia and probably had been called off because of this. In these days of delicate new international balances quite a thing could be made of a buzzing on the public highway by a foreign aircraft. It was the kind of incident which could easily lead to an exchange of notes between Kuala Lumpur and London, and almost certainly someone down in that British base had thought of this and got cold feet, sending out the come-home signal.

Beyond the town, mist lay in fat tentacles across the road. I walked on the verge for silence, thinking about that cry for help from Betty which had reached me the night before I left on my excursion to Thailand. She was quite right. My response then hadn't earned me anything like the return service I was asking.

Clem had moved to the back seat of the vintage model, where the springs had stood up better to long service. He was curled up, with his eyes shut, his bad arm tucked in against his stomach. The bandages were still caked with jungle slime, which had dried off earlier, but was wet again from blood. He didn't speak at once and when he did it was without looking at me.

"Well?"

"Everything's fixed up. A plane coming. No sign of alarm out for us. We just have to wait. I've remembered I put some chocolate in that pouch. Like some for breakfast?"

"No. And don't ask me how I'm feeling."

"I didn't tell our pilot to bring morphia. Thought it might discourage him from coming."

"That's all right. A portion of pain is man's lot."

"There'll be a first-aid box in the plane. But if we try to use it that'll mean questions for which I haven't any answers."

"Stop worrying. Just get me to that private doctor. You've laid that on, too?"

"Yes."

"Once again let me congratulate you on your organization in this country. I wish mine were as good."

I ignored that.

"Mickey shouldn't see your arm. I've got a windbreaker we'll fit you into somehow."

"I'm in your hands," he said, without gratitude.

I sat down on the wide running board which was a feature of the Fiat, putting my chin in my fists. A few rows over from us, a Tamil was making the day's first incisions in tree trunks and lowering the drip cups to catch the latex. If he was interested in an old car parked with two men waiting, he had long ago learned to mind his own business. The Tamils have polished up the art of strict neutrality in a country where they are a racial minority not much liked by either the Chinese or the Malays. The tapper might be excited about the plane when it came in, but telephones weren't part of his world at all and he would never think of running to one.

58

I thought about Betty going back upstairs and into a cool box just large enough to hold twin beds. Tom and she lived in a sprawling wooden house of the type it isn't practical to air-condition; the best you can do is establish refrigerated areas. I wondered why they bothered even with that box. The temperature in their marriage was already cool enough not to require any artificial sixty-five degrees. She would be too angry at me to sleep again. Our relation, such as it was, continually provoked positive reactions of this kind, which was probably the main reason why she kept on seeing me. If what we had was love, then there's not much coziness in that state.

The sound which reached me was like a sewing machine motor under whining strain from a loose driving belt. I identified it and stood up. As the 'copter came low over the screening roof of rubber trees Clem said:

"They haven't even taken time off for breakfast."

The road out beyond us, which was wide enough for Mickey's Piper, was just perfect for a 'copter, and once they were down on it we had no cover at all. The area under these cultivated raw producers is kept neat and tidy, with visibility stretching for long distances down geometrically planted rows. And if we tried to drive out after their landing, I suspected they might now be irritated enough to use bullets, at least at our tires.

"What do we do, friend?" Clem asked.

"Hold our breaths."

The green above was being flayed. I decided right then that I hated helicopters; you can do too much with them.

The Tamil saved us. Not a lot happened in his patterns and that clattering just above the crop he worked was too much; he had to see. He ran over thick leaves, stumbling once, then almost falling out onto the road just at the moment a wheel of the undercarriage came dropping into our line of vision.

The man might have been killed. He was certainly caught by that downthrust and put flat on his face against laterite. This enraged him. He got to his knees, a very black face lifted, one arm gesturing, indicating fury at this interference with quiet routine.

All books of service rules have passages in small print about how to treat the natives of a country you are patrolling, and those wheels suddenly went up again. The Tamil got on his feet. He seemed remarkably unafraid for someone of a race which is on the whole timid. And that presence beneath them of a man clearly interrupted on his lawful pursuits

59

changed the pilot's mind about a ground check of this area. The choppers continued their lift and the noise diminished.

"Search resumed at dawn," Clem said. "Mist and all. Who says the British Navy goes home at the first excuse these days? This calls for an overall reassessment."

"Have you thought how interested they are going to be in a private plane landing here in a matter of minutes?"

"I told you hours ago this wasn't going to work."

But I thought it still might. The helicopter couldn't have a forward speed of more than a hundred knots, which meant that if the Piper was able to land and take off again without interference, we could get away in it from air pursuit. At the same time it would be easy enough for the 'copter to pick up the light plane's markings and all kinds of messages to all kinds of people could result from that, which might mean that we were met at Kuala Lumpur airfield. If I had been on my own it would have been simple enough; I'd have asked Mickey to put me down somewhere over the mountains, from which point Ohashi could have come to fetch me in the Mercedes. But travel arrangements involving delay to establish alibis weren't the answer for Clem at the moment. I didn't like the way in which, between efforts to talk, he kept closing his eyes, as though without light pain was more endurable.

I climbed into the driver's seat and switched on the engine.

"We're going someplace?"

"Back into cover. There's scrub over at the edge of the rubber. I can nudge the car in and hide it."

"What's the good of that when our Tamil friend has only to gossip over his lunch break?"

"I'll deal with the Tamil," I said.

"He knows too much to be allowed to live?"

Clem's cracks were beginning to earn the silences they deserved. It was bumpy driving and almost beyond the Fiat's capabilities, but we made it, finding a clump of bamboo young enough to bow and let us in. Whether anyone would get that car out again under its own power was another matter.

"That was a horrible ride," Clem said.

I left him, hidden with the car, and walked toward the Tamil, who was back now at his rubber tapping but saw me coming. Long before I was really near I noticed the whites of his eyes. He was a senior man, entrusted with cutting the trees, a specialized job, and one he did on his own. Any excess of human activity in his area made him jumpy.

60

My Malay greeting didn't seem to be reassuring, either. He was old enough to remember the troubles in the country and to associate the European with these. Already he was quite certain that a machine skimming his trees had something to do with two people sitting in a car. He wiped the palms of his hands on the lower part of a white shirt and faced me, a finely featured little man, almost coal black, with a feminine delicacy in slim wrists, thin arms, and enormous, sensuous eyes that would be a good feature for his daughters to inherit.

The southern Indians are a much nicer people than they are given credit for being either in their own country or abroad. They have been used for centuries to domination by tougher specimens than themselves, against whom their main resistance has nearly always been a pliant gentleness as though, like well-rooted reeds, they had learned to bend and let the rough winds blow over. They are still, however, capable of sudden, explosive surges of anger, which have proved the sharpest embarrassment at times to their bosses in New Delhi or in plantation bungalows. The ones in Malaya were brought in as indentured workers long enough ago to have allowed them two and even three of their shortish generations in the country, after which they are still in a sense aliens and highly suspicious of any attempts to intrude on their tightly coherent immunity. They remember that the Japanese chopped off a good many of their heads and suspect that the Chinese and Malays might also do the same if the right opportunity arose. The white man has left their heads alone but has a long record of exploiting their labor for big company dividends. He, also, is looked at without love.

"I'm in trouble," I said, again in Malay.

That was *my* problem. A direct appeal brought no warmth into liquid eyes. His lips moved, but not for words.

"I need your help and I'm willing to pay for it."

The very slight altering of his expression said that money is always useful.

"I can't give you cash. But I'll send it. Do you have an address I can use? I'll send a postal order for two hundred dollars. All you have to do is say that you saw no one in this rubber. A plane is going to land soon, and you can tell them about that. But not that you saw us getting onto it. Understand?"

He spoke then.

"They wouldn't believe me."

"Then say you were in another part of the wood and saw nothing."

"My work is here today, *Tuan*."

"You went off to have a look at the work you had done yesterday. You just heard the plane. Two hundred dollars for that. And you can make it the truth by going away."

"For this you pay me?"

"Yes. Have you a pencil? Write your name and address on a piece of paper."

"The *Tuan* will not pay after," he said with simple cynicism.

"I can only tell you that I will. I do not lie."

He smiled. It was a comment on his experience of the West. But in the end he produced a notebook, in which were jottings, probably notes on his trees, and with decided reluctance at the extravagance, tore a sheet from the back. He put down his name and address carefully, wetting the tip of the pencil with his tongue before writing. I put the paper in a trouser pocket and when he saw me doing this he was frightened of having committed himself, of allowing greed to triumph over prudence. He wanted then to run away. He turned back to his tree as to a norm for comfort, putting out a hand to bark he had himself scarred with a sharp knife. My need for his help was something alien, intrusive.

The Tamil was put to the test almost at once. I was just back at the bamboo screening when there was a noise from the main road, the grinding of gears as a car turned off onto that wide laterite estate track. Clem was sitting up straight on the back seat.

"Planter's jeep?" he asked.

"No, police."

"Sure?"

"Inspired guess."

"Hope you've dealt with our friend the woodcarver?"

I hoped so, too. From behind bamboo we saw one of those long, low cars which are official status symbols in emergent nations. Out of it got three men in white uniforms. Almost at once they spotted the Tamil and there was a shout of the kind which means business. The Tamil went at a trot. He stood with a drainage ditch between him and the police while I just waited for an arm to lift and point straight at us. I thought about tire tracks; there were plenty of them, a churning up of leaf mold which the slightest excursion under rubber would have revealed. But the morning was getting warmer, and the car certainly had an air-conditioner. The police got back into it, not thinking much of Tamils, reversing up the road with gearbox whining.

The tapper stood watching them go, then turned slowly and stared in our direction. I considered adding a bonus of fifty dollars, but decided against it. There was no need to start an inflation in the price of good deeds.

Mickey was late, for which I was thankful. The chopper was now completely inaudible, probably bumbling over some other estate looking for a dangerous Red called Harris known to be on the run with an American security man who, though wounded, was going to bring his man back to base in his own way and in his own time. Now that I had the minutes in which to assess things, I realized that this was a pretty black Thursday morning for me, in fact just about a rock-bottom morning in a career which had known a fair number of totally joyless days. I leaned back against that old car, longing for a cigarette I didn't have. I don't know what Clem was longing for—probably sedation and a bed with white sheets.

"I'll take that chocolate now," he said some time later.

I turned.

"Feeling better?"

"No. But my blood sugar is low."

He ate slowly. Watching him didn't make me hungry. He had good teeth for his years and crunched without any nervousness about fillings, looking into the middle distance as he did this. I marveled again how little time had battered Clem's face. It wasn't just the youthfulness which still shone through pain and mud splashes, but youth's total self-absorption as well, which gives massive insulation against any outside penetration into a sealed core of private thought processes. He was a man who would, in the end, be too much for any woman, no matter what enthusiasm she brought to the task of training him to heel, and I remembered that his wife had left him. I wondered if tears had come into those Prussian blue eyes that day.

"I know you hate Europe," I said. "But what's your ancestry in it?"

He swallowed.

"I don't hate Europe, just limeys. My father was one. Everything good came out of England, according to him. And everything bad from the rest of the world. He was a college professor in Omaha. Which is a strange place for an Anglophile. It made for a curious home life. And turned me into a

63

hundred-percent flag-waving stars-and-stripes boy, which lasted until I went into journalism. Then I lost my wild patriotism, probing American motivations."

"Your mother was English, too?"

"Oh, God, no. She was a Polack married in a moment of aberration by the professor. How do you like my neurotic background?"

"Not much."

"I didn't, either," Clem said. "But I'm right where I should be in this service. It takes a real nut case to get past the psychiatric screening we're subjected to."

We heard a plane engine. Carefully I fitted Clem into the windbreaker. In this he looked like a wrapped-up but still not disguised casualty of the wars. Pain had again bleached his tan.

"How much did you pay that Indian to go away?" he asked.

I told him.

"Private enterprise certainly can hand it out."

"Saving you is becoming more than a legitimate business expense," I said.

He looked at me.

"Send the invoices to Washington. You'll get a printed letter of thanks back from the head of CIA. But no money."

He was just slightly wobbly on his feet.

"Lean on my shoulder?"

"No."

We plodded out into rubber and along under it, me watchful, Clem passive. The sound of the plane engine grew louder. The laterite road I had chosen wasn't in itself very wide, but it was a dead straight along the edge of a good half-mile of rubber and with enough clearance beyond two ditches for the Piper's wingspan. Any error of judgment on the pilot's part in landing would see him with a total wreck on his hands and I didn't know a great deal about Mickey's flying experience beyond the fact that he always seemed able to get home safely after a big night at the club, back up into his mountains in time for that first muster. And people who travel around in planes after high alcohol intake either pick up some sharp subconscious skills or die early.

We stood just in the shade, watching him come in. He flirted with the tops of rubber trees, throttled back, came down at about seventy to a few feet above the road, chose a new area on it, went up, then down again, skimming along packed red clay without even a bounce, the wings wobbling a shade but everything splendidly under control. The final braking stopped the plane a hundred yards up from us and we were making slow progress toward it when Mickey jumped down to come running back with all the eagerness of a puppy just let out for its morning walk.

"Hello, chaps. Sorry I'm a bit late."

We weren't. He stopped then, gazing at us, and I got the impression that the way we looked gave him something of a shock.

"Engine was a bit gummy," he said, with a few degrees less brightness.

He had an almost round face under remnants of what had once been sleek blond hair. His eyes were blue, but pale, washed with gray from the English skies of his youth. The tropics and years of gin had mottled a once delicate skin which had always gone pink on exposure, never brown.

"What do you mean—gummy?" I asked.

"Plug, I should think. Have it seen to in K.L. I say, you two look as though you'd been having it rough."

"We have."

He stared in at the dark rubber aisles, suddenly uneasy about having taken on this hire.

"There's no one with a gun in there," I said. "Our troubles are over now you've arrived. Just get us home and accept our grateful thanks."

He hadn't made the trip to earn thanks and this showed on his face.

"Together with the commercial price per flying hour," I added.

The Piper had been bought secondhand from a Singapore *towkay* who had thought it would be a good way to avoid the professional kidnappers lined up along the route to his summer palace, but he had got cold feet on this form of transport after being caught in a violent heat thermal over Johore Bahru, and had returned to armored Cadillacs. The plane had been a bargain once, but had flown a great many air miles since, and you could see quite clearly a number of places on the bodywork which Mickey had touched up from a can of quick-drying enamel.

While Clem and I climbed thankfully up to the cabin, our pilot fussed around outside like a used-car owner who has decided to make the old job do for another season. We heard him kicking the tires.

65

Clem's breathing began to get noisy again, and just at the sill of the door he sagged. I caught him round the waist and swung him inside, past the front seats to the back, where he would be less conspicuous. I got him down and saw that his eyes were shut. Fastening a seat belt took some doing and in the end Clem was more or less propped upright by it, not looking at all like a happy traveler. Mickey still hadn't joined us and I peered down to see him worried, as though he had finally confirmed a hairline crack in wing metal.

"Let's get going," I said loudly.

He swung himself up slowly, and as he was doing it I glanced down the road that was our takeoff runway. Turning onto laterite from the highway was a car I had already seen that morning, the one containing men in uniform.

Any discussion of the situation, to say nothing of explanations, would have taken time we didn't have. I dropped into the pilot's seat. As the prop began to revolve, I caught sight of Mickey's face in the doorway—astonishment, then outrage. I gunned the motor and what he said was lost.

"Shut that door!"

I got the brakes off and had us moving before he had quite done this. He seemed to be struggling with a lock in a kind of lunatic frenzy before turning on me. I counted on sheer stark terror as my ally to keep him inactive, and got it.

"No!" he bellowed. "No!"

The car, as I'd hoped it would, stopped. Then it began to reverse, rocking from side to side on the estate road in an escape bid. Jolting vibration eased as I got one Piper wheel off laterite, then stopped altogether. We were airborne. Mickey screamed. I saw that he was worried about what was happening to the wings. So was I.

We cleared the car roof by a foot or two and the jungle beyond the highway by some inches.

"For God's sake don't hold this angle!" Mickey howled. "You'll stall her!"

So I leveled out a bit and the engine note altered. I was sweating. I got a glimpse of Mickey's face. It was awash, a kind of livid green underneath wet. The altimeter said two hundred feet. That seemed to me quite an achievement.

"You take her," I said.

"Not now! Get some height!"

So I got some height, trying to remember everything I had been taught at the Singapore flying club before I became a dropout. And that was some years ago.

66

At about a thousand, and with the engine only knocking slightly from strain put on a faulty plug, Mickey said in the voice of a broken man:

"Level off."

So I leveled off, rather neatly. Mickey said:

"Never in all my life have I had a couple of minutes as horrible as those."

"You've led a quiet life for the Far East, old boy."

He produced a handkerchief. It was clear he hadn't yet got back enough strength to fly his own plane, much as he wanted to.

"Who were they? The car?"

"Police."

"What?"

"I don't think they were able to take down our markings. You'll be all right. Did you tell anyone you were coming up here?"

"No."

"Well, it's a long way off your beat. If you put us down somewhere and fly back to the mine, you'll be all right. I think we'll give Kuala Lumpur airfield a miss, though."

He didn't comment on that, just signaled me with one hand to vacate the seat of power, and reached over for the controls as he slithered heavily across my body. I could smell his fear. For a long time we seemed to go trundling straight at a mountain on a flight course of one thousand feet. Then he banked and we ascended spirally, the menacing rough country slowly spinning away beneath. The airspeed indicator said ninety knots. I glanced back to see Clem still with his eyes shut, apparently spared all excitements.

"Do you have a flying license?" Mickey asked, his voice grim.

"Not now."

This was stretching the truth slightly, since my flying credits consist of one twenty-five-minute solo up over a flat field. And when I landed that time my instructor, who had been wearing his crash helmet on the ground just in case I missed the marked places and swung over to take him in even where he stood sheltered by a shed door, came over and said very politely, "I think maybe you ought to stick to boats and fast cars, Mr. Harris." I have always listened to authoritative advice, though my experiences at the controls still enable me to be critical of the way a captain of a Boeing 727 brings in his ship to the tarmac. There are good, indifferent, and bad land-

67

ings, and as an expert on the last I recognize these when I feel them.

It was nice to just sit in that plane with our troubles behind us and the pilot alongside being extra careful. We were high enough to avoid serious bumps and the flight was suddenly tranquil, if a shade on the slow side, still around ninety. Over the main spine of Malaysia to the starboard there was a bank of what looked like thunderclouds, these spiked by peaks and held apparently motionless. We were in bright sunlight and I glanced down at the jungle below, at once seeing a shadow traveling over it which was a little too far ahead to be ours.

The 'copter was doing more than our ninety knots and, while I watched, it decided to come up. The way they did that was unnerving, a straight ascent at speed.

"Mickey, what's your ceiling?"

"About twenty thousand. Why?"

"Get to it."

"I will not."

"We're being followed. Look down."

He did.

"It's just the Army," he said.

"Navy. And get up. As steep a climb as you can."

"Paul, what the hell is this?"

"If he picks up your markings, you're in trouble. With us."

"What kind of trouble?"

"Quite big."

"I'm not risking any steep climbs with that plug." Then he added bitterly, "Thanks a lot for involving me in all this. Thanks a lot."

We began to climb, the angle not impressive. That ascent below us, coupled with forward progress at the same time, was much more so.

"What's the Navy got against Harris and Company?" Mickey shouted.

"At the moment more than I like. Can't you risk a bit of speed?"

"I don't want to have to walk out of primary jungle. If we survived the crash."

"Make for cloud cover over the main range."

"That cloud's rough."

He was thinking about hairline cracks, and all the holes he had filled up with plastic metal.

"If we head toward the high peaks they won't try to come up with us. And you could fly over that cloud."

"Not this morning I couldn't. I'll take you to Kuala Lumpur. And I've never had a load I'll be happier to dump."

He wasn't a man for the little emergencies. I looked at Clem. His eyes were open now. What he was thinking was not available for public issue. What I thought was that a little further delay in getting Clem medical attention was now unavoidable. At K.L. we might easily be arrested on touchdown. If you irritate the police in one place they send out quick messages to colleagues in the place they think you're making for. Our flight south had been observed.

"Change of plan," I said. "We'll go over the main range to Kampar. You can land on the edge of the club course. I've seen it done. Name your price, Mickey. I'll pay."

"That's right, rub my nose in how you can buy anything. Well, you can't buy me another life."

"Seven hundred and fifty dollars to Kampar."

He said something I didn't hear. I guessed that he was thinking about that house in Majorca he and his wife were building against an early and permanent escape from the Far East. The place was costing much more than he had expected because he was being forced to put in an artesian well. With all the people from northern Europe squeezing onto those Mediterranean islands, it won't be long before the limited water on them is more expensive than whiskey in Scotland. You go to the sun to have a swimming pool and then can't afford to put anything in it. Escapism is becoming a highly complex proposition these days. California has got "no vacancy" signs all over it like a rash and the French won't allow anyone but millionaires approved by de Gaulle into Tahiti. As for the West Indies, the only place where you can still buy land is on one of those small islands with a large volcano which the estate agents hope isn't going to erupt before the development is all sold out. Mickey needed money for his little slab of paradise where the brandy may still be cheap but nothing else is.

"One thousand dollars," I said.

"Damn you!" he said.

I was losing another friend. It seemed less important than losing that helicopter.

Slowly we began to swing around toward the west and the altimeter went up to ten, then twelve, then fifteen thousand. Mickey was intensely worried about the noise his one little dependable engine was making and I couldn't really blame him. Our forward speed, even into the climb, reached a hun-

69

dred and eighteen, which was much better, and I peered down to see the helicopter looking discouraged. It had a full complement and a pilot who had already shown reflexes heavily conditioned by basic caution. I was fairly certain that they had not seen our markings and Mickey ought to be safe enough if he flew home at once with enough brush-on enamel to cover the whole Piper, converting it from cream and black to an all-over more muted color. I would probably have to pay for the paint, too.

"Mind if I use your phone?" I asked.

It was an extremely expensive piece of additional equipment and I wondered what had made him decide to install it. Possibly the handy instrument had been put in before the Majorca project had been decided on.

"Twenty dollars a call," Mickey said, surly.

I took up the handset. Contemporary electronic devices never fail to astonish me. In less than half a minute I was through to the Lipis exchange and the girl down there asked for my number as if I had been in a booth around the corner.

"And you are calling?"

"Kangar 2-274."

":Hold on, please, for your connection."

All telephone girls seem to have taken the same charm course. Maybe they are only rude to other women. While waiting, I noticed that the altimeter had touched sixteen thousand. We were about level with the top of the cloud bank over the main range and heading toward it. The 'copter I couldn't see anymore.

There was a sound on the line.

"Hello? Can I speak to Mr. Teng Ching Wok, please?"

"Speaking. As well as he can at this time in the morning."

"It's nearly eight o'clock."

"That's yesterday. Who are you?"

"Paul. I need your help."

"Oh, bones of my ancestors. That man again. Don't you have any respect for civilized habits? I'm still in my bed. Where are you? Down in a bazaar disguised as a Tamil holy man?"

I told him where I was. He gave no sign of being impressed or curious, only sounded disturbed that we were headed in his direction. I asked him to lay on transport to be waiting at Kangar, hinting that in my present circumstances it would be unwise for me to attempt to arrange my own.

"You mean the cops are after you?" he asked with brutal

70

frankness. "Ready to pounce on a Mercedes driven by your Japanese gunman?"

"Perhaps. Only we won't go on about it. This call might just be monitored, though I think it is a bit early for them to have thought of that. What I need is some kind of well-sprung vehicle that is closed and can travel fast. Meeting us at your racecourse. With a lilo or stretcher in it."

"You got a girlfriend with you?"

"Just an associate who needs his rest. I want a good driver. Not one of your truck men."

"What's the risk to me?"

"Not much, if you watch it. I hate to mention this, but you are slightly in my debt, remember?"

"I remember, you blackmailing bastard."

There was a moment's silence, then Teng added:

"I think I've got the very thing."

That Piper was valiant, even with a sticky plug. She got over the cloud bank, keeping in sunlight all the way and only having to make the descent through a thin blanket of gray over on the other side of the range. Kangar gave us sun again and Mickey, concentrating on technique, put the plane down onto grass in a gentle three-point I could never have achieved in ten years of practice.

"Thanks," I said. "You'll get your check."

There wasn't a word from the pilot. I looked out of the window. The transport was waiting. The Teng family money had been built up by a process of slowly acquiring all the businesses around the town which were still likely to flourish even in a recession year. One of them was undertaking. He had sent us a black hearse without windows.

FIVE

I sat out on the lawn of my house in Kuala Lumpur waiting for the results of surgery. Betty had made no suggestion that I function as her assistant, having already organized my houseboy for that role. The cold calm of her reception of us had held a strong hint that I was to be dealt with after the patient. Clem had showed no signs at all of any prejudice against women doctors, just very glad to see someone in a white coverall who looked qualified to get to work on him.

Home felt extremely restful. I stared at the view while chain-smoking cheroots, feeling human again after a cleanup, if very short on sleep. Far below in Batu Road the traffic was thick, car windshields flashing heliographs up to my hill. There were a lot of things to be done immediately and I didn't want to do any of them, for all that Ohashi, as one of the reception committee waiting on the veranda, had sent me a number of facial signals about an urgent need for top-level action in the affairs of Harris and Company. I hadn't sent any messages back. Whatever the crisis my number two had been faced with in my absence, I could top it with disaster so nearly total that it seemed to defy any kind of treatment. Dashing down to the office now for an emergency conference would only result in two, instead of one, being sharply unhappy about future prospects.

For the first time in my commercial life I had a certain sympathy with the man who has left his London city office on a Friday knowing that on Monday morning that horrible tradition of ringing a bell to announce a company liquidation will be brought into play for him. This afternoon, like that poor wretch's weekend, was my respite, a short space of ticking time in which a long-established norm appears to be continuing, tea on the lawn, neighbors in for drinks, the happy laughter of expensive children, the pedigree dog yapping. The imminent bankrupt can still mix a very dry martini in the solid silver shaker which won't be his next week. He can even go for a drive in the outsize Mercedes which will shortly be in the hands of the receiver. His garage will allow him credit for petrol and he can still cash a check at his grocer's, getting the usual smiles, soon to fade.

Clem's bombshell had hit me at a time when what the Singapore press had somewhat exaggeratedly referred to as my financial empire was stretched very tight indeed. Business in the Far East these days is much more of a gamble than it is anywhere else, and the shrewd executive spends a very large portion of his active hours sniffing the air for political change of the sort which can have acute effects on his trading interests. As a result of some concentrated sniffing I had decided, together with two Chinese gentlemen in Singapore and one rich Dane, all of whom had been notably good wind-of-change prophets in the past, that the end of the Malaysia-Indonesian "confrontation" was about to happen, which meant the termination of what was really a state of war between the two countries. A new peace is a good time to get in on the ground floor with a fresh enterprise, and to the bold in such a period can come rich rewards. Harris and Company, together with its affiliates, had decided to be extremely bold, and we had pooled our resources to build up a fleet of seven small cargo vessels of about three thousand gross tons which it was our plan to operate out of Singapore through all the vast network of Indonesian islands right to eastern Papua. We were out to capture the trade which had once made very prosperous indeed a subsidiary of the Nederland East Indies Line, an area of commercial activity sadly neglected for the past decade as a result of Sukarno's deep prejudice against doing business with those he calls so charmingly the "neocols."

The Lindquist, Harris, and Hok Lin Shipping Company had been incorporated in Kuala Lumpur with the idea of trying to operate out of now independent Singapore, but, if this became too complex, using Penang as our home port. We had been lucky enough to get hold of three slightly too old ships of the right tonnage and draft in Europe and were building four more in Norwegian, Dutch, German, and Japanese yards, having been priced out of Britain by rising labor costs. Already the new company was facing problems. Our three old ships were on the way to us and general conditions over in Java hadn't improved to the point where we could start trading, due largely to Sukarno's fantastic skill at holding onto office even when apparently stripped of power. "Bottoms," as the trade calls them, not in active use, are a steady financial drain and it was beginning to look as though we might have to wait quite some time for any returns at all to balance a massive outlay.

My personal bill for a fourth share in all this had come to three-quarters of a million sterling, which is more money than I keep in post office savings. I had gone to my bankers for half a million, offering as security Harris and Company's junk trading together with my shares in the Dolphin engine consortium of Johore Bharu, in which I have a 45 percent interest. Security was good and the banks had played with me, smiling. The remaining quarter of a million totaled all my private funds for old age.

We had issued no public stock in the new company, keeping this as a reserve for the future, but if there had been a market quotation it would have remained sound enough despite delays to a trading start. Time was clearly on our side. What would certainly not be on our side was any disaster to Harris and Company which forced my major bread-and-butter activity into liquidation. And Clem, now my reluctant house guest, had the power to bring this about simply by issuing one public statement that I had been gunrunning into North Vietnam.

I was still too dehydrated from the jungle to be sweating as I sat under a sun umbrella, but in my normal physiological state I would have been. The facts were gruesomely simple. The news that I was dealing in arms to the Far Eastern Reds and, in consequence, sharply out of favor with Uncle Sam in the Orient, wouldn't now put me in any jail, but it could still mean the cancellation of contracts by nearly all the small traders who regularly shipped in my junks. There were other bottoms available—it is a competitive field—and no Chinese or Indian merchant wants the label of being a user of vessels blacked by the United States. It could be very bad for their business in the years ahead. And because of this I would soon have my entire fleet of motorized junks lying empty and silent in their home ports of Bintulu, Penang, and Alor Star, with the crews clamoring for severance pay.

I tried to take a little comfort from the thought that the death of Kim Sung had eliminated Clem's solid evidence against me, but I knew perfectly well that an unofficial leak about one of my ships caught gunrunning could still mean the end of Harris and Company.

If this were to happen, what about my partners in the new

74

L.H.&H. Shipping Line? I am old enough not to nurture too many illusions about business associates. I am fond of old Lindquist down in Singapore, who is, in the private areas of his living, a sentimental man, doting on his grandchildren and prone to easy tears. But when it comes to his commercial interests those tears just dry up. I would have his deep sympathy freely given and he would almost certainly come up with a solution to my problems, sorting these out for me like a benign daddy.

It was the benign daddy I was afraid of, because I could foretell Lindquist's plan right down to the small print. He would point out that a respectable new business venture just set on its feet could naturally not afford to have the name of a gunrunner on its notepaper, therefore I had to be bought out. But buying me out wouldn't involve any actual payment at this stage. He would therefore, from the goodness of his old heart, take over my indebtedness to the now snarling bankers in lieu of that directorship and as a personal obligation in memory of his old friend, my father. As for the cash I had sunk in what would now be known as the Lindquist and Hok Lin Shipping Company, I could expect, in due course, to receive a handful of shares when there was a public issue of these, which could be any time in the next fifteen years providing trade was good.

As I now saw things extremely clearly indeed, I was about to be stripped of my junks and left stark naked out in business areas where I had long been accustomed to moving about expensively clothed. It also seemed highly probable that I would somehow be squeezed out of my holdings in Dolphin Engines. When a business of my kind starts sliding, this process almost invariably turns into an avalanche.

It was getting near to one of those situations in which a man sometimes decides not to stay in a world where he can no longer reach out for the silver shaker. But that wasn't my reaction. I was beginning to get good and angry.

Betty Hill was good and angry, too. She stood in front of me suddenly, with all traces of her recent professional activities peeled away, a woman just touching thirty, wearing a simple green linen dress and about to give someone a piece of her mind.

"You look relaxed," she said, still acid.

People in the medical business are not always as highly observant as they like to believe. I stood.

"Sit down."

75

"No, thank you. I must go home."

"How's the patient?"

"He'll live."

"I was afraid of that," I said.

Betty has brown eyes. It's not a color in which ice is usually noticeable, but it was now.

"So he's not a friend of yours?"

"I've had guests I loved more."

"Doing your duty by him?"

"Put it like that."

She took a deep breath.

"I'm not going to say anything, Paul, about your involving me in this. I came after all. The choice was mine."

"Betty, I'm sorry."

"You're not in the least. You've never at any time really stopped to consider other people. It's the secret of your success."

She was being unfair. I had been considering her husband for over a year. Betty and I were not lovers. Tom had always seemed to me the major reason for this.

"Your friend," she said, "is going to need a few things. A nurse for one. Night duty at least."

"He's as bad as that?"

"Yes. He must have plasma soon. I can get it, but I can't get the drip apparatus. I mean, I can't just walk into my hospital and borrow the gadget for an unspecified use. A surgeon's black bag doesn't contain very much these days. As a matter of fact, I don't carry one. I use sterilized instruments kept in the theater and I don't have a personal bone saw with my initials on the handle. All this creates quite a problem when it comes to treating patients illegally."

"I'm sure I can get hold of everything you need."

"I'm certain you can. So here's the list. I want all these things waiting when I call again this evening. And the nurse arranged for."

"The nurse must be here by tonight?"

"I have no intention of sitting up with the patient myself."

"This is going to be tricky, Betty."

"I'm sure."

"You haven't a lead for me?"

"None. There are three private nursing services in Kuala Lumpur. If you try to use any one of them I should think it will mean the police in your house by tomorrow noon at the latest."

"Couldn't I get hold of someone who had retired from practice?"

"Not through me you couldn't. I'd say that this is a time to get in touch with one of your shady Chinese friends. How about that outsize playboy you once introduced me to? Who lives up north somewhere. I forget the name."

"Teng," I said. Betty hadn't liked my friend, which perhaps wasn't surprising.

She nodded.

"I'd have thought him just the man to arrange something like this."

She had a point; he was.

"Betty, you'll be coming back again yourself?"

"I've said I would."

"Perhaps one more visit from you will be enough?"

"I've taken this on, Paul, and I'll come as often as I feel is necessary. You have a patient in your guest room who should be in a hospital. He'll be very weak for at least ten days. What I did on that arm was really major surgery. I took out two bullets. I thought you might want them."

She opened a white plastic handbag and took out something wrapped in cotton.

"Police evidence," she said, handing it over, "which could have me disbarred."

I put the cotton in my trouser pocket, where it felt heavier than the small change.

"Will . . . the patient be able to use his arm again?"

"You avoid using his name out of consideration for me? Thanks. If he gets proper treatment, that arm should be functioning normally in about six months. I'm good at my job. But I may say I don't like acting as my own anesthetist. That, too, is a complete specialization these days. We all work in our specific compartments with very little overlapping. Only abortionists form complete units in themselves. I suppose I have that career in reserve if my name is scored off the medical register."

"That won't happen."

"Your guarantees don't amount to much in this area, Paul. There are some things your money can't settle. And I've just one more thing to say. When your house guest doesn't need me any longer, you and I are not meeting again."

"In a place like Kuala Lumpur that will cause more talk than if we did."

"I don't care!"

"I have an invitation to your cocktail party and I'm coming to it. Tom would think it odd if I didn't."

"What Tom thinks is no concern of yours."

There was something else on her mind. She had meant to hold it there, but suddenly couldn't.

"Paul, I bitterly resent what you said on the phone about my having wailed for help that night."

"I didn't say you wailed for help. And I know I shouldn't have mentioned it."

"You did, though. Piling up my debt to you. Laying claims against it."

"Betty, I've said I was sorry."

Her eyes were wide.

"You think I needed you that night as a frail female, don't you? That I had to have the right shoulder to cry on because of what had happened?"

"Not exactly."

"Yes! I rang you after eleven that night because I had a deep human need of your company."

"What's wrong with that?"

"Just the fact that it wasn't the reason why I suddenly asked you to take me down to Morib. I just couldn't go home to Tom, that's all. I needed to get down to the sea for a swim and I didn't want to go alone."

"Betty—"

"Shut up and listen to me! Do you really think I was personally torn to shreds because that girl died on the operating table? Do you really believe that after all these years of practice I would go totally female about my job in that way?"

"Why shouldn't you?"

"Damn it, a surgeon can't! You don't tie yourself personally to a patient. I was sick, all right, sick and angry. But not because the girl died under my knife. It was not my fault. What happened wasn't because I was inefficient."

"I never thought so for a moment."

"Really? Then let me tell you who did have that thought. My assistant at the table. And my anesthetist. I saw their eyes above the masks. You know what their eyes were saying?"

She stood very erect on the grass, arms at her side, the white bag dangling from one hand, the other a fist. She might have been at attention for interrogation before a very senior officer, that hint of service experience in her bearing though I knew she hadn't had any.

"Their eyes were saying, Paul, that the girl just mightn't

have died if one of my male colleagues had been in charge of the operation."

"You imagined that."

"Imagined it? God! I wonder if you can have the faintest idea of what a woman in my job is up against? And not only in this part of the world. All right, my assistant was Chinese and the anesthetist a Tamil, and they don't really believe in women surgeons, or women anything. But I've had exactly the same looks in England when the responsibility was mine. An operation produces tension, but not emotional, nervous. This is true with every surgeon, male or female. But the woman has to contend with something more and that's a continuing male suspicion, however it may be disguised, about our basic capability in the role. When that girl died I looked up and saw exactly what I was expecting once again. The complicated operations of mine which have been successes didn't count at all. The thing right at the front of their minds then was that if Kemp had been operating, that girl might have lived."

She took a deep breath but held the rigid pose.

"Kemp! We're not supposed to say anything about our colleagues. But I'll break the rule. When Kemp is called out to an emergency at that time of night, he has had a good dinner. And a good dinner with him consists of three whiskeys first, a wine with food, and a fair whack at the brandy bottle after it. I've seen his hands shake, and not from nerves. Oh, no. He's a controlled alcoholic. But under those just slightly shaking hands the girl might have lived, because Kemp has got a slight extra something that is part of male mystique, which is so bloody well propped up by other males. That's what those eyes by the table were saying to me. And that's why I went to a phone and wailed to you and got you to drive me to the sea. I was angry. I had to cool my anger."

I remembered her tears.

"Betty, what's wrong with caring about your patient?"

She stared.

"I've told you! In that way the patient doesn't exist to the surgeon."

She swung around and walked off across my lawn. It is a wide lawn and it took her some time. She had the trim figure of the tennis player she was. The game strengthened her wrists, something she needed professionally. She wore her brown hair in one of those short, chopped-all-over haircuts which only require a comb run through them to look smoothly sophisticated, if you can find the right cutter. Betty had, probably a little woman she had trained herself, demonstrating what she wanted done with a pair of dissecting scissors.

I waited until I heard her car drive off and then sat down again. I remembered that the thing which had struck me at our first meeting was that Betty didn't care whether she was looked at as a woman or not. It was her big act for the world.

Ohashi shared with his age group, and behind certain Japanese mannerisms, that remarkable confidence in his own powers which is something that seems to be pretty universal these days, skipping lightly over national frontiers. It is fine that the young are sure of themselves and able to claim the rewards that this state deserves, but it might be finer if their assurance weren't based on the apparent assumption that their generation has inherited from us a unique shambles, something that could never have come about under their control. Further, there is a considerable resentment that they have to spend so much of their valuable time rejecting our mess, either by protest or in more positive reorganization. Behind Ohashi's carefully groomed politeness I had detected this impatience often enough, and it was in his voice now on the phone from our office.

"Oh, I'm so glad you are now calling, Mr. Harris."

I had made him a partner but he hadn't accepted the invitation to call me Paul. His deliberate avoidance of the casual might be due to a Japanese need to have someone on high toward whom a continuing obeisance of respect was almost obligatory, but I suspected that it was more likely to be his desire to keep the line of age demarcation firmly drawn between us.

"Well, what's up?" I asked.

"Not good things. Mr. Lindquist in Singapore has rung me up many times in the last two days. Always he is asking where you are."

"Did you say elephant hunting?"

"I say nothing."

"Give me the crisis."

"It is most serious. Government in Java is playing the field in connection with inter-island trading."

"How?"

"Last week arrive in Djakarta, German mission from

Hamburg Bremen Lloyd Company. For negotiations regarding small ships built especially in German yards to do job planned for our shipping company."

"But they have no ships yet?"

"True. At the same time grave dangers of signing contract to build these with German efficiency. To operate under profit-sharing arrangement with Indonesian government."

"The devil," I said.

"Most serious," Ohashi agreed. "Mr. Lindquist in much distress. Over the telephone he is shouting."

"And what's his idea?"

"That you must go to Djakarta yourself. At once. On behalf of new company interest."

"That would be fine. Only there is still officially a price on my head over in Indonesia."

"I beg your pardon?"

"Something from before your time, Ohashi. But those people boast that they have long memories. I think if I showed up in Java I'd land in jail, at least. So for the time being this neo-col isn't risking it over there. One of the other partners will have to represent our interests. I suggest Mr. Hok."

"I also make this suggestion. But Mr. Hok say political climate still unhappy for Chinese."

"That's true enough. It'll have to be old Lindquist himself. It wouldn't hurt him to get off his behind."

"You will phone Mr. Lindquist now?"

"No, I won't."

"What?"

"I'm not back yet, officially. You don't know where I am."

"Mr. Harris, you cannot be understanding me correctly. This is *most* serious matter."

"I'm capable of my own assessment, Ohashi. It just so happens that I have something on my hands which is considerably more serious."

"Is this possible?"

"I'm sorry to say it is. Though I wouldn't have believed it forty-eight hours ago. Now listen: I don't want you ringing me up here, or directing any messages to this house. If I want to see you I'll come to the office. Meantime you are in complete charge. If you like, you can tell them in Singapore that I rang you up from the north, where you can't get in touch with me again, and suggested that Lindquist deal with this problem himself. It'll make him angry to have to leave his air-conditioning, but he'll do it. And he'll do a good job when he gets there. They like grandfather figures over in Java. And no one has anything against the Danes, lucky people."

After a moment my codirector said:

"I am most unhappy."

"That makes two of us. Good-bye."

It took considerably longer to reach Kampar on a land line than it had from the Piper. Then I ran into the collection of secretaries which Teng Ching Wok keeps around him, all good looking. Finally I got the town's big man himself.

"Teng, I'm stretching my credit just a little further."

"You haven't any left," he said.

"What's the matter? Didn't your van get home?"

"Sure, it got home. And that's a debt settled. Anything more I do for you needs a cash down payment."

"I need a nurse," I said.

"Your nerve cracked at last? I thought your voice sounded shaky."

"A nice reliable nurse who is the soul of discretion and who doesn't know anyone in Kuala Lumpur. A trained nurse."

"I didn't think you'd adopted orphans. Why should I have nurses available?"

"You have everything available. I want her by tonight. I'll send a hire up to you to collect. The nurse will probably be needed for two weeks. An older woman. Knits in her spare time. Live in and no shopping excursions into the big city."

"I don't like this," Teng said.

"I don't like it myself. Have the woman down at the *padang* so we won't involve your offices. Fanning herself under one of the palms. She'll be picked up in a couple of hours. I'll just have time to settle her in here before leaving for that new roadhouse up at the Gap where you will be my guest to dinner."

"What?"

"We haven't had a good chat for a long time. And I'm told they got a good cook up there. A Dutchman, but trained in near French cuisine over in Saigon."

"Thank you, Paul, but the Gap is much too long a drive for me. And I have an appointment for this evening."

"Tell the girl you'll be with her tomorrow. I'll meet you up there. And give my love to your wife."

After a moment, and before hanging up, Teng said grumpily:

"Which one?"

82

I went along to look at the patient. The air-conditioning had apparently been turned up during surgery and the room had that clammy chill I don't like. I dialed sixty-five for the sake of Clem's health, then turned to the bed.

It was easy to see that blood plasma was called for. He seemed to have shrunk physically, with all the basic menace of his personality in temporary abeyance. What was left on that bed was a reminiscence of the boy who had once been, the high school cheerleader suddenly struck down by a first serious illness. He was propped up against pillows and a bandaged arm was laid across his chest. His eyes were tight shut and his breathing rate confirmed a withdrawal artificially induced. Betty had left a basin handy for postoperative sickness when he came out of a drugged sleep.

Clem would be immobile and incapable of any really positive action for about a week, if I was lucky. That was the time allotted me in which to get on good terms with the United States of America again. It wasn't a lot of time for the job involved, which meant finding out who was the Reds' top undercover man in Kuala Lumpur. The computer said he was me. I had to be the first man in the world to successfully prove a computer wrong. I didn't, right then, like my chances.

I'm a sucker for advertising, even though as a businessman I ought to know better. A really good toothpaste commercial has me switching my brands and the cigarettes I've cut down on have a special filter which takes the smoke through a new de-tarring compound not yet endorsed by any medical association. I gladly pay more for this brand than another that would let me furnish my house with free essentials like hi-fi equipment and collapsible electric underpants dryers.

I bought the Audi because I was challenged by the advertising, which wondered if I dared drive one. I didn't need another car and it isn't faster than my Mercedes, but it is a kind of personal toy and to a near bankrupt offers the additional advantage of not using a lot of fuel.

The Gap is halfway to the east coast from Kuala Lumpur, at the peak of the pass through the mountains, and my time up to it even on that twisting road was very good indeed. You drive that little front-wheel job into corners as hard as you like and she goes round them as steady as a ship fitted with stabilizers. The steering takes a little getting used to, so precise is it, and it's the ditch for the man who is casual with his hands on the wheel, but I am never casual about driving; it is an art in which I claim to be something of a perfectionist. So far I had met that advertising challenge: I had dared, and was still alive.

Teng Ching Wok believes that success in this world is something which ought to be underlined and he has a new Cadillac every year, trading in the old one with a lot of scrapes on its paintwork. I tucked my neat little box alongside the hood of a status symbol and went toward the door to the bar, pausing for a minute to sniff the mountain air, which at four thousand feet held an almost north-country coolness. A couple thousand feet higher, at Frazer's Hill, they light log fires in the evening. Malaysia is that kind of country: you can drive into near temperate zones for a few hours to escape from the tropics. This is a stimulus to clear thinking, and one I needed.

Teng had bought himself a triple whiskey and was looking gloomy over it. His outsize Chinese frame was covered by a white silk suiting over which some serf in one of his houses had labored for an hour but which was already completely rumpled. He was a man for whom the drip-dry creaseless had been invented but they weren't expensive enough. He looked up and his heavy, un-Oriental face had even more blood-hound sags in it than usual. The only thing really neat about the man was his black hair, which looked as though it had been plastered to his skull with half a pound of scented axle grease.

"Hello, old friend," I said.

"Don't give me that. I've been waiting here for twenty-five minutes. This whiskey is one of your Scotch rejects, only good enough for Oriental playboys."

"I was settling in the nurse."

He almost smiled.

"How did you like her?"

"Just what I ordered. And I'm not the one who needs her. What's her history?"

"Shady," Teng said, and drank. Then he looked at me. "My hearse driver thought your friend was an American. That right?"

"Yes."

"Are you entertaining him by force?"

"Force hasn't been necessary."

"But held in reserve?"

"I'm not making any statements."

"Which means yes. Who is he?"

84

"A tourist."

"Since when has Kelantan been tourist country?"

"Who said anything about Kelantan?"

"The newspapers," Teng told me, unfolding one from the seat beside him. "Been too busy to read?"

I had been. It was all there, right on the front page, much sooner than I would have expected. A British Navy helicopter, based on Singapore, but making a goodwill tour around Malaysia with a two-day stopover at Kuala Lipis, had been busy giving free flights to local schoolchildren in a bid to have them grow up pro-Western in outlook. Most nights it also took off on nonpropaganda short training flights for new personnel and while on one of these over the main massif had spotted a fire. Investigation had revealed a newly crashed plane burning on the runway of a disused airfield. There were no identifiable markings on the smoldering wreckage and there was no mention of anything found in that pyre. The whole thing was billed as a mystery of jungle country and was markedly lacking in any reportorial guesswork. Even before a second reading I got a strong feeling of an official handout which might or might not be followed up with more news later. There was not a word about a large number of men leaving the runway at high speed or the pursuit of two others.

"Your guest a passenger on that plane?"

I thought a moment before answering.

"Yes."

"Were you up there meeting it?"

"Yes."

He smiled, an effort his cheeks resisted.

"You must really need me to be so friendly," he said.

"I do."

The bar was empty except for a British couple having their fortnightly evening out. I knew them slightly from the club in K.L., the husband in the rather dismal job of trying to sell agricultural phosphates to bored Malay farmers who operated on the principle that when a piece of land wore out you cut yourself a new slice out of jungle. The couple had exhausted all common small talk twenty years earlier and had since taken to the bottle. They weren't even interested enough in anything anymore to listen to what we said. The wife kept lifting a cigarette to unfashionably red lips which dated her, but the husband had reached a dangerous age and wasn't smoking. In a couple of years they would be settled in Bournemouth and no happier. The days of the British raj had terminated before they were able to get in on the final pickings and the husband gave the impression of brooding about this a good deal.

Behind the bar was a Malay boy who looked a stern Moslem and therefore a total abstainer, carefully mixing Western poisons with a certain relish at the thought of what they were doing to his customers' livers. A radio played, a continuous low whining which seemed to offer the performer no break for air at all.

"What makes you think the food's good here?" Teng asked. "It doesn't have the feel of a place where the food is good. Do you know how many miles I had to drive to get here?"

A typical well-heeled Chinese, always thinking about his stomach when he isn't thinking about business. Women he never thinks about at all; just has them. I cut out all skirmishing.

"Who would you say was Mao's top man in these parts?"

"Eh?" He stared. "What kind of a question is that to ask me?"

"I couldn't think of anyone better qualified to answer it. As the headman of your own big village, and the richest *towkay* for twenty miles in all directions, you'll be down to have your throat cut if the Reds ever become ascendant again. And as a Chinese you'd make it your business to find out who was likely to authorize that throat-cutting, in order to buy him off. Unless, of course, you're Mao's man yourself."

"Very clever," Teng said. "But do you mind keeping your voice down?"

"Is Lum Ping active again?"

"How the hell would I know?"

"Teng, let's not play pat-a-cake. You'd know, all right. Kampar isn't all that far from where the man who would like to be the leader of the Malaysian Soviet Socialist Republic still lives. Are any of your people being tapped for money again?"

"Not that I've heard."

"Which probably means you make regular contributions to Lum Ping's pension fund."

"If you think paying for my dinner also pays for that kind of talk, I don't."

"Lum Ping's men attacked and burned that plane when it was on the ground. They killed everyone in it except the man in my house."

Teng had gone very still. He seemed suddenly to reject both the whiskey in front of him and his role as the man of two worlds. The bloodhound sags from good living were still there, but the sadness was synthetic.

"So you see," I said after a minute, "I know the old chief is active again. Just as you do."

He put out the delicately boned, ridiculously small hand which most of their big men still retain, fingers prodding at the mat under his glass.

"What do you want from me?" he asked, in scarcely more than a whisper.

"Information about the Red feed line into this country."

"I don't know what you mean."

"Don't you? It's this. Supplies for the Reds are coming into Malaysia, in a big way. I know it because they are going out again."

"In your ships?" he asked.

It could have been just a lucky shot, but I didn't like it. I didn't like, either, the way he turned his head to look at me.

"You haven't been caught?" he asked gently.

"I've been framed."

Teng took time to fill his lungs, then he began to laugh. He made such a row doing this that the phosphate wife looked up, more than a little shocked, and suggested to her husband that they go in to eat. The Malay boy came out from behind the bar to clear away empty glasses and then, for the first time, moved over to ask if I wanted anything, and perhaps to get in on the joke. I ordered one of his bad whiskeys.

Another boy from the dining room arrived carrying those vast menu cards which are an almost certain guarantee that everything on them comes out of tins or the deep freeze, and in haste at that. We each got one and I glared at it, trying to remember who had told me about the new chef up here. Teng, at the suggestion of food, had become deadly serious again. Even his curiosity was in parenthesis for a time.

"Oysters?" he said. "Oysters?"

"Australia," the dining room boy told us.

"Which means they'll be big and coarse. No. Rainbow trout? Ah! You know where I last had rainbow trout, Paul? Scotts, in London, a year ago."

"How am I supposed to cap that?" I asked. "With papaw in Mooréa three months back?"

Teng became absorbed in ordering, but I knew that he was also using the recess to assess how things were with me, and how change might affect the slightly curious relation between us to his advantage. It's nonsense that rich men seek each other's company in plush surroundings in order to relax with their own kind. They do it to keep their eyes and ears open while pretending to be *bons vivants*. The unguarded moment over the *flambé* has seen the start of many a commercial slide.

We went in to dinner. It seemed a long meal, with Teng watching me through most of it, and the food was undistinguished. The same radio voice had followed us through on wire, and that girl was setting an all-time record for soprano warbling. The phosphates munched without much enthusiasm on the other side of the room. There were no other customers and the claret was hot, almost mulled.

"Next time," Teng said, "take me to eat in a night stall, will you?"

We skipped liqueurs and went out to sit in the back seat of the Cadillac, where there was a liquor cabinet with cut-glass decanters, a little custom feature inserted at the customer's request. Teng did without traveling television because he drove himself, but he kept his cigars in a fitted electric humidor and they were still indifferent Manila leaf. These gourmets always slip up somewhere.

"So the Americans are after you?" he said.

I knew he now had everything worked out. The chances were that at almost any time in the last five years he could have told, without reference to his files, what my assets were down to the small change I was carrying around in my pockets. And he certainly knew the extent to which my reserves were now stretched. He knew, also, that the slightest rip in the taut fabric of my affairs could see the whole thing tearing right across, with the impressive tent collapsing smack on top of the commercial Arab who sat under it smoking his water pipe and pretending to be at peace with the world. It would be absurd not to expect a rival Arab to get a certain private satisfaction out of a neighbor's disaster. It would also be foolish not to count on Teng nipping over to see if he could steal some of the cushions out from under the unhappy victim of sudden calamity.

"What have they got on you?" Teng asked, skipping any detailed interrogation, which wasn't necessary.

"Very little, thanks to Lum Ping and a few murders."

"Was the plane some kind of confrontation?"

He was a great guesser.

"Yes."

"I see. And you now have the only man who could really damage you tucked away in your house?"

"I do."

"How long do you think you can hold things?"

"Long enough for my purposes."

"Always the optimist," Teng said.

"Sure. And I've survived some time in a fairly hostile climate. I intend to hang on. This is my country and no one is pushing me out—the Americans, Chinese, Malays, or Reds."

"Brave words."

"I can afford them, with you by my side."

He laughed again, the noise loud even in that roomy car. I decided to chill his mirth just a little.

"Look, Teng, there is a noticeable change in the climate these days in our beloved country. Coming from on high in Kuala Lumpur. Too many foreign interests have too much power still to please the local politicians. And one of the effects of trouble with Indonesia coming to an end is going to be a great upsurge of pan-Moslem feeling. Moslem ascendancy, in other words. Your people may control the economy of this country now but the break with Singapore has threatened that happy state for the lot of you. The Chinese in Java damn nearly controlled that economy, too. And look what's happened to them. The lucky ones are getting to Mao's China as refugees. That has struck me as very interesting. You wouldn't really expect so many of those free-enterprise Chinese, who made their money under capitalism, to be making a beeline to get back under the Red umbrella, but they are. Which suggests that their loyalties were pretty mixed while they operated in Java."

"You're talking about the small shopkeepers," Teng said.

"I wonder? As I see things, what happened in Java could be happening here in a few years—your people on the run, even the ones who have been here for generations."

He didn't deny this; it was one of his nightmares.

"The time may come when you'll need all your friends, Teng. At the moment I'm one of them. So stop rubbing your hands to glee over my present distresses. I want you to tell me whom you suspect to be the Reds' big man in this country."

After a moment he said:

"I couldn't even guess at that. I don't know who their man in Kampar is."

"The man I'm looking for wouldn't even have to be a resident in Kuala Lumpur. It might be safer for him not to be. It's a small country. He could do his job from anywhere in it. Do you agree?"

"I suppose so."

"But you won't help me with a hint?"

"I can't give you one."

I looked at the side of his head and didn't believe him.

"He's likely to be one of your *towkays*," I said, angry. "There are sound profits to be made out of selling out to Mao. With insurance for the future thrown in as well."

Teng said nothing. I reached for the door handle and pulled it down. Standing out on tarmac, I looked back into the car.

"It's going to be a sad day for this country when the bulk of Chinese influence in it decides that the only hope for the future lies in backing the Reds against Moslem ascendancy. A very sad day, because it won't work. Just as it didn't work in Java. A lot of you will be butchered. Good night, Teng. And if you change your mind about letting me have information send a messenger. My phones won't be working."

In the Audi I lit a tipped cigarette while doors banged as Teng changed seats. I let him away first, and followed down the mountain. The Cadillac lurched around bends designed by British engineers who were thinking of smaller cars. Teng drove with what he thought was style, but was really an invitation to an early death, the performance perhaps exaggerated by the knowledge I was tailing him and watching. With my window down because I hadn't air-conditioning, I could hear the screaming of brakes ahead. I also heard rushing water sometimes and the lights of two cars kept swinging out over black drops tapestried with jungle.

On the flat we both began to go fast, with the Audi hanging on at braking distance even when the needle climbed to eighty, eighty-five, and then hovered near ninety. I began to let him have a little more room just in case an angry man lost control, but he flashed into the Kampar fork in a glitter of rear illumination which didn't respond to the good-bye flickers from my headlights.

Kuala Lumpur glowed in the sky ahead, my home, a new nation's touchy capital, the sleepy-seeming tree-shaded city with its little hills a setting for old angers in new forms. I was alone on a long road as I had been so often before, not unhappy in the again hot tropic dark, but conscious of it as a vast area for concealment.

And I believed what I had said to Teng, that the peace of sorts we knew now could be but a respite between two horrors.

SIX

In spite of all that Western man has done in the last hundred years which is shaming, I believe that he has nonetheless done a great deal more which is not, and that in the contemporary world our role shouldn't be based on any apology for the past or paralyzing guilt from it. The guilt only earns us laughter, and is invariably interpreted as another symptom of decadence. It is probably a very good thing for the West to be burdened by conscience, but extremely bad policy to let this show when dealing with races who haven't yet evolved one.

I see the situation in Southeast Asia in terms of basics, and for me the basic in dealing with Red China, at least at the moment, is a line drawn and a firm statement: "Not a step beyond this." Such a statement may be morally indefensible in terms of enlightened liberalism, but against the plain, cold facts of continuing Chinese aggression it is effective. Further, it is something that the old man in Peking, and his generals and their successors, can't possibly misinterpret. I would be the first to admit that much of the Southeast Asia Mao hasn't yet taken over is in a mess, but I don't think the answer to that mess is to withdraw and let him have it. My stake is here, of course, which certainly prejudices me.

As someone very far indeed from being against general US policy in this area, it made me angry to be rejected by an American computer. I drove the Audi toward my suburban residence still very much in the mood of saying to hell with the CIA and also to its man from Vietnam, for whom I was providing free board and lodging, not to mention the best of medical care, while he—with returning consciousness—would be back at plotting my ruin.

Nothing sharpens to a finer point a man's appreciation of what he has managed to build up in this world than a sudden threat to it all. I drove the little car up my driveway, and past those huge jungle trees I had preserved with such care, feeling that if I lost all this I lost my roots. And I liked my roots.

They were well dug in to pretty fertile soil, watered regularly by heaven and sending out up above huge, top-quality leaves as an end product.

The steel-mesh gate recently installed stopped me halfway on a sharp gradient and a flick of headlamps brought out my Sikh watchman, who was trying not to yawn. He took one look, then reached back into the concrete sentry hut to pull down a lever which released the gates and broke the electric current running all around my hilltop through steel fencing. Such precautions may seem a shade elaborate, but it is a country in which kidnapping the prosperous for ransom has become a top profession, and sometimes the mood hits me to sleep out on the lawn under stars, where I used to be rather exposed to this form of free enterprise. I also like to have my visitors properly announced, leaving me with all of five minutes in which to think up a good reason why I'm not receiving them.

I asked Gian Singh if there had been any callers that evening and was told that the lady doctor had been allowed through, no one else. Gian Singh's duty relief was at that moment doing a circular inspection of the fencing along the path inside it before he took over at the sentry box. My private world seemed expensively peaceful as usual.

One advantage of an adquate perimeter defense is that you can leave the house behind open to the night without worrying about bolts pushed home. Since my bungalow was of the sprawling type with arches onto verandas, it had, before the fencing, been a very bad burglary risk, but I now had my premium cut by 60 percent. The inspector from the company had been particularly impressed by the electric current.

"Would kill?" he asked during our tour.

"Not unless you had a weak heart. Only meant to knock you out."

"Children dangerous?"

"They couldn't possibly climb up. There isn't anything to climb on."

The mesh was far too fine for finger holds and the well-spaced support columns were each wired to an alarm device which rang a bell in my bedroom and the guard box if anyone leaned a weight against them. The live wire ran ten feet above the ground and though a patient man with the proper cutters could have carved himself a hole into my grounds beneath this, he would have been sadly disappointed when, after patient effort, a hidden cable in long grass announced what he had been up to. I had put a good deal of thought into my defenses and so had the security company who sent in the bill for them. In a troubled world if you want peace of mind you have to pay for it.

In my dimly lit hall there is a Japanese wax warrior, life size, picked up cheap at a Singapore auction, and now standing guard in full fighting armor with spear up at the ready. Looking at that defensive equipment of another age suggested that my own system might have also been designed to keep house guests from straying. When Clem was recuperating out in the garden, still pretending to be feeble, he would find a sudden dash for freedom and contact with his own local agent a somewhat frustrating procedure. Though he probably knew all about my fencing, along with everything else.

I went down to the sickroom. Teng's nurse was there, and I had to admit, looking at the woman, that I wouldn't have enjoyed coming back from a private dark to find her in attendance. Whatever had blasted her professional career, and I was sure from a first meeting that something had, she accepted the twists of fate with a gay spirit. Under black oiled hair pulled to a bun on her neck, and decorated with a pin ornament, her broad, just slightly greasy face at once suggested the comedienne. For death she had laughter, and for total disability giggles.

There was a plasma drip apparatus which would be charged to me—or my receivers—standing by the bed, but no longer in use. Beneath it Clem seemed unchanged, still with that rapid breathing, the pallor under the tan, and closed eyes.

"How is he?" I asked.

The nurse got up from the cot which had been provided for her. It creaked and so did her bones under a covering of heavy flesh. She smiled happily and told me in Malay that Clem had been conscious for a time. This was apparently both unexpected and amusing. The fact that the patient had been able to drink a little beef tea provided by Chow, my houseboy, was also entertaining. There was clearly nothing for me to worry about.

To indicate that she had everything under control, Mrs. Hasmah waddled over to the bed, tugging at a sheet and light blanket, thereby clearly demonstrating her training in a calling which demands that the patient, whatever his condition,

94

must be strapped down into an invincible tidiness. A mussed-up bed and true professionalism can never live together and we are most of us doomed to die surrounded by grim, aseptic neatness. There was already a strong smell of disinfectant in the room, as though this had been sprayed about straight from the bottle onto Chow's highly polished teak floors. I felt an intruder and quite useless. Tomorrow would be time enough to see about the one bunch of flowers permitted to someone off the danger list.

I went to my own room, where I was greeted by Taro, my Tosa hound. The dog opened both eyes and thumped his tail twice against the mat which is his bed, but didn't rise because he disapproves of late hours and anything outside of a placid norm. I had noticed a certain slacking off in his sense of responsibility recently, as though he realized that the new fence relieved him of most of his job, and was quite pleased about this. He was also putting on a bit of weight, which meant that his walks were being adapted to Chow's convenience, something on which I would have to take action.

Taro watched me getting into pajama trousers, certain that I meant to read in bed, which he doesn't like at all. When all I did was put the Colt I had worn to dinner on the table near my pillow and then switched out the light, he sighed. Five minutes later there were snores.

I lay in the dark considering the possibility that I had been followed up to the Gap, but decided it was unlikely. My route out of the city had been devious and on the straight to the mountains the Audi had gone fast enough to shake off any pursuit. Teng didn't seem to have been tailed, either; at least there had been no one behind us on that descent of hairpin bends. I thought about Teng's ready laughter, deciding I didn't like it at all.

The dog's growl woke me. Taro is no alarmist, but he is also a great dreamer, and when there was no repeat I relaxed again, though listening. My house was built all of seventy years ago, and entirely of wood, which contracts in the cooler hours, this resulting in a small, steady orchestration of nocturnal noise. Wide board floors seem to creak under ghostly visitations from former owners and more than once I have been quite certain that the planter who originally built the place was back, pouring himself a triple gin and squeezing the fresh limes to put in it. I don't often use the air-conditioner in my room, preferring the night's own easing of heat and the subtle pleasure of stirring at about three in the morning to reach down for a blanket. Now a slight chill from the open window told me the time. There was almost no noise from the city.

I was just dropping off again when Taro bellowed action stations. His bark, when angry, seems to come from well down in his guts, a special tone. I heard him make for the window, then the thud of his paws on the veranda beyond it. I didn't follow that route, but took my Colt to the door. In the passage was a faint glow from the lamp near the Japanese warrior. I ran to another door and banged it open.

Mrs. Hasmah wasn't in Clem's room, but someone else was. A heavily shrouded light burned, enough to show Clem in the bed and a shape in front of a closed window. The shape had an arm extended out, pointed toward the bed. I fired at that arm, the Colt noisy. The plasma bottle crashed to the floor. Taro's baying seemed to be in the house again, as though he had come back to look for me. I hurled myself across the room but the shape didn't wait; the window behind had only been pulled to. I fell against the empty frame of it, one foot sending a revolver slithering across boards.

"Taro!"

The dog came from behind me, still baying. I cleared the window space for his jump through. He went out into the night again, shutting off the loud protests in his leap, switching to the hunter's growl. I didn't do a follow-up. The intruder no longer had his gun, which meant that Taro could deal with the situation on his own for the time being.

"Mrs. Hasmah!"

There was a shuffling from the corridor. I locked the window and swung away from it. Clem hadn't moved. He was still breathing at jerky speed. I went to the hall and switched on the lights. The nurse coming toward me wasn't finding this an amusing situation. Her plump face had sags in it.

"*Tuan!*" That was a wail, followed by near English. "I go pee-pee. *Tuan*, I go pee-pee."

"Just at the right moment! Why was the window in here open? The air-conditioner is switched on."

She had nothing to say, and brought plump hands up to her face, the gesture defensive.

"Look after your patient," I ordered.

She started a bleating in Malay and this followed me to the front hall. Out on the drive there was no sound at all, nothing from Taro announcing a quarry cornered, stillness until the distant rumble of heavy night transport climbing a hill some-where.

I called the dog again, then began to run down the drive toward the gates. Taro could be beyond the range of my voice, down in the heavy undergrowth on steep slopes.

Ranji Singh was emerging from his little guardhouse, an impressive white-turbaned figure, black bearded, a retired policeman with the dignified air of a man who has long defended law and order by a sheer massive weight of personality. He cerebrated slowly, and if he had heard the shot hadn't yet permitted himself alarm. The sight of me in half a pajama set didn't spark this off, either. He merely stared, as though he found something unseemly in my activity.

"Someone's inside," I panted.

He shook his head, denying this as a possibility, and was still at it when I reached him.

"A man with a gun tried to kill my guest."

Shock opened his mouth. I went into the hut. There was a lever for the gates and above this a box like those for electric cookers, in which a light glowed red when the current was running through the fence. The switch was still down but the light dead, which meant that the current had been cut from the second control point, in my bathroom. I remembered Taro's growl. It could have been someone passing through my room, a presence tolerated by the dog because my night visitor was accepted in the house.

Ranji Singh breathed heavily behind me, staring at the box with its dead eye. The light came on again, a glowing ruby. The Sikh gasped. I grabbed a flashlight and pushed past him.

Taro's silence didn't make sense. I couldn't believe that a running man had dealt effectively with my dog. The Tosa was trained to make a noise before moving in to the attack. Further, when it came to bringing down a running man, the dog knew his business. He had come out with top marks from a six-week police training course, a quicker learner than the Alsatians or Dobermans.

I ran along the path inside the wire, shining the flashlight ahead, trying to check soft earth for any signs of a landing from a jump. Getting over that fence with the current off was relatively easy. I could have designed a gadget to do it quickly enough, a telescopic aluminum ladder fitted at one end with extending bars onto which could be hooked runged rope for the getaway. All that was needed was an accomplice inside the house working switches to a synchronized timetable. With the current off, my defense system was useless.

I stopped to get my breath back halfway around my hill, just below the vegetable garden. It was very quiet.

"Taro!"

Almost at once the dog came into the light, trotting down the path, wagging his tail. I stared at him. He had cost me a lot to buy, import, and train, and I was fond of the brute as well. But right then I considered a replacement. It was his sheer happiness over inefficiency which shook me.

"And where the hell have you been?"

Taro didn't like my tone much and the tail slowed down. He paused, thoughtful, aware suddenly that the boss was a bit worked up. Things became still between us. Then there was a sudden crackling in the scrub growth not twenty yards away.

"Get him!" I said.

To redeem his reputation the dog at once leaped into action, but without a hint of a growl. I heard him thrashing up the slope and followed fast. There were loud sounds of canine joy and another noise suggesting that this wasn't being too well received. I found myself looking down on the back of a man who had suddenly given up crawling, who had, in fact, given up.

While Taro stood by with tail metronoming happiness, a head came slowly round. The man on his hands and knees was my former personal assistant in Harris and Company, now codirector, Seki Ohashi.

Taro loved him, which perhaps wasn't surprising since they were both Japanese.

I had a long drink from my double whiskey but Ohashi hadn't touched his. He kept looking at the Webley fitted with silencer, a bulky instrument found in a corner of Clem's room, solid evidence.

"All right," I said. "There was another man in the gounds and you chased him."

"Dog chase me," Ohashi complained. When he wasn't looking at the gun he stared at a Persian rug just beyond his feet.

"So you didn't see what happened to the other man?"

"No."

"I still have to find out how you got in here. Don't tell me Ranji Singh took a bribe?"

"I . . . I come in doctor's car."

"As her guest?"

98

"No. I am hiding. In trunk."

"How did you get into the trunk?"

"She stops car by gates. Waiting to open. She talks to guard. I am waiting in bushes. Trunk not locked."

Ohashi's English is normally very good these days, but slips a bit under stress. It was slipping now. He isn't a man who ever seems to sweat much, either, but his forehead was bedewed even though his chair was directly under one of my antique revolving fans.

"The doctor called about ten P.M. What have you been doing since then?"

"Sitting in Mercedes. In garage."

"What sent you out on patrol at just the right moment?"

"From time to time I am going round the house."

"A guard I hadn't asked for? An extra?"

"So."

He bowed slightly from the sitting position.

"Come off it," I said.

He looked at me.

"Pardon?"

"You don't expect me to believe that? The extra watchman, self-appointed?"

"Also . . . I greatly wish talks with you."

"I see."

"It is most important that I speak with you, Mr. Harris. From what you say on telephone come many questions. It is my feeling you deliberately neglect vital business. I cannot understand. You do not do such things. So I must meet you."

"Ohashi, I'm afraid you haven't really thought through your alibi. You should have put in the time in the Mercedes doing this. If you wanted a business conference with me in the small hours, why didn't you appear when you heard the Audi drive in?"

"I not hear. I think I am sleeping."

"Worn out from the responsibility of running things while I was away?"

He was beginning to look almost forlorn and might, in other circumstances have made me feel a brute.

"I am needing sleep . . . yes."

I could have made a crack about his three-month-old marriage to a girl from Yokosuka, but didn't.

"Let me get this quite straight, Ohashi. You were wandering around my house at three in the morning hoping that my conscience was keeping me awake and that my light would suddenly go on. You'd then say a polite Japanese 'Excuse me' through my window?"

"Perhaps," he said.

"Perhaps is about it. Perhaps maybe not."

"The telephones in this house not working!" There was despair in his voice. "I think surely some trouble is happening here."

"So you decided to play faithful *samurai* with a personal check?"

His eyes remained fascinated by rug patterns.

"Thanks," I said. "Thanks a lot. And I'm grateful, too, for your having worked out that car-trunk trick. We'll watch this in the future. Tell the Sikhs to check trunks as well as whether something is huddled under a rug behind the driver's seat. We'll have real security up here provided I'm prepared to live entirely alone and shoot at sight anything that moves."

He watched me drink some more whiskey. A single drop of perspiration left his forehead and ran down one cheek, leaving a shiny mark like a snail's journey.

"Mr. Harris, you think I am lying?"

"Yes. And so badly it makes me regret having given you a seat on the board. I don't believe I've ever seen you frightened before. What's so terrifying about being a good *samurai*?"

"It is shameful . . . to be discovered like a sneak thief."

"You're not ashamed, Ohashi. You're scared. And I know why."

It was as if I had hit him. His body jerked upright. He looked at me from slits magnified by thick lenses, black-framed glasses so much a part of his face that without them his personality seemed almost alarmingly diminished. I have watched the man standing polishing his specs, wanting to beg him to hurry up and put the things back on his minuscule nose in order to give him a recognizable identity again. The lenses were in place now but I still wasn't looking at someone I knew well and a full realization of this made me feel a little sick.

I went over to a side table and refreshed my glass, deciding to do my talking looking at a Chinese painting on silk of the Kwangsi Mountains.

"You didn't come through that fence to see me. You had to contact someone else."

He made no sound.

"I said . . . there was someone else you had to see!"

"Mr. Harris, please . . ."

100

I turned my head. He was bent over as though to ease a stomach cramp. If something was paining him it was no worse than the pain I had, too. And it was no moment for mercy.

"Ohashi, you once told me about your family's *samurai* background. I took that to mean loyalty to anything to which you had committed yourself. I thought I was lucky to have some of that loyalty for my affairs. And for myself. I've gone on thinking I was lucky . . . until now. You little sod!"

His breath came in with a hiss.

"Please . . . please . . ."

The wail didn't impress me. I didn't raise my voice; there was no need in a room held by early-morning stillness.

"In the last twenty-four hours it's been made plain to me that some remarkably detailed information has leaked about the workings of Harris and Company. I admit the leak was to people I was working for . . . just as you have been. For that's true, isn't it? You have been working separately for an American called Clement P. Windburgh? And the man you had to get in touch with inside this wire was him, not me. He's your real boss. And you've been feeding him facts about how we operate that should have been known only to you and me. Isn't that so?"

He made no attempt to defend himself. I stood looking at a bent back.

"Why in hell's name did you do this to me? Wasn't I paying you enough? Did you need money on the side to help cover the expenses of a new marriage?"

"No, no!"

"Then why?"

"I do not betray. I do not!"

"Most company executives would consider the feeding of confidential information to an outside source as pretty massive betrayal. What was your motive? I could perhaps understand it if we had been operating in any way outside the law. But we haven't been, as you know damn well. Further, I've never operated that way since you came into the firm."

For a moment Ohashi kept the silence. Then he said:

"But not always so, Mr. Harris."

"I see. The gunrunner accusation again. That's going to follow me for the rest of my life. But even you know damn well why I was in those operations. I was against the then government of Indonesia. I tried to help considerable numbers of people in that country who were also against the government.

And when I helped them over in Sumatra the place was already in armed revolt."

"What a man does once . . . he may do again."

I wanted to see Ohashi's face then. I came back to my chair opposite him and sat in it. And after a minute his eyes came up, as though to explore my face for the depth of my anger.

"So you were employed by the Americans to watch my current activities? From inside. From your unique position. They must have been delighted when I gave you that directorship."

He swallowed. What I saw in his eyes reminded me suddenly of that curious aggression from Kim Sung.

"You say I am inside, Mr. Harris. But I am not so sure. Often I am feeling I do not really know how company operates."

"What gave you that feeling?"

"You make me partner and I am no longer employee. But partner is not told everything. When Kim Sung comes to see you it is always a private meeting in your office."

"Kim Sung was an old friend. I treated him as such. But we never discussed anything that was kept from you."

"I see," he said, almost with a reserved politeness, as though he had received the statement expected.

I was conscious then of a considerable weakening in my position as the man who has had his hand bitten by a favored pet. The plain facts were that Ohashi, almost from the moment he had come into my business, had done as much for me as I had for him. There was no doubt that he had earned his right to be touchy about not being totally in the boss's confidence. In fact he *had* been in my confidence, but it was almost impossible to prove this. I swung off on a new tack.

"How did the Americans approach you?"

He was quite candid.

"In Kuala Lumpur restaurant. I think man is tourist with camera. He asks me about the city. But soon something else is plain. He makes me listen even though I do not wish. He tells me I am working for man who is dangerous. I am angry, but I have also doubts in my heart. You understand?"

"I suppose I can. Go on."

"We meet again. It is difficult for me not to do so. I have many questions. He knows much of our business. He tells me that it is most dangerous for Japanese to become involved in such situation. He say to me that Japan must now play strict neutral role. And all her people also."

"That man wasn't Mr. Winburgh?"

"No."

"But you have met the man now in my house?"

"Yes."

"Where?"

"Singapore. Last month when I go on business."

"Fascinating. What did he tell you to do? Watch me?"

Ohashi nodded.

"Mr. Harris, by this time I am greatly troubled. There are things for which I can find no explanation. It seems to me possible that the Americans speak the truth. That Harris and Company front for other things."

"What exactly made you feel this?"

"While you are working on plans for the new shipping company I am left in complete control of old business, all the matters of junk trade. I get the returns for this, routes of ship movements, all that. You hand it over. I am really running Kuala Lumpur office."

"Not very sensible of me if I had something to hide."

"This I also consider. But you are very confident man. Perhaps you think you are quite safe from Japanese assistant. Too clever for him."

"I see. In what way?"

His hands were trembling slightly. He held them out in front of his body as though to watch that.

"Well . . . I discover serious discrepancies. In timing of junk voyages from captains' reports. I notice things like four days to load twenty tons of copra in small port. There are explanations for this, but they do not convince. Like delays in delivery. But these ports are collection points, where copra is stored to await shipment. So I add up and come to big totals in wasted time. One of Kim Sung's voyages spent nearly half of its trading days in port. The junks have fast engines. So it seems to me clearly that junks have other, unreported activities, even long voyages. You understand?"

I understood, all right. Ohashi had probed into an area in company affairs where I had been too casual by half. The profits had been sound and that had been quite enough for me. It was highly probable that when Kim Sung needed more time for his gunrunning he simply pushed in false returns on ordinary trading and allowed a cut on his dirty racket to pass

103

through the books of Harris and Company in order to keep me happy.

"You took what you had found to the Americans, Ohashi?"

He nodded.

"It never occurred to you to raise the matter with me? Or did you think it was dangerous to? That I might eliminate you for knowing too much?"

"I . . . I'm not sure. I am much confused. Also, the Americans are strong. In Japan they are still powerful influence. For me to challenge such authority is dangerous."

"In what way?"

He shook his head.

"I'm not sure. Only troubled."

"About your mother in Kamakura?"

"Maybe."

He had been a boy during the occupation of his country. That time had left its marks. And it had also left a potent respect for power, however well this might be camouflaged by goodwill. Ohashi's response to the authority of his youth wasn't surprising.

"You recognized Mr. Winburgh at once, of course, when I brought him here?"

"Yes."

"And you got orders to contact him as soon as possible?"

Ohashi nodded.

"And you got orders to contact him as soon as possible?"

"That is so."

"Well, you didn't manage to do that. Let them know about this, too. And suggest that any further attempts to get through to him are unlikely to come off."

He stared.

"You mean . . . I must make contact with Americans as if . . . you know nothing."

"Exactly. Just a little demand on your old loyalty. To Harris and Company, now somewhat bedraggled."

Ohashi seemed to notice his drink for the first time. He lifted it in both hands, sipped, then put the glass back on a table.

"To be married makes man more timid," he said.

"The responsibility?"

"So. My wife will have baby."

"Congratulations."

He looked at me.

"My heart very sick, Mr. Harris."

"I know the feeling. If it's any comfort to you, and you can believe it, I had no knowledge of how our junks were being used. And that's the position from which I'm trying to fight back. It's not going to be easy. At the same time they've lost their key witness. Kim Sung is dead."

His face showed no surprise. For a subagent on special assignment he was being kept well in the picture, much further into it than I had been, which perhaps wasn't surprising since with me they had merely been paying out rope.

"Go home now, Ohashi. Back to your wife. I'll give you a chit to the gateman so he won't ask questions."

"But . . . how can I help you?"

"That's a nice thought, in the circumstances. You can get in touch with all our junks. Every single one, in all the fleets. I want them collected at their base ports. They're not to leave without orders."

"What are you going to do, Mr. Harris?"

"Sack all the crews," I said. "From the captains right down to the cook boys. Harris and Company is starting from scratch again, major assets a fleet of junks collecting barnacles. It's going to play hell with our dividends. Only a miracle can save us from total liquidation. Do you believe in miracles, Ohashi?"

He just stared at me.

"Most miracles," I told him, "call for a great deal of support sweat from the beneficiaries. They're not just a free issue."

SEVEN

The self-confidence Mrs. Hasmah had built up over the years from her career as a successful sinner had been shockingly undermined by the events of one night. I saw Ohashi off home to the Japanese wife who is always waiting—no matter what the hour—with a smiling politeness for the return of her lord, and went straight along to the sick bay. Teng's nursing discovery, if not in a state of total collapse, looked very near to it. Something had happened to her face, a rapid deterioration from well-being, muscles gone slack leaving pouches of hanging flesh. She sat on the cot bed, her feet just touching the floor, in an attitude of dismal waiting, as though for some considerable time now she had been going over her alibi only to find this as totally wanting as I did. Certainly a nurse on duty has to answer the calls of nature like anyone else, but she doesn't need to unlock a window in an air-conditioned room before she goes off. It might have restored the woman's morale just slightly to know that I had no intention of notifying the police about an assassin in my grounds, but I saw no reason to give her hope.

"*Tuan*," she said in a near whimper, as though I had been the executioner arriving with the dawn.

I looked at Clem in the bed. He was certainly having a long rest, even for a man who has undergone surgery, still with eyes closed, and that look on his face of someone currently out of this world who may, or may not, be returning to it. His breathing continued unnaturally rapid. Mrs. Hasmah's one positive action appeared to have been a clear-up of the mess made by the shattered plasma bottle, and the contraption for holding this was now pushed back against the wall as if to make a reminder of sudden violence as inconspicuous as possible.

I stared at the patient for some time and my total immobility allowed the nurse to rally slightly. She tried out a few cautious words in Malay:

"He's sleeping well."

I looked at her.

"Where's your suitcase?"

"What, *Tuan?*"

"The one you brought with you. Brown leather."

She went down on her knees to get it from under the cot, that position for a moment suggesting an alien piety.

"Just my things," she said, halfheartedly stalling.

"Open it."

She pulled the suitcase up after her and sat with it on her knees, her arms across the top, as though defending some basic totem of privacy. Then very slowly her fingers went out to the catches, releasing first one and, after more hesitation, the other.

One-third of the contents were personal, but the rest suggested a first-aid kit for an ambulance, remarkably complete. I inspected a number of items, lifting them out to do it. One of these was an unlabeled bottle containing enough morphia to poison a stable of horses. There were also at least a dozen interesting-looking ampuls without identification marks and a syringe. In a little box padded with cotton wool were some not too sterile-looking needles.

"You always carry all this?"

"I'm a nurse," she explained.

"Nurses administer drugs only under a doctor's orders. Did Dr. Hill tell you to go on keeping the patient under sedation?"

"What, *Tuan?*"

"Were any of these drugs left by the doctor?"

"Well, no. But I'm a nurse. I must have them. For accidents."

"The law doesn't say you must have them."

But there really wasn't much use in threatening Mrs. Hasmah with a professional disbarment, which had almost certainly already happened. The lady was now a free lance in areas untouched by ethics.

"Did you give the patient any sedation not instructed by Dr. Hill?"

She considered carefully the advisability of a lie, but decided against it.

"Only a little. He needed to sleep."

The little accounted for that pumped breathing. It had also been designed to keep a target quite motionless against pillows. To this woman's credit had to be put the fact that she plumped for the truth when a situation rendered anything else useless. Mrs. Hasmah was a realist opportunist. And she was peeping at me now from this stance in life, rather hoping— from all she had heard—that it was my own position and as a result we could plot out some sort of working arrangement. It is slightly unnerving to be offered an alliance by a total sinner, as though the evil in you had suddenly surfaced and been identified.

I thought about putting her under interrogation. She was in an emotional state which might have made this productive, but there were two counts against it—first, that I had just ended such a session and felt slightly spent from it, and second, my questions would inevitably reveal to this woman the limits of my knowledge. Further, though she might confess a good deal, there was a point beyond which she wouldn't go. Even under stress Mrs. Hasmah was enough of a trained operator to reveal nothing about the people of whom she was much more frightened than she could ever be of me. It seemed policy for the time being to discipline her with only minor terrors. I picked up the morphia bottle again, feeling it fat in my hand.

"Are you in the retail business?"

Her eyes, which had been willing to meet mine, changed focus and moved around the room. She moved the suitcase slightly, as though finding it heavy on her knees. The lid back against her body made an exhibition bust of head and shoulders, and she was as soundless as bronze.

"There is a drive on to stamp out morphia addiction," I said. "I forget the exact sentence for local vendors, but it's stiff. As much as three years. You'd have been wiser to stick to raw opium instead of trying to move into the class trade. And you should have left your samples at home."

She swallowed. Plump hands were suddenly added to the bust around the sides of the suitcase lid. The effect was odd.

"I am a nurse," she insisted. "I need these things."

"So you always carry enough to deal with the injured in a major train wreck?"

There was no reaction to this cynicism about her role as a healer.

"Mrs. Hasmah, you're not going to get out of this house until your patient doesn't need you anymore. And you're not going to get any messages out, either. I have a dog here who is very highly trained. He allowed you to pass through my bedroom to turn off the electric current in the fence because you had been accepted in this house. But I'm going to tell him now to watch you. Taro!"

I hoped my hound would take his cue and make an entrance. We both listened. There was a padding out in the passage and at this sound Mrs. Hashmah's hands disappeared behind the lid again. Her mouth opened. She had heard enough about the training of Western dogs to believe that this involved a kind of witchcraft. And Taro, standing faintly bewildered in the doorway looking at us, was certainly impressive. He was still conscious of an earlier failure to match up to what was expected of him and his eyes retained a hurt from this.

"See this woman?" I asked in stern Malay. "You're to let her go to the bathroom, but nowhere else. If she tries to get out of the house, stop her."

A tail wagged to placate me, but also suggested message received. Mrs. Hasmah was now only visible from a plump chin upward.

"Go back to bed," I said, in English.

"*Tuan*, do not put the dog on me!" That was a wail. "Please, not the dog!"

"He won't touch you if you do what you're told. But don't try to get out of the house. And no more attempts to shut off that current. He's a big dog, Mrs. Hasmah."

"No!"

"It might be wise to call Chow as an escort if you have any reason to move about in the house. In here you'll be quite safe. Though when I'm not at home Taro becomes very keen about his duty."

I felt fairly certain that I had the woman, for all her resource, nicely nobbled. Witchcraft still has its uses. Nurse obviously believed in it. She might even practice it herself as a spare-time activity, but there wasn't going to be any counter-spell to Taro.

I kept the morphia and helped myself to the ampuls.

"The doctor will give you what you need. And this stuff is going down my toilet. All you have to worry about now is getting your patient well again. When you've done that you'll be allowed to leave this house. But only then. Understand?"

She nodded. I went along to my bedroom, where the dog offered me a couple of tail thumps from his mat, but continued to watch me with sad eyes.

I was out on the lawn having a late breakfast when Betty's

Ford Consul groaned up the steep gradient in a lower gear than was necessary. Like so many doctors, she treated a car with almost no respect, changing it every year before the thing started to fall apart from brutal use. The second-hand trade hates having to find customers for these medical discards, none of which have the life left in them that the speedometer mileage would seem to indicate. I heard the driver's door slammed in a test of lock and hinges, then a silence. I had another cup of coffee and lit a cheroot, sitting there with the feeling of a man taking a deliberate use of leisure he hasn't got because a time bomb is ticking away under his life.

When Betty came down the front steps I was near them. She was wearing a white linen sheath, on top of which would soon be a white coat for her round of surgical wards. She sent me a look which was very like the other ones I'd had from her since my return from the north.

"Pleased with your patient?"

"No, I'm not. That wretched woman must have given him some extra sedation, though she denies it. I made her open her bag but I couldn't find anything. He should have been conscious by this time."

"He's lucky to be alive."

Betty resented that professionally until I put her in the picture. Then she said:

"I'll go back in there and deal with that creature!"

"She's only an accomplice and I've dealt with her."

Betty stared.

"Don't you feel that this has become a police matter?"

"Not exactly. The police mightn't be friendly to me."

"So you're prepared to go on risking my patient?"

"Yes. He's getting more than he deserves as it is. And there's no medical danger, is there?"

"With that woman beside him anything could happen."

"She was a nurse once."

"*Once* is the operative word. I won't speculate as to what she does for a living now. All I'll say is that she isn't the type with whom I'm used to functioning. Paul, I feel very much like washing my hands of all this."

"You've been saying that ever since I asked for your help."

I held out an ampul.

"Any idea what this is?"

Betty took it, broke off the plastic top with her fingernail, sniffed, then looked at me.

"Where did you get this?"

110

"Mrs. Hasmah. Confiscated. There were ten more and a bottle of morphia. Do you recognize the drug?"

"Helcramine, I'd say. Proprietary."

"And you left those ampuls?"

"Certainly not. I left nothing. He'd had all necessary sedation. And further, I wouldn't have given any nurse Helcramine. Are you sure that's all she's got?"

"I think so. Though I haven't shaken her to see if anything else falls out."

"Paul, it's a shade disturbing to be treating unofficially a patient some people want to assassinate, including probably the nurse in attendance. It's my suggestion that you put your guest in a hospital ward at once. The fact that surgery has already been done can be explained somehow. I'm prepared to do that. And he'd be safe in a hospital."

"I don't feel that. Wards are fairly accessible. I think the risk to my friend would be greater."

"I see. You refuse to consider me at all? I must warn you that I can't keep coming here twice a day."

"Don't do it then. Clem's tough. The bullets are out; he'll survive."

"That arm has to go into plaster soon!"

"All right, come back and do the job when you think it's about the right time. I agree that if you keep showing up morning and evening it's going to look more than social."

She stared.

"So now I'm dismissed? I did what was essential and that's that." She took a deep breath. "You sit up here on your hill in the middle of the city and think because you're Paul Harris and have a wire fence around your place you can get away with anything!"

"Not anything. Just this. And privacy is what my guest wants, too. Very much. How long before he'll be sitting up with his eyes open?"

"I just don't know. It depends on how much Helcramine that lying bitch pumped into him. At the moment he looks about ready to be wheeled in for major surgery. Let me tell you something: I'll never do anything like this again, I don't care who it's for. I didn't sleep last night, sick with worry. And I'm not fit for hospital this morning."

She did look stretched tight.

"Betty, I'm really sorry. I honestly didn't think about what all this involved. There was a lot else on my mind."

"You knew a doctor and you got in touch with her?"

"Something like that. Look, I'd like to make this up to you in some way."

"What way? I feel like a criminal at the moment. And nothing that I can tell myself alters the fact that I really am."

"You've been giving help where it was needed."

"Oh . . . hell! You're impossible."

"Lunch with me at Yung Ching Wa's today."

"What? Our little session just as usual? Heaven give me strength! You'll be lunching alone!"

Betty walked over to the car. The Consul door slammed again. She held the starter button down long after the engine was running, then managed to do something remarkable to the reverse gear and the car swept backward in a lurching arc which slung its weight over onto the nearside wheels, sagging the tires. She rolled down a window while noisily groping for first, and shouted: "I've a damn good mind to crash through your gate and wreck your defenses!"

"You'd be fried in all that metal," I called back. "The heat's still on."

The car went down my drive at some speed and I turned back into the house, making good time myself toward Clem's room, but taking care that my feet didn't announce this. In a trouser pocket the Colt I had decided to wear permanently for troubled times felt chilly through thin nylon.

Betty had arranged for another transfusion to thin down that extra Helcramine in Clem's blood, and the drip apparatus was forward by the bed again, with the feed line leading down into the normal arm. Mrs. Hasmah was in attendance, her broad back to me, and then she moved her stance slightly, bracing her body, leaning over. I saw the glint of a syringe.

"Push that plunger down," I said, "and I'll put a bullet in your hand."

She went limp. The syringe fell to the floor. Before I could stop her she had put a foot on it, and there was a crunch of glass. She turned like an old witch from her brew, fury livid in her face, now no act of shocked humility, no excuse, not even a hint of fear.

"You go right on trying, don't you?"

She said nothing. Her eyes were chilly brown pebbles.

"It would be a public service to shoot you," I told her in English.

The message reached her, showing that she understood English a lot better than had been admitted. But the defiance continued. She was an active combatant in a war which has a

112

steady death roll. If you died doing your job you died. An earlier whimpering had been part of a false image of herself.

"Why bother with an assassin when they've got you on the job?"

She wasn't talking. She watched the gun, for a moment of slackening on my part.

"Chow! Come here."

Taro arrived first, but his usefulness was over. I sent the dog away again.

"Get away from the bed, Mrs. Hasmah. Right away, over there."

She moved slowly. Chow put his completely shaven head around the door as she was doing it, his pleasantly stupid face now marred by the resentment he felt at having his well-run house turned into a hospital featuring alien women.

"*Tuan?*" His voice was slightly sulky.

"We're going to lock Mrs. Hasmah in the small bathroom. The one with the grille over the window. She'll have everything she needs in there. You can feed her if you want to but I wouldn't bother. Let her coast on her fat. And if you do open that door, see that you have Taro beside you. Because this woman is going to try very hard to get out and would think nothing of killing you to do it."

Chow looked at the nurse for all of half a minute. Then he offered one of his rare opinions.

"I knew she was bad."

It was spoken with the quiet confidence of a man who is guided by intuition and because of this has never needed brains.

I lifted the gun slightly.

"Walk, Mrs. Hasmah."

The lady's movement down the passage wasn't too graceful, a somewhat heavy swaying, as though her legs hurt from varicose veins. Even healers are afflicted by the common ailments.

Though I sell engines I'm not very mechanically minded and when I have to do something with a gadget I haven't dealt with before my fingers are slow. But it did seem logical that an empty plasma bottle should be disconnected from the patient. I set about removing that tube with what I thought was careful intelligence, but my technique jerked Clem out of his coma. It was startling to find his eyes watching me.

"Enjoying yourself!" he asked, through slightly blue lips.

113

I had my non-friend back again and was strictly conventional about the reunion.

"How are you?"

"Uncomfortable."

He looked down at the feed point on his arm. I swabbed that hole with cotton and alcohol, he watched as I did it. It seemed highly probable from his expression that Clem was one of those people who have a deep-rooted dislike of the idea of someone else's blood in his veins, never quite able to shake off old wives' tales about how you acquired some of the donor's personality characteristics via plasma. Though in his case any change could only be for the better.

"Fancy something to eat?" I asked.

He thought about that.

"No. A cigarette."

After a healthy rest from poison smoke his lungs protested and he coughed. This seemed to shake him back into life.

"What about my arm?" he asked.

"In time it's going to be all right, provided you get the proper treatment."

"Sure?"

"The doctor's word."

"Apart from being a girlfriend, how good is she?"

"Kuala Lumpur depends on her."

He frowned.

"I've never rated European medicine all that high."

"Sheer Midwestern prejudice. I think you ought to have something in your stomach. Perhaps beef tea?"

"I had that boiled cow juice before. No, thanks."

"Something more solid?"

"Sure. A boiled egg."

If I had loved him dearly I'd have been cheered.

"Not an underdone steak?"

"No."

He had a small brandy, however, after I had brought in bottles highly unsuited to the sickroom. The hand which lifted a glass shivered but steadied down once a contact with lips had been made. Clem was doing much better than he would have in one of Betty's aseptic wards, and though brandy may have been totally wrong for his post-sedated state it certainly put a touch of color through waxy pallor.

"When I was awake before," Clem said, "I had a nurse. She looked like a walrus without tusks. Where is she?"

"Locked up."

"You couldn't stand her face, either?"

"She tried to kill you."

He took that without any sign of sudden palpitations.

"How?"

"With a syringe. I don't know what was in it but it smelled bad. And there's a permanent stain on the expensive piece of Peking carpeting around your bed."

"What made you think she wasn't just administering normal medication?"

"Because she was assistant to the assassin who tried to kill you earlier this morning. With a gun that time."

"Oh," Clem said.

He moved his bandaged arm slightly, testing whether the upper muscles still functioned, and seemed faintly pleased about the results of the experiment.

"How did you stop her from putting a needle into me?"

"By saying I'd blast her hand off."

"As close as that?"

"Yes."

"Thanks."

"Don't mention it."

"What about the gunman?"

"A bullet from my Colt knocked a silenced Webley out of his hand."

He smiled for the first time.

"You been getting any sleep at all?"

"Not much. And take note that the nurse is now locked in our third-best bathroom. That's the one with the key on the hall side. If you should be up testing your legs I wouldn't advise you to peek in. Beyond those panels is a lady killer. If I read things right, your enemies have issued an emergency order to all personnel that you are not to be allowed to leave Malaysia alive."

The news didn't seem to do anything to check his convalescence.

"What happened to the gunman?"

"He got away."

"Through your electric fence?"

As I had expected he was well-informed. He probably even knew which picture my bedroom wall safe was behind. He asked for another small brandy, which I gave him, and then he wondered if there had been any contact with the police while he was resting.

"None at all. Our isolation from the world is complete.

And I've hired two extra Sikhs to give us a double patrol around the wire night and day. I'm thinking of putting them on a bonus basis, so much for every hour that passes with no unauthorized characters getting inside."

"How about essential services and the postman?"

"They're let through."

"So I can write my mom. What about a long-distance call?"

"The phones are dead."

"You're a suspicious guy. Isn't it all terribly inconvenient for you?"

"I'm living in a dream world pretending that the last few days haven't happened. And Harris and Company is still just as solvent as it was last month."

I lit a cheroot, a really brusque Java leaf likely to prolong any lingering nausea. Then I filled in more detail of a busy night, slowly, building up to the dog story, noting a certain tightening of his interest.

"Ohashi?" he repeated gently, as though he had heard the name somewhere but couldn't quite place it.

"That's right. My codirector and your man in Kuala Lumpur."

Something flicked in blue irises, but that was all. After a moment he said:

"So it's checkmate?"

I leaned forward in my chair.

"You're damn right it's checkmate. I've got you cooped up here like a chicken in transit to market. If you're good I may ship you on to Saigon later. But not until I'm quite certain you can't do me any harm over there."

"Don't shout, Paul. I'm still frail. And actually I'm quite happy about all this security around my sickbed. I've been needing a real rest like this for a long time. You'll find me absolutely quiescent and docile."

"Well, I'm not counting on it."

Chow came in with the boiled egg, wafer-thin toast, coffee, a starched napkin, and the morning papers on a tray, just like room service at a Hilton. There is a strong maternal streak in Chow and his first real look at the patient set this twanging. He made clucking sounds as he set down the tray, hauled up a small table, tidied the bed, and saw to all those other little details which are supposed to be a loving woman's role but can also be bought by a monthly salary to a carefully chosen domestic. I left them at it and went for a walk in the grounds, having a word out there with my head gardener, who was one of the privileged allowed through the gate and whom I caught, happily, hard at work digging, to the surprise of us both.

Like nearly all Malaysian mornings it was a fine one, the hard sun making damp earth steam, with suddenly exposed worms wriggling like mad to get under cover again. A dragonfly hovered over my head in blessing and the taint of exhaust fumes from the city beneath was only very slight. The Tamil with the spade talked away about his plans for a new bank of bougainvillea as though nothing could ever threaten his totally stable world. My home was a kind of Valhalla for resting warriors and the only trouble was that very soon I had to drive down into the fray again while Clem lay in comfort with his too active brain back to fast ticking.

I had now saved the man's life three times but there wasn't the slightest hint that he meant to put my name up for a citation. Quite the contrary, in fact. I was still public enemy number one on those computer returns, and the thought of this made me angrier. I went back into the house.

A lightly boiled egg and coffee can work wonders, and Clem, propped up against fresh pillows, had the world under his hands again. Smoke trickled down from his nostrils onto the jacket of my best Hong Kong silk pajamas.

"You certainly can pick servants, Paul."

"If not crews," I said.

He appeared to miss that.

"I had him turn up the air-conditioning. I hope you don't mind the extra current?"

"It'll be debited against my assets."

"You're gloomy this morning?"

"Yes."

I sat down again, sharply conscious that my guest room was no longer that at all; it belonged to Clem. He hadn't moved from the bed and had no possessions scattered about, but everything was still his. The dog hadn't made this his base as yet, but that could start at any time. Before long Taro might go out for his walk with a screwed-up message to the world under his right ear. Without any doubt at all Clem would have a way with dogs.

"What's eating you, friend?"

I looked at him.

"Just that I am still the accused and you are still the prosecution."

117

He gave me the charm smile that had stayed with him ever since he was six months old.

"A kind of trussed-up prosecution, wouldn't you say? But still terribly interested in hearing the whole of the defense's case."

"You know damn well I haven't got a case."

"But you're working on it? Well, I can wait. It must be my British blood gaining control at last. I'm prepared to do absolutely nothing while others run around. You're planning on doing some running around?"

"I need a sporting chance to make it effective."

He grinned. "I'm a great sportsman."

"OK. What do you know about Red supply lines into Malaysia? Just assume for a minute that I'm as innocent as I say I am."

"Why, certainly."

I glared at him. "What I *guess* is this. There must be a central dump somewhere, fed from outside the country, with one supply line leading away from it up to Lum Ping's mob in southern Thailand and another to the west coast and from there in junks to Vietnam. I can see, too, why the Reds chose Malaysia as a central distribution point. It has direct access to the Indian Ocean for one thing, and your Navy isn't watching sea routes to Europe on that side of the country. Further, Malaysia is a heavy importer from the West just now, which provides cover for arms coming into the country hidden in normal-seeming shipments. Am I right in all this?"

"So far remarkably."

"Clem, it's pretty obvious that your boys are fairly thick on the ground in this country. Which means you've had a watch on our ports and at least a fairly accurate check on what came through them. Have you discovered any arms at all hidden in shipments?"

He looked at the ceiling. "Ah . . . no. Put like that."

"You've checked Port Swettenham, Malacca, Penang, as well as Singapore?"

"To the best of our ability, which, in spite of your suggestion that we're well dug in, is limited."

"With negative results?"

"So far, yes."

"Have you actually opened crates in bonded store and that kind of thing?"

"No statement."

"All right, I'll pass that. Have you followed goods about which you were suspicious to orderers in this country?"

"On one or two occasions."

"With no results?"

"Nothing conclusive."

"Have you any idea at all of the location of the Reds' central supply dump in Malaysia?"

"We have some guesses."

"But you can't point to a place on the map and say it's there?"

"I wouldn't do that."

"How do you think the Reds are getting supplies to their central dump here?"

He reached out with his good hand for another cigarette, making a play of the invalid's helplessness, which forced me up to help him. He sucked in smoke, let it out slowly, and then lifted his eyes.

"Actually, Paul, we had settled for your junk fleet based on Alor Star."

I sat down again.

"So that's it? I'm in on the deal wholesale and retail? I shove the stuff in at one side of the country and take it out again on the other?"

He looked at the tip of his cigarette.

"You have a reputation for efficiency."

"And just where are my junks on the east coast supposed to be picking up arms from Europe, or wherever they are coming from?"

"We thought Burma. Your Alor Star fleet operates up the peninsula in Thai waters."

"But we don't go beyond them to Burma!"

"So you say. But you do go as far as the Andaman Islands, and Burma would be on the way back, just a small detour."

I could see what Clem was driving at. Freighters from Europe, Russian or Polish, could unload their cargoes at Tavoy in southern Burma, or perhaps even farther south at the little port of Mergui, from which point my east-coast junks could filter the arms down into Malaysia. It was certainly a tortuous route, but this was called for if the object of the whole exercise was total secrecy. And, of course, it would be. A Red plan for a sudden and major flare-up in southern Thailand meant that the guerrillas in that area had to be supplied and with no leak as to how it was being done. Any direct shipments from Mao's territory would have to use the risky route through the American-patrolled South China Sea. But the lanes between Burma and the West weren't patrolled by anyone, just a vast area of empty sea. The only east-coast portion of that long peninsula stretching from Bangkok to Singapore that would be watched at all was the strip of Thailand coast on it. And all that my junks with hidden arms would have to do as they were passing this was stay well out to sea.

I sat there with the unpleasant thought that Clem just might have stumbled on something which incriminated my east-coast fleet. I simply didn't know whether those junks had been running guns or not. Kim Sung could have been in control over on that side, too. And he might well have confessed to this during his interrogation.

"All right," I said. "The guerrillas in southern Thailand need to get their arms through Malaysia. But Vietnam doesn't. Why send junks from this country to Ho Chi Minh when Iron Curtain ships are carrying all he needs direct to his ports?"

Clem nodded.

"Sure, they are at the moment. But supposing the war escalated some more and we blockaded Haiphong completely? Bombed out the docks? It's right on the cards. And that would leave Ho entirely dependent on the route from Red China to keep going, which is the last thing he wants. Ho's idea is to play the field with his allies, and to keep European Communism very much in the direct-help picture. That man looks ahead. He means to keep going even if we do stop big ships from getting to his coast. He then turns to the little ships. And before it is actually vital to his interests he has an alternative system of supply by junks worked out."

"Meaning me?"

"And a lot of others now held in reserve. You were the pilot scheme. Malaysia was the natural base for such a scheme, really the only one, with Indonesia now out of the picture as a potential Red ally. This country is good cover, too; as you pointed out, touchy about foreign snoopers on its soil. Don't imagine that we think Kim Sung's little cargoes were much of a contribution to Ho's war effort; they were nothing really. But they were establishing a route in. And it's mighty hard for us to control junk traffic, as the Reds know well. Which is why they are putting more and more emphasis on it."

120

"And you saw me in total control of this operation through Malaysia?"

"Yes. It looked like we had everything worked out, except the matter of your central supply dump."

I looked at him for at least half a minute.

"I'll pick some holes in all this, Clem."

"By all means."

"First point. I have only six junks operating out of Alor Star. None of my other ships go around to that coast at all. I'm sure you've found that out through Ohashi. That leaves six small junks with limited cargo capacity doing a ferry service between southern Burma and somewhere on the Malaysian coast. Each round trip couldn't be under a thousand miles. How the hell could six ships operating in this way bring down enough stuff to supply a small army in southern Thailand and still have arms left over to send out on Ho Chi Minh's emergency junk route through the South China Sea?"

"Easy. You're using a lot of other junks besides your own. Your whole career has been starred with occasions on which you have happily collaborated with Chinese merchants, and to mutual advantage."

That was a gentle kick in the teeth, but I ignored it.

"By your information, how many Chinese merchants have junk fleets trading regularly between Malaysia and Burma?"

"Three or four," Clem said.

"With enough ships to do a big-scale job?"

"It's possible. A number of unscheduled sailings even by small steamers could be thrown in for good measure."

"Have you any record of such unscheduled sailings?"

"No comment."

"Have you any evidence against Chinese merchants in the Burma trade?"

"Again no statement."

"You're bluffing," I said. "You haven't a thing to back up desk theory. Now let me tell you something. If arms are coming into Malaysia in the quantities you suggest, then they have to be coming direct to ports here from the West in big freighters. Since you haven't been able to discover how that's being worked, I will!"

He laughed. The shaking hurt his arm and he stopped.

"Delighted. Just you carry right on with that assignment."

"Before I do I need all the help you can give."

"That seems fair."

"Clem, you must have a general idea of where this central dump is. Even if it's only guesswork."

"Deduction, actually. We think you'd have your dump somewhere in the center of the country, and in the northern half. It would have to be accessible to road transport and also provide a legitimate excuse for a great deal of traffic to it. There are a lot of projects in the country at the moment providing this kind of cover, but I will say that so far we haven't connected you with any of them."

"That's a comfort."

"You can't say I'm not putting my cards on the table. And in a way I'm really admitting partial failure." He grinned. "We feel that you looked for someplace that gave you access to Thailand but not by any obvious route. Which sort of puts us near jungle country, possibly the main ridge. There could then be a secret covered trail all the way, ending up just beyond the area which you investigated for us. It's probably a long walk, but what's that to Chinese manpower specially imported for the job? They've had plenty of training at that kind of thing, down through Laos into Vietnam."

"Are you suggesting a hidden road good enough for trucks?"

"No, not in that country. It'll be porterage all the way. Except where they use boats on that river. And porterage over the mountains down to the east coast as well. For that rendezvous with your junks. In both cases just a track, but well hidden from the air. And all this has been going for quite some time, too. There are indications that the big blowup in southern Thailand is scheduled for soon."

This had been a local bogey for some time, America's main ally in south-Asia suddenly squeezed from two sides—in the north by direct infiltration from Red-controlled territories, and in the south from the new guerrilla army it was known Lum Ping was building up. Clem had been up against a very acute intelligence problem. The Thais have allowed American troops into their country, but Malaysia remains highly touchy about independence and neutrality, a situation which makes the building up of a good undercover network difficult. It seemed probable that there were still a lot of big holes in Clem's spy net, even if it had caught me.

There was a sudden intrusion into the picture I was beginning to build up, and that was from the thought that Teng's enterprises would fit into it rather well. The town which he practically owned wasn't quite in the center of Malaysia, but it was well north, and also directly at the foot of the main range, which meant that jungle came down practically to its suburbs. It would be a long hike from Kampar to the east coast or to Thailand, but Chinese coolies could do it on rice bags hanging from their belts.

I was conscious of Clem trying to read my thoughts, but telepathy hasn't yet been put on any training schedules. When they get the technique of that perfected, spying as a business is going to go into total eclipse, which will be a great relief of tension all around. And think of the money that will be saved.

"Time for a beer," I said, getting up. "Like one?"

"Sure. Talking has scraped my throat. Paul, I do admire your admirable control."

"It's from a clear conscience."

When I had fetched two glasses of Carlsburg, I stood looking down at him, sipping mine.

"Clem, why did you want to run from that helicopter?"

"It was British," he answered simply.

"And this country is still a British-intelligence sphere of influence? Americans keep out?"

"No. Mostly we have the happiest cooperation."

"Mostly but not always. And you wouldn't be too keen to have certain British parties still functioning down in Singapore know that you had arrangements to clear small landing grounds around this country for quick private business trips in and out?"

"Well, you can put it like that."

"You bet I can! The helicopter was out looking for you on information received. The papers say it was up north showing the flag of mutual defense to the cheering natives. But that was one big blind. A craft on a goodwill tour rests at night, it doesn't go out on patrol."

"I'd have thought that," he agreed.

"Singapore got the word about cute little village girls you hire to keep the grass down on certain remote selected strips. And they decided to pounce the next time the grass cutters went out. To catch you. And return you, via Singapore, to Saigon. Just a nice friendly little gesture to cut the CIA down to size. You know something? I sense a certain conflict of interests going on over the body of prostrate Malaysia."

Clem's one good hand crushed out a cigarette, grinding the butt down onto porcelain. He might have once again decided to give up the vice.

"Paul, don't start waving your new-found patriotism at me.

123

It's one of your acts which I find yawn-making. Because if I ever met up with a good going neo-colonialist, it's you. Though the rudeness may make you wince, you're in this country for the trading and damn all else. And, friend, I've got a fat file to prove it."

It pleased me to see him irritated.

"I have to go now," I said gently. "I'll be away for quite some time, possibly overnight. But Chow will look after you."

"Sure he will. Depart with my blessing. I always like that Japanese ceremonial farewell, don't you?"

"What?"

"Kindly have deep regard for your health."

The electrified gates clicked shut behind the Audi. There was always an odd little sizzling noise as the current went into circuit again. I drove slowly down the rest of my hill, the road curving through thick undergrowth topped by massive trees, each bend perfect for an ambush even though traffic lights were only five minutes away. I had thought of putting the fence right down at the edge of my property, but it would have been too conspicuous and also cost twice as much. No one shot at me but as I approached two stone pillars marking the entrance to the public highway, a man stepped out from among the traveler's palms where he had been sheltered.

I knew him well. He was a Singapore police inspector called Kang who, in these days of the island's total independence, should have no excuse at all for spending so much time in Malaysia. His answer to this was that the police forces had to maintain close liaison despite new and somewhat artificial national barriers. It was my belief that the man was paid more than his municipal salary for work done on behalf of interests who preferred to be nameless, but had their headquarters somewhere in London.

Kang wasn't dressed like any loiterer, but was impeccable as usual in his expensively tailored white suit with knife creases down the trousers. He wore a formal collar with hand-knitted scarlet tie, this in no way indicating his political convictions, which had been tempered by years and seniority. Though you can never be absolutely certain, I was reasonably sure that the Inspector did not see his future in terms of Mao Tse-tung.

"Good morning, Paul." His English was as smooth as the rest of him.

He opened the car door and got into the seat beside me.

"I'd like a lift into town, if you don't mind. I sent my taxi away. I was calling on you for morning coffee, but you're not being very hospitable these days. And I seemed to notice a slight excess of Sikhs. Surly ones, too."

"I've been getting threatening letters."

"I see. So now no one is allowed up there? Not even old friends?"

"That's right. I meet old friends by appointment at the club."

"Difficult to make arrangements when your phone is disconnected."

"There aren't many people I want to see. I'm living the life of a recluse while I give my liver a rest."

"And you have no one staying with you?"

"I hate house guests. They upset routine. What are you after me for this time?"

"Flying an airplane without a pilot's license," Kang said sweetly.

I nearly put the car in a drainage ditch; that steering is dangerously sensitive.

"Ridiculous."

"You were seen through the cockpit windows by some very unhappy policemen up in Kelantan. Definitely at the controls and unmistakably identified."

"Even if this were true, what has it got to do with Singapore?"

"I was called in for consultation."

"Like hell you were! You got the word that I had gone to ground in Kedah and turned up two weeks later in Kelantan. A lot of suspicious minds decided that this might be dangerous to some security or other and sent you haring up here to look into things. On one of your overtime duties."

"So you admit to being in the border jungles?"

"Yes."

"What were you doing?"

"Prospecting for gold."

"I didn't know the Americans were interested in Malaysian gold potential."

"They're not. They've got all they need in Fort Knox. I wanted it for Harris and Company. I'm greedy."

"You deny working for the Americans?"

"I work for myself."

Kang sighed. It was audible above a very quiet engine.

Then something extremely hard made contact with my left rib cage. I know a gun when I feel it.

"I hate to do things this way Paul. And to an old friend. But you're driving us both to the airport. There are two seats reserved on the Singapore plane. It was considerate of you to come out from your fortress just in time to let us catch it."

EIGHT

I drive fast enough to make fastening the seat belt a necessary precaution and had clipped the buckle at my waist on
getting into the Audi. Unclipping it again for a sudden escape
from that gun was an impractical proposition. Kang had kept
himself completely mobile by not bothering about his belt.
We moved into traffic in the direction of the airport with the
silence between us chill enough to bring down the temperature even in the tropics and under a steel roof.

"Let's see your extradition order," I said suddenly.

"It wasn't necessary to go to all that trouble."

"I'm a citizen of Malaysia and you can't export me to Singapore in this manner. I have my rights."

"Actually, in this case you don't. All the formalities have
been arranged. It's relatively easy if you are a policeman.
We'll be able to avoid customs, too."

"Is this an arrest?"

"Nothing like that. You're coming south with me of your
own free will to answer a few questions."

"Thanks for defining the position," I said.

He kept the gun against my ribs.

"Not at all."

I took a deep breath.

"I have always suspected that under the smooth exterior
you were at heart a twisted two-faced bastard."

The Inspector produced a modest little cough.

"All policemen become used to abuse early in their careers.
It has no effect on them at all."

We came to a red light. If Kang noticed that I had brought
the Audi to a halt behind a very large truck loaded with scrap
iron, he made no comment. I hated to do what was coming
next to my nice little car, but there was no alternative. The
truck began to move on amber; I waited for green, which put
five yards between us. I slid into first, then jammed the accel-
erator hard to the floor.

In five yards lengthened to nearly six by the truck's movement, we reached thirty miles an hour, smashing into the lumbering mass in front with force enough to sprawl me over the wheel and whack Kang's head hard against the windshield. I don't know what happened to his revolver, but it ceased to threaten me. I got the belt buckle loose and jumped out into the road, blared at by a taxi and just touched by its offside fender. I made it to pavement and continued running. Behind was some considerable din, shouting, then the peep of a whistle which I didn't think came from Kang.

Batu Road offers a splendid selection of tributary lanes and I swung into one of them, then another, with such hue and cry as had been started soon left well behind. I walked, mopping my face. In the first shopping street I stopped a pedicab. I don't like manpowered transport and normally never use it, but one of these contraptions was the last thing a man on the run would be expected to jump into in order to get anywhere fast and it seemed policy to suggest that I was one of the world's leisured. So was the downtrodden Malay who did the pedaling. At one point he got up to seven miles an hour, but thought better of this and dropped back to five. He was also a bell addict and rang this continuously, which almost guaranteed that no one would take the slightest notice of our passage.

Movement created a breeze and I sat in it wondering just what police procedure was likely to be in the case of a driver who hits and runs, but is not in his vehicle. Their evidence was a crumpled Audi and identification of the owner would be a matter of about ten minutes even if Kang was in no state to assist them. They could try to phone my home, which would draw a blank, or visit it, which would draw another, for I was quite certain that my retired policemen would never allow active members of their service through those gates without a search warrant. The offense in question simply didn't rate the issue of such a warrant. I had the feeling, also, that the Inspector from Singapore wouldn't be spending any more time with his Malaysian colleagues than he could help, wanting to get clear to start up a personal hunt, and without official assistance. Kang wouldn't expect me to be thinking about food at a time like this, which made the restaurant I was making for seem the safest bet. It was certainly early for lunch but the place would be quite ready to give me discreet sanctuary at any time. I paid well for their discretion.

Yung Ching Wa's is a six-story Chinese house of pleasure,

which means that it is mainly concerned with serving food. A lot of other things besides eating go on in the building during the twenty-four hours a day it is open, but all such minor activities are put in proper perspective by a continuous and splendid aroma of vast meals either being served or in the process of preparation. The building is nearly always noisy, with fat women waddling around in the passages amiably flashing gold teeth. It has a lift, which is in constant movement, and around the open cage of this twist concrete stairs, also bearing a heavy traffic, these latter being regarded by contented clients as a suitable place in which to spit. Western standards of hygiene are unknown and would be thought ridiculous. Once or twice I have glanced through an open hatch into the kitchens, only to avert my head at once. The duck and mushrooms in chili sauce are a gastronomic triumph for which the place is celebrated as far north as Sungei Patani, and Betty and I usually settled for that *plat de maison* on our weekly luncheon dates.

I paid my languid pedal man triple the correct fare, but to keep his mouth shut, not out of any extreme of humanity. The stairs were strangely deserted and I reached our fourth-floor private room without meeting anyone at all. Even the usually continuous clattering of a rope-operated dumbwaiter was silent and there were no high-pitched cries from the thousand or so girls who were connected with the establishment in one way or another. By accident I had hit Yung Ching Wa's only siesta time and it was interesting that the cooks and others did take a period for rest, something I hadn't suspected. A little mental arithmetic suggested that this reduced the average working week in the place to a mere hundred and sixty hours. The Chinese restaurant business has sweated its labor for four thousand years and always will.

As a setting for romantic secret meetings the private room left a few things to be desired, the chief of these being a comfortable sofa. I wouldn't have thought that well-heeled Chinese businessmen had any masochistic streaks at all, but that expensive privacy was furnished with a hard wooden bench along one wall, two upright chairs and a table. There was also a mirror suffering from eroding damp, a Chinese pinup-girl calendar, a spittoon, one pot holding three dying calla lilies, and a telephone with a place of honor all its own on a little stand, for much business was conducted from these compartments for high living. The one window looked out on a ventilation shaft in the middle of the building and was the chief source of cooking smells. An electric fan on a bracket whirred day and night, stirring the tepid air but never managing to push out an under odor of stale tobacco smoke.

Europeans almost never came here, using garden restaurants with tinkling fountains more suited to their fancy even if the food was greatly inferior. The phone which I lifted at once wasn't a pay instrument; local calls were on the house and though you were supposed to leave the price of long distance, the average dinner check appeared to include six minutes to London. I got the airport at once and asked for a seat on the three-o'clock flight to Penang.

"Name, please?"

"Bonder," I said. "Eric Bonder."

Eric is my banker, a full-blooded man, most of it in his face from whiskey intake, who has a tendency to clap me on the back when we meet at the club bar, but I have always suspected that it would give him a kind of fiscal pleasure, if the day ever came, to let me know in the nicest possible way that Harris and Company were no longer considered a good bet for an extended overdraft. He would resent the liberty I had taken, but that didn't trouble me.

Service always happened at Yung Ching Wa's, if not in any rush, and during the siesta hour it took twenty minutes. The girl who arrived, yawning, was our usual attendant, little Miss Spring Anemone. It is a pretty name, but that was about all the waitress had got as her heritage, and coming from a hungry home, she had settled in at Yung's to eat her way into the future. The result of a steady application toward this end was that, though only four feet eleven inches in height, she had to come through the door sideways.

"Oh, it's you," she said in Cantonese, and with controlled surprise. She was chewing something. "What do you want?"

"Tiger beer."

"All right. You eating later?"

"Probably."

"Your woman coming?"

"I don't think so."

"Don't take the duck today. Pork."

"What's happened to the ducks?"

She shook her head, keeping the chef's secret, edging her way back into the corridor, and pulling the door shut again, which was an automatic reflex.

Without a meal to occupy me, and the company over it, sitting alone in that box was a little like making use of the

130

waiting room in a station on a railway line that is about to be closed down. Time didn't appear to move at all. Anemone brought me my beer, gossiped about the latest murder, and then decided that she wasn't paid to be a hostess. At ten minutes past twelve the phone rang, and the bell made me jump.

One of the things which are efficient at Yung's is the switchboard; it has to be to keep the clientele. Calls are put through at once, and to the right cubicle, just in case a guest, as a result of the news, has to make quick use of one of the seven separate exits provided. The building has so many annexes probing out in different directions that it is improbable that even a detachment of police could properly surround the place to plug all escape holes. An irate wife is simply no problem at all, and the staff are geared to deal with this routine. An acquaintance of mine had even been assisted to travel down from the fifth floor in the dumbwaiter, with girls at each hatch level spinning the ropes through their hands.

"Ching Wa Tsu here," I said in singing Cantonese.

"What?" It was Betty's voice.

"Well, correct that to Paul. It's nice you're coming after all. But you didn't need to ring up."

"I am *not* coming. But a very odd thing has happened. I'm glad I've got you."

Somehow that made me uneasy.

"Brief me quickly, dear."

"Paul, what's been going on this morning?"

"Tell me about you first."

"I was called down to casualty about half an hour ago. Normally I have nothing to do with it. If it's a surgery case I'm simply notified and—"

"Betty, I'm not interested in hospital procedure. Why were you called to casualty?"

"To meet a Singapore police inspector who had been brought in unconscious."

"Did you say *meet* him?"

"Yes. You could say it was semisocial."

"Oh."

"You know about him?"

"Yes. Was he—ah—badly hurt?"

"Apart from an egg on his head, no. And no question of concussion."

"That's a relief."

"You mean you had something to do with the bump?"

"Indirectly."

"Paul! You haven't hit a policeman?"

"No. Though I've done worse things. What did he want?"

"That's what I don't understand. Though I do understand enough to make me feel a little sick. Your friend was very smooth."

"He always is."

"They'd given him some tea. He was sitting there sipping it. He just looked up and said, terribly politely, 'I'd be most grateful, Dr. Hill, if you could give me the name of the restaurant where you usually lunch with Mr. Harris. I find it has slipped my mind. Probably something to do with this bump.' And then he laughed."

"You told him?"

"But I *had* to! And why should I try to cover up from the police?"

"No reason. How long ago was this?"

"About half an hour. I couldn't get to a phone right away. Paul, he knew all about us! Have we been watched?"

"I have been. You're all right. Just forget it."

"*Forget* it?"

"Look, Betty, this has nothing to do with my meeting you for lunch here. It's just certain parties keeping tab. It's one of my career hazards."

"And you don't think something like this happening is a career hazard to me?"

"Not in the least. But we'll go into that later. Just now I can't linger. And thanks very much for calling."

"Paul!"

Her cry seemed to linger in the little room, even after the click. I opened the door. The passage was still empty, though there were now some feet on the stairs, echoing from concrete. The lift was droning, too.

Inspector Kang had made the tactical error of incarcerating himself in a very slow-moving metal crate. He looked out at me between floors, and through two sets of decorated steel netting as I passed down. I nodded, then started taking three steps at a time. Above me I could hear the self-operated lift go into an emergency stop. High up in the building the wheels of the mechanism clanged, then the counterweights changed direction. It was going to be a slow descent.

Mr. Eric Bonder, slightly less red in the face than usual, was passed through the barrier onto the tarmac without a hand coming down on my shoulder. The alien policeman from Singapore had held to his lone-wolf act and couldn't be everywhere at once.

I had a delightful flight north in a three-quarters-empty plane in which the hostess, who could effectively swing her hips even coming down a narrow aisle, seemed much more concerned than these girls usually are about the comfort of her male passengers. And since I was for once a good deal younger than the other businessmen on board, there was a truly personal touch in everything she did for me. She had tiny hands which fluttered like butterflies and then settled suddenly on a man's arm, or thigh. When I offered her a drink she said it was against the rules and accepted. We sat together for some time without bothering much about the view. It is a pleasantly informal airline in which the staff are permitted to be human in their approach, and Miss Lin told me all about her ambition for a career as a cabaret artiste. She had trained as a contortionist and did her act in two little strips of tiger skin, but was heavily handicapped by respectable parents who wanted her to marry and have a lot of Chinese babies. The air service had been a compromise, but a dream of true glamour still prodded her. She wished, she said, that she could show me the bit where she brought her head up under her buttocks and smiled at the audience. Miss Lin was certain this would be a show stopper, and so was I.

Disillusionment about my personal appeal came only as we moved into sight of Penang Island, when it turned out that the hostess had mistaken me for another European whose photograph she had recently seen in a newspaper and whose life work was booking floor shows for the big Singapore and Bangkok hotels. She gave me a smile as I got off, but this tinged with sadness, as though life was always letting her down.

I went over in the ferry from Port Wellesley, thinking once again how much Penang reminded me of Hong Kong, the same island out in the water, the same high ground behind the city dotted with the homes of the prosperous, these getting bigger toward the peaks. The British have left curiously indelible marks and a tone of colonial life which refuses to be extinguished. The port has always just missed becoming a major one because Singapore is too near and sucks away the trade, but it has a certain charm from this, bustle moderated, the tempo of any day broken by long pauses for refreshing recreation, which has tended to be based on alcohol. I had once, when uprooting from Singapore, contemplated moving my business headquarters to this island, but decided against it, chiefly because of that infectious tempo.

Not all empires have been built by hard unremitting toil. In portions of theirs the British quite often gained power and from it riches, simply by being first on an unexploited spot and then socially ostracizing anyone from other western lands who tried to muscle in, until the wives of the interlopers forced their men to give up and go home. All of which makes the contemporary insolvency of the old motherland, now stripped of dividend-earning colonies, less surprising than it might seem. I know my secret weakness for the good life and in Penang could easily have gone to seed, taking Harris and Company with me.

From the bund I took a taxi to the offices of Lung Fing and Partners, Ltd. Lung was an old associate of mine. It would be too much to call him a trusted friend, but in the past our interests had coincided often enough for an understanding to have emerged to which Lung had come to attach some of the trappings of a blood relation. He always greeted me with a tear in each slightly rheumy eye and had on occasion said I was like a son to him. How long this intimacy would have stood up under no profits I don't know, but it had never been put to real test because all our deals made money.

When I had been engaged in close support of insurgent forces in Sumatra, Lung had handled the supply end, and very deftly indeed, which was why I had come to see him now. This, plus the fact that he was the biggest contractual employer of lightermen in Penang, as well as owning half of the bonded godowns. There was no lift to his third-floor offices; you went under cool and massive arches into cool and dim corridors and then walked up.

The old man didn't seem to me a day older, but then he had always been too ancient to age. He rose shakily from behind a massive teak desk which ought to have emphasized the mortality of the frail creature who used it, but somehow didn't. The Ho Chi Minh wisp beard he affected was blown back toward his ears from a central parting by a portable fan.

"Paul Harris!" he squeaked, holding out skeletal hands in a demonstrative gesture unusual with his race. "My boy."

"Hello, Dad."

He liked that.

"Always you call me Dad, eh?"

"You were always a father figure worth watching."

"Sit down, sit down. There."

I sat on his side of the desk, where he could see all of me, old eyes taking comfort from still unwasted muscles. It took a long time to get around to business; in fact, I never did get around to the real business at all, which would have been a sharp error in strategy. Instead I gave him information he already had documented about the new shipping company to which I was committed, indicating that I was out drumming up trade even before we had funnels repainted in the new line colors, which were to be red, white, and blue with a green strip zigzagging through all three of these shades to indicate that we were canceling out the bad old days. Penang was to be a major port of call and Dad, out of quasi-paternal sentiment, was going to see that a lot of crates in his sheds were stamped for shipment in our vessels.

He thought this very funny, one of the best jokes he had heard in months, good enough almost to bring on his asthma. When he had recovered sufficiently, he wiped his face with a silk handkerchief and then practically whispered through it in Cantonese that, alas, his business had nothing to do with shipping as such, only unloading and storage. I ought to know this well enough, surely?

"My dear Lung Fing, the fact remains that you are the president of the Penang Chinese Chamber of Commerce, a director of the Ho Kwa bank, you own half the more ruinous property in the town, to say nothing of that new hotel. You're the big man, in fact. Everyone bows when you come into a room. It's why I feel so proud when you call me your son."

The agitated rat noises came again. After them he said sweetly:

"You know I'll do what I can. And I wish you every success, Paul, every success. But a new company must establish itself. It must offer a unique service."

"By which you mean cut rates outside of the local maritime agreement?"

He didn't confirm that, exactly, only stroked his beard down into place on his shirt.

"Just what do you want?" That was cautious.

"At the moment I'm our company's promotion man. I'm contacting personally every potential customer of any size. And it occurred to me that the one person who could give me a clear lead as to what companies are using a good deal of shipping at the moment is you. After all, you unload for them. And you dispatch out to Malaysian destinations. Nothing moves in or out of Penang that you don't know about."

135

"True, yes. But to give this information . . . I'm thinking of business ethics."

"Business ethics are something to insist on against your competitors. I'm not one of them. I'd never be such a fool as to set up in opposition to you."

He liked that, too. After another half hour of palaver he agreed to give me a session with his head clerk, also aged, a man with whom I had dealt before and if not liked, respected.

It was an interesting hour out in that main office, where they had to use electric light in the afternoon. When it was over I went back and took a ceremonial farewell of Dad. He didn't kiss me good-bye, but there was a moment when I thought he was going to.

I went down those stairs wondering how the old man ever managed to get up them. Perhaps he didn't; perhaps he lived in his office, the head clerk unrolling a bedmat alongside the teak desk at 11:30 P.M., when it was time to bring a routine business day to its close. People who resent Chinese efficiency generally overlook the hours these Orientals put in to amass their profits and spread their influence in the world. There are moments when I am unhappily certain that the swelling hordes of Western clock watchers are due for some really nasty shocks in the next couple of decades.

The street outside still held the last light and was full of Chinese who hadn't managed the first rung in the success ladder and were without any expectations of charity from those who had, but remained undepressed about what life had done to them. Perhaps it is the climate; you may starve, but you won't starve cold.

I emerged from a long colonnade onto pavement flanked with huge palms, walking with a lot to think about and in the general direction of the old hotel, where I was going to treat myself, after a series of gin Collinses, to a good old-fashioned apoplexy-inviting dinner starting with oxtail soup and ending with Welsh rarebit, all nine courses served in the downdraft from one of those vast bladed fans which look like propellers from obsolete aircraft. I had missed lunch and Lung Fing must have seen signs of this, for he had asked me whether I was hungry. When I said yes the old skinflint ordered scented Amoy and a plate of half a dozen of the thinnest rice biscuits I had ever seen. He had then smoked my cheroots, inhaling them to stave off the craving for his daily pipe of opium.

I was fairly certain that I hadn't let Lung's head clerk see just how interesting I found an area of the facts we uncovered jointly, but they had certainly sent me off on a new line of speculation. I would never have made much of a scientist because I like to get my theory first by a kind of clutching intuition and then shape the facts to fit it. It's a much more entertaining course than a plodding progress to an inescapable conclusion. Anyway, a considerable number of inescapable conclusions just aren't the truth, like Clem's on my activities. Perhaps I've been lucky, but at least six times out of ten my approach has worked out, and with some pretty wild theories as the original premise, too.

There was much to keep me preoccupied as I walked along, and I paid no attention to the traffic, not noticing a car that must have been slowing down to pull in parallel to my progress. Attention was smacked back to the outside world by a burst of submachine-gun fire with me as the target. The fact that the first round of seven or eight high-velocity bullets didn't hit target must have been due to the gunman not taking enough time to get his range, or perhaps someone in the car accidentally joggled his elbow. At any rate a great deal of irrelevant glass shattered beyond me. The second burst would have zeroed home all right if it hadn't been for the palm tree I was suddenly behind, a blessedly plump old specimen shaped rather like a sprouting pineapple. I could literally feel, so close had the two of us become, lead whacking deep into a fibrous core, and after that second burst fronds crackled above my head from the poor plant's trembling.

Someone started to scream, though it wasn't me. My throat was parched dry as a prairie after a seven-year drought and not a whisper could have worked its way up over arid roughness. The car was just moving, and I kept moving, too, around that splendid generosity of nature deeply rooted in among electricity cables.

I'm glad to say that I rallied to the point of putting one bullet from my Colt through a side window of the Austin saloon, 1957 vintage. The hired killers had been told there would be no resistance and they didn't like this development. The Austin leaped away, leaving me and the palm, and someone screaming, though the road seemed suddenly remarkably empty.

I have a career allergy to police interrogations and a taxi traveling south was my next target. I didn't actually stop this with my Colt, but the driver braked noisily and let me in. If he had seen any of the action he didn't want to admit this, just accelerated fast, which was exactly what I wanted.

137

I leaned back on cushions and found a handkerchief. Dear, quiet, ex-colonial Penang. Dinner was off. I was getting out of the place.

And then, rather late in the day, I remembered that Lung Fing's first cousin's son was Teng, that man who practically owned his town near the main mountain range.

I went south by train, even though this would mean getting up at an ungodly hour when no one would have any kind of breakfast ready for me. There is something infinitely soothing about a first-class, air-conditioned sleeping compartment. You are in transit, moving in life, but in a manner which puts no subconscious strain on the nerves, rolling on wheels toward a destination, with all the cosy certainty of arrival which kept the Victorians so happily immune to contemporary tensions. My door was locked and at Port Wellesley station I had bought a packet of British potato crisps, a half-cooked chicken, and a bottle of eight-year-old Glen Grant malt whiskey which was miraculously sitting up on a shelf behind the cash register. I had also bought a paperback Gideon of the Yard, which promised to tell me more about police methods than I really wanted to know.

Another night I would have finished the Gideon before switching out the berth light, but I was suffering from a slight reaction to a day of some activity and I had also been generous to myself with the malt. It wasn't perhaps a deep sleep which took me, and I was waked from it by a heavier rumbling than had been the background noise, plus a loud, metallic clanking from just outside the carriage wall. I needed a moment to realize that all this din meant we were on the bridge which crosses the South Perak River.

It was then I noticed a crack. The door I had locked was open an inch, admitting a dim light from blue corridor bulbs. I remembered that a passkey allowed the attendant in with morning tea. I watched, more frozen than alerted for action, as the crack widened. A hand came in for the switch on wall paneling. Something else came in, too, the snout of a heavy service revolver. There was going to be sudden light and then sudden death.

Probably a man with nerves in better shape would have waited until a door opened wide enough to reveal more of the assassin's body, but I had the sharp feeling of having used up my uncertain ration of luck for some time ahead. I fired at fingers on a switch, but from an awkward shooting position. The noise of the gun sounded loud enough to panic a train, but it probably didn't even wake neighboring sleepers if the bridge crossing hadn't already.

The door shut. I didn't hear the click. I got the berth light on and for a moment had the feeling of waking from a nightmare. Then I saw splintered paneling about the switch. The air-conditioning was dealing with a slight smell of toasted rubber. There was no one in the corridor and no one opened a compartment door to look out as we moved onto quieter track.

If the police decided to dig that bullet out of teak veneer and start up an investigation on the evidence it offered, this was going to mean some embarrassing moments in the manager's office at the Kuala Lumpur branch of the Chartered Bank of South Asia and Australia. I was still traveling as Eric Bonder. The name was printed on a little card in a door holder.

I reached home decidedly red-eyed. You get that way sitting up through the small hours with a Colt on your sheeted lap, staring fixedly in one direction. Clem, however, against pillows, looked as contented as a baby who has had a really good 4 A.M. feed and been properly burped for sleep after it. His blue eyes, clear and innocent, fixed on me. He concentrated for a moment, then said:

"Welcome home. How are things?"

"I've been looking after my health."

"So I see. You might have had a shave before waking me. What time is it?"

"Six-fifteen. And all seems well up on the hill. No alarms, according to the guards."

"None that reached me, at any rate. If I had a more placid home environment to offer, I'd lure Chow away from you. I get the feeling you've never really made full use of the man's talents. Take a week off sometime with your feet up. I like it here."

I looked at Clem in dead silence for some time. Then I said:

"Do you still believe I'm operating for the Reds?"

"Why do you ask?"

"I need a friend."

He smiled.

"You've come to the wrong department. I'm not allowed to cultivate them. Though I'm prepared to be neutral even if I can't offer love."

"Thanks."

"Shave and have breakfast with me," he suggested generously.

So I did that. It was early even for Chow's service, but he rallied to the occasion with a holiday offering of hot scones and bacon and eggs, though I couldn't see a holiday ahead. We ate out on the veranda. Clem, in my absence and against doctor's orders, had become walking wounded. It was only with the second cup of coffee that I remembered my other guest in the bathroom.

"No trouble with your ex-nurse?"

Clem shook his head.

"Absolutely none. She made a bit of noise yesterday afternoon, perhaps for food. Probably Chow fed her, because there was silence again. It looks rather as though she has opted for sleep in the bathtub."

"I see your arm's in plaster?"

"That's right. The nice lady doctor. We get on fine. I've recovered from prejudice. I think she knows her job. But she was a bit irritated about having her car searched on the way in."

"What did she say about no nurse?"

"Incurious. I told her the lady had gone. And from the state of my pulse and so on it was clear that Chow was doing a good job as substitute."

"No sounds from the bathroom while Betty was here?"

"None that I heard. Anyway, your doctor wasn't in a very observant state. I think she had something on her mind. It could have been you."

When I made no comment Clem prodded.

"How romantic are things?"

"Not very."

"Because she has a husband?"

"There is that. And a lot besides."

"Come on, come on, it does us all good to bare our hearts. And we've nothing in your file on this."

"Betty isn't relevant to my file."

"Everything is relevant, including your dog. Incidentally, that's a nice dog, but he's not properly integrated. You ought to get him a bitch and start breeding Tosas."

"He does all right in the park without a home life."

"Like you?"

"Shut up, Clem. I don't feel like talking about myself this morning."

"We were talking about the lady doctor, remember?"

"What about her?"

"I'm interested in her background. She's good. Why is she out here?"

"A challenge to duty."

"I didn't know people had those anymore. This grows fascinating."

I stared at a groomed lawn, part of the total tidiness about my domestic patterns.

"Betty came out here because . . . well, it was a new opportunity."

"Is she under contract?"

"She had one for three years. It's been renewed."

"Let's get back to motivation. The British woman doctor coming out East. And not as a missionary, or anything."

"You mayn't be so far off it with that missionary idea. She's the daughter of a fundamentalist parson up in the English Midlands. Brought up to strict Bible punching. There was an inflexible moral rule for everything. She lost faith, but still wants the moral rules. God is dead, but good works remain. No, that's not quite it."

"What is?" Clem asked.

"I suppose the need for a purpose remains. She found her purpose in medicine. But the practice of it in Britain blunted the purpose somewhat. She came out here to get back to first principles. Also . . ."

"Yes?" Clem said gently.

"I think the distinction of being a woman surgeon in an Eastern country appealed to her. She's a bit of an actress."

"And we're not actors?"

"Not as much. I don't think you see yourself as Clement P. Winburgh from the CIA posed against a blood-red Vietnam sunset."

"You don't know me, boy. That's in my mind all the time. What the hell do you think I do it for? The pay?"

"All right. You and Betty Hill."

"Not a Harris girl at all, I'd say."

"She's nobody's girl but her own. That's been the trouble. I thought at first she didn't give a damn what other people thought of her, women especially. But that's all the act. She comes into a room deliberately not seeing anyone in it. She

141

has to be claimed, she never claims. You go out toward her and maybe after a time she moves a bit toward you."

"You've spent some nights gnawing the edge of your sheet thinking about this?"

"Maybe I have."

"The attraction is just raw sex?"

"I don't know. We haven't tried it out."

"What? Oh, fellow, you need help. What's her husband?"

"A poet. He came along as Betty's guest. Then got a job lecturing in English literature at the University here. Tom's a simpler case, or at least seems so to me. A bottle-a-day man because the world hasn't recognized his genius. Only the *New Statesman*."

"Any children?"

"One daughter aged seven. Totally spoiled by Mummy, Daddy, and the Chinese amah. When Penny doesn't get her own way she kicks everyone in sight. I've seen her do it. And no one has ever tried to stop her with a good clout."

"You resent the child as a challenge to your plans?"

"I have no plans," I said.

"Why can't you choose a nice simple emotional setup and be comfortable?"

"It's not in my nature."

Clem asked me to butter and Frank Cooper marmalade him another piece of toast. While I was doing it he made a polite inquiry about what I had been up to in the last twenty-four hours. I told him most of the truth. From his expression it might all have been any subagent's normal day.

"The situation is clear up to a point," I said. "Either the Americans, the British, or the Reds are trying to liquidate me. I thought for a time of including on the list some of my business rivals, but have left them out. Homicide is an admission of commercial defeat. Still, the Americans, the British, or the Reds make up quite a large field for one man to play on his own."

"Isn't it nice you've got a real fortress to come home to," Clem said with his particular brand of inhumanity. "Aren't you worried about helicopters at all?"

I looked at him.

"You don't mean you think that Kang might call in that good-will flight again?"

"Why not, since he's tried all other ways to get you and failed? And there's plenty of nice smooth grass out there to land on."

"But we're right in the middle of a capital city."

"It wouldn't matter about them being seen. They just use temporary rotor failure as an excuse for a setdown and apologize later. The whole operation wouldn't take long. By the time there was any real interest from the local police the machine could be twenty miles away. The weakness of perimeter fortifications in our time is that the chopper just pops over them."

"I don't like this," I said.

"Well, don't worry about it too much. If they land I'm going to tell them that I've been held prisoner here for the last six weeks and got shot by you when I was trying to escape."

I got up and left. As a staff to lean on in time of trouble, Clem was a piece of collapsible rubber. I went to my bedroom, reloaded the Colt, and took it along to a bathroom door. When I had unlocked this I kicked it open.

Mrs. Hasmah had opted for sleep, all right, the long one. She was lying full length in the bathtub, clothed, and from each of her wrists was a trail of dried blood to the drainpipe. The razor blade was half hidden under one of her thighs, a Wilkinson stainless.

NINE

The dead nearly always seem almost unbelievably diminished, as though personality had been let out like air from a lilo, what is left pitiable in its unimportance. Mrs. Hasmah would have killed me without compunction if it had been in her orders, but there wasn't even a reminiscence of menace in that slumped body. Coffined by the tub, she looked composed in final immunity, ready for collection and disposal. In her case the collection had to be delayed for a time.

I checked that the passage was empty, turned the key, and locked the door. The nurse's case was on the floor. In it I found a dispenser packet of blades, as though the woman had traveled about equipped for all eventualities, even the need to slash her own wrists. It was impossible for me to assess time of death, though the body had passed beyond rigor mortis, already in that process of dissolution which made leaving it here for long out of the question. The little room didn't have air-conditioning, but there was an extractor fan which would have its use, and I switched this on. The sound of the motor might be heard by Chow but would only suggest that the prisoner wanted air. It would also add a little to the time I had, though it was quite plain that the situation up on my hill had changed sharply. Clem might be nobbled for as long as I needed, and happily quiescent in this state, but a body in a bathroom left me with only hours before electrified gates had to be opened to allow in the police. I didn't in the least fancy the idea of a secret grave somewhere in my grounds; the law had to be brought in when I was ready, or at least when I hoped I was ready.

In the meantime it was important that no one else in the house find out about Mrs. Hasmah. Concealment ought to be relatively easy, demanding a small performance from me, then a key turned. Chow was fully occupied in his role as substitute nurse, my cook never came into the main bungalow, and his wife, who cleaned, was far from bright. The two gardeners stayed in their domain.

Clem, of course, was another matter. He was well enough again to be acutely observant but I didn't feel that his shaky mobility would be up to any search of the premises. The bathroom he would use didn't adjoin this one.

As I was relocking the door from outside, Chow came out of the sickroom carrying a load of breakfast dishes.

"We'll have to feed the woman," I said, making my voice loud enough to carry through an open door and out onto a veranda. "Fruit, milk, and biscuits should be enough. Get these ready and I'll take them in. You haven't given her anything?"

He shook his head.

"I never went in. Why should I?"

It was clear from his expression that Chow's humanity was spasmodic and unpredictable. He had none to spare for Mrs. Hasmah at all. He mumbled something else as he went off but ten minutes later I had a tray on which were arranged modest little offerings for the dead and I took charge of it, feeling rather like an animist who believes that those who have left this life need solid sustenance for that first trying journey into another. I put the ceremonial food on a stool and left it, taking the key of the bathroom door along to the wall safe in my bedroom, locking it away. I then set my alarm for 11 A.M., swallowed a sleeping pill, and lay down on my bed to build up the strength I was going to need.

But I didn't get the two hours I had rationed myself. Chow literally shook me awake.

"*Tuan, tuan,* the guard! He wants to see you."

Ranji Singh was already through the door, standing just inside it, turbaned and self-consciously dignified as always. He waited until Chow had left us and then launched into a policeman's account of his activities, this designed to show how strictly he had been adhering to duty. I knew it was useless to interrupt.

Ranji had been on wire patrol and had reached a point below the vegetable garden when something came out of the jungle wall beyond the fencing, flew over it, and landed very near his feet. Before bending to pick up the object, which he could see was a piece of paper wrapped around a stone, he had inspected the heavy growth for any signs of movement from it, but had seen none. He had then called out in Malay the equivalent of "Who goes there?" but, not surprisingly, had got no response. Since wire mesh made pursuit impossible, my guard had listened most carefully and then, after making quite sure there was no sound of any kind, he bent down for the paper.

"The note, Ranji," I said, butting into this placid, comprehensive report.

"It is for you, *Tuan*."

"I guessed as much."

The Sikh came stiffly over to the bed and stood as though it embarrassed him to see me relaxed, extending an arm with a sheet of paper at the end of it. This had been torn from a notebook, with the crumples now carefully smoothed out, probably all of five minutes taken over this proceeding. The letters were in square block printing designed to fool a handwriting expert and written with a ballpoint.

PAUL HARRIS,
    The eagle's nest appears to be under very complete observation by birdwatchers. Police? I can't get in. If you can get out meet me in the Botanic Gardens today at 1 P.M. By the duck pond. Vitally important information. T.

Teng had certainly not sweated up to my wire in person to deliver this chit, which meant that he must have organized the whole operation of an approach to my house very carefully indeed, keeping his big Cadillac as a control center a long way off, dispatching first scouts to reconnoiter and then using a trained tracker who could get through jungle growth without being heard. He really wanted to see me.

I was inclined to agree with my friend's suggestion that it was the police down there, and not waiting to serve a summons for car wrecking in Batu Road, either. Kang could so easily be in control of proceedings now, assigned local plainclothesmen as the result of a sudden order from a very high level indeed, which wasn't a pleasing development to contemplate.

"Ranji, isn't this the morning for the baker's van?"

"Yes, *Tuan*, it comes between twelve and one."

"Be on duty yourself when it passes the gate. When you check it do you open those back doors?"

He claimed that he always did this, despite the fact that the whole van, behind the driver's seat, was fitted with racks right up to the roof in which were closely set sliding trays full of our local French bakery's goodies.

"This morning keep those doors open for long enough to let anyone hiding down the drive to see the trays."

"Who would be hiding, *Tuan?* Do you wish me to hunt in the woods for someone?"

"No, no, there may be no one there. But just do as I say. Open those doors wide."

"Yes, *Tuan.*"

The order was understood, the reason for it was not. I could see that my guard, trained for long years to uphold the strict letter of the law, was beginning to have some doubts about his present employer, and only the need to supplement an inadequate pension still held him loyal. It was one thing to protect your boss from kidnappers, quite another to collaborate with him in outwitting former colleagues now lurking about the place. That word "police" in the note had really upset him.

It was possible, of course, that the men in the woods weren't locals at all, but a detachment of US Marines dropped in the night to rescue Clem and now hard at it digging a tunnel under my wire. But somehow I couldn't see this. Back in that plane cabin I had been given a strong impression that my now happy prisoner was under a big enough cloud with his own side to have him rated expendable, or if not quite that, at least no longer placed high enough on personnel charts to make him worth saving at the risk of an international incident.

Ranji left, taking with him doubts about my probity, and I got off the bed to get ready for a day in town which could so easily involve a need for my Colt. The baker's van eventually came grinding up the hill and I left the bungalow without saying good-bye to anyone.

There is a short stretch on the drive where neither the house nor the new gates can be seen, and I stood waiting there from twenty past twelve to a quarter to one while the driver gossiped with my cook. The bulky vehicle quite suddenly put in an appearance above me, free-wheeling in dead silence with engine off down a sharp slope. Brakes applied resulted in a terrible squealing and brought the van to rest almost sideways across tarmac.

The driver was half Indian, half Portuguese, which gave him the lilting Welsh accent that has taken over India, Southeast Asia, and now threatens the whole of England via the British Broadcasting Corporation.

147

"My goodness me, sir! But you have given me a terrible shock!"

"Sorry. I need your help."

"But I am not understanding? I am supplying bread and cakes to your establishment. Is there some dissatisfactions?"

It is a mistake to envy the well-heeled. They have overheads undreamed of by the lower- and middle-income groups. I was waving money again, quite a sizable sum, too. The driver stared at the notes and only when what I wanted began to penetrate did his eyes shift to me.

"You cannot be meaning this, sir? I am to put my bread and my cakes in the bush-shes?"

"Just the two lower trays."

"But what will happen to all the ba-king?"

"My dog will get it. I'm paying you for loss. And something more besides. You can pick up the trays next week."

Persuasion involved a transfer of notes to the man's hand. Even then he sat immobile and I went around to the back and began to pull out the trays myself. The scraping brought him, with an idea.

"Look, sir, we can put the ba-king in the other trays."

"That'll take time."

He had already started to work, frenziedly, forgetting that the buns were mine. Keeping them was sheer profiteering but a sudden crusade against waste had me at a moral disadvantage and in Asia one can't be casual about food, even from an expensive French bakery. I let the driver hide his emptied trays to his own satisfaction and while he was doing it, squeezed myself down into the space these had left, roughly a foot and a half between floor boards and a rack of tea cakes. The man came back looking happy, as well he might.

"You are quite comfy, sir?"

"No. Get moving."

The van was old, the back doors only just shut, and something had happened to the catch, which meant this had to be carefully reinforced with a piece of looped cord. I had limited visibility through a gap, about a quarter of an inch, and lay there peering out, suddenly hit by gloom from the thought that my current prodigality in handing out money, a new development, was very likely a clear clinical symptom of impending financial disaster. No one has ever called me a mean Scotsman to my face, and I don't feel I've earned the classification, but I've never forgotten that my grandfather started up in Shanghai almost ninety years ago with total assets of sev-

148

enty pounds sterling, which, by diligence and a careful watch for sinful waste, he managed to increase some five thousand times before his demise, the good work carried on by my father at a much lower but still healthy rate of multiplication, this trust duly handed over to me in my turn. The race I belong to still secretly believes in that old saw about three generations from shirt sleeves to shirt sleeves and here was the third generation wildly handing out bribes to Tamil rubber tappers, private plane owners, and bakery wagon drivers, as though seized by a kind of compulsive madness. What my legal partner and fellow Scot in Singapore was going to say to all this I could well imagine. Russell Menzies can laugh off most things except extravagance with money.

We bumped down to the wire fence, were allowed through it without incident, and then coasted the rest of the way to the main road without benefit of engine because the driver, even after his killing on the bakery market, couldn't shake off a habit of saving juice whenever possible as part of his fiddle on the running expenses of his vehicle. I lay there expecting the old crate to resist the starter when we reached the highway, which would probably mean that I had to lie under loaves of bread and the eyes of my besiegers for two hours while a tow-truck came out from the city. But we were spared this; three and a quarter cylinders came to life with a jerk from second gear and our turn up the main road gave me a moderately clear view down it.

Parked not five yards from the stone pillars marking the beginning of my property was a rent-a-car Ford in which sat a man I knew well. Inspector Kang was smoking a cigar and looked fresh, as though he had only recently arrived to take over from an underling after a night in the city's most comfortable hotel and a very leisurely breakfast. As the distance between us slowly widened I waited for the Inspector to reach out a hand to the starter button and pursuit. However, his usual sharpness seemed a little blunted this morning and he continued to sit motionless, apparently placidly waiting for a quarry who just might possibly walk away from his home, but if he rode, would certainly use the Mercedes.

I found it a shade disturbing that Kang wasn't in the least furtive about this watch at a mousehole. He looked like a man who has been given carte blanche authority, even to the point of a temporary command over a section of the local police. If this was the case, it meant that the friends I thought I had in high places in Kuala Lumpur weren't so friendly anymore. I was Harris the great unloved, and it was entirely possible that word had leaked already about a threat to my business interests, which meant that the smiles money puts on surrounding faces would now be gone.

Near the entrance to the Botanics I severed my connection with that purveyor of starch heaviness. He was cheerful, I wasn't. Like an overtipped taxi driver, the man came around to help me out.

"Oh, my goodness me, sir. You have flour on your suit-tings."

I stopped that cloakroom-attendant act.

"The money I gave you means no talking about any of this. Can you cover those missing trays?"

"Oh, yes indeed. There are many in store at the ba-kery. And my lips are sealed forever."

He would squawk, of course, the moment half a degree of heat was applied.

The Botanics are always interesting, visited by exotic birds, but the featured attraction was a tribe of monkeys grown exhibitionist from being stared at. These put on a nonstop parody of intimate human domestic and other behavior which is more unnerving to the unprepared than the sickest late-night review. Sometimes, too, there are accidents of the kind which occur even in the best-trained circuses. I was walking my dog once when a simian beatnik started to act a junky high up in his tree, swaying about on top branches, then slowly overbalancing to come plummeting down with ear-piercing shrieks. The trick, of course, was to catch the lowest limbs seconds before it was too late and then jerk upright to leer at a startled audience. But that little monkey didn't manage to catch the lowest limb. It was rather sad. The rest of the troupe gave him a full two-minute silence before carrying on with the show.

Teng wasn't watching the monkeys, he was sitting in the Cadillac by the duck pond, looking like a small-town tycoon who always gets an inferiority complex when he comes up to the real bustle of the big city. Through the curved windshield he observed my approach, but gave no sign, the scowl on his already marred face not lifting at all. Possibly it upset him that we weren't entirely alone in that part of the gardens, though I couldn't see any great threat to security from two Chinese amahs supervising three flaxen-haired children who had the high treble British voices which somehow suggest an inherited residue of racial arrogance.

These kids had certainly been born far too late for any easy confidence about their automatic position in the world, but when you are brought up with an amah always handy to kick with impunity any time you feel like it, this tends toward an isolation—during formative years—from the real facts of our time. I've often wondered what happens to the little amah-kickers when they get back to the second-class English suburbia which is on the cards for most of them, but I've never been in a position to find out.

The largest child, tall and rather bony, had lost interest in the monkeys and was throwing stones at a very Chinese-looking drake, who continued a leisurely circuit of his domain, completely ignoring the little Western barbarian. The girl turned toward me. She had a big-featured face which seemed unlikely to fine down later into anything remotely approaching good looks and I had felt at our first meeting that her father's genes had been heavily dominant at conception, and that father couldn't by any stretch of the imagination be the poet she now called daddy. It was an uncharitable thought to have, but these do rise unbidden from time to time with most of us, unwelcome byproducts of our natural powers of observation.

"Hello, Penny."

The child didn't smile and the tone of her response suggested a bored deb at a pre-wedding cocktail party.

"Hel-laow."

Betty's daughter was growing up a long way from her mother's heritage of British nonconformism. When I opened a door of the Cadillac the girl was still watching me, with a line between her eyebrows indicating concentrated attention, as though she had learned early that a precocious intelligence could offer a real threat in her contest with the adult world.

"Who's that?" Teng asked, his stare leaving no doubt as to what he meant.

I told him, and he at once started the car, driving away from the ducks, pulling up again under a vast durian tree where shade diminished the conspicuousness of the Cadillac. Then he heaved a very deep sigh.

"You can't have anything like my reasons for feeling sad," I said.

"Paul, I've only just found out about that nurse I sent you."

"Oh?"

"You must understand that I had to get someone in a hurry and did. There was no question of looking into credentials.

151

Though I knew she was no longer a registered nurse and . . . the reason. What I didn't know is that she is active in the Communist party. One somehow doesn't expect this with Malays. She comes from a village outside Kampar. And I can tell you I didn't get much sleep last night after I found out about her past. But there just wasn't any way of getting in touch with you."

He looked at me.

"The American? He's all right?"

"Coming on nicely, thank you."

"Oh. Look, go back to your house at once and throw that woman out. It's not safe to have her."

"You came all the way down here to tell me this?"

"But of course, I felt responsible. That so-called nurse could have been a deliberate plant. It's more than possible she has orders to see that the American doesn't leave your place alive."

"What a good guesser you are, Teng."

"You mean . . . she tried something?"

"Oh, yes. And failed. She's dead."

I watched for a reaction. It came with elaborate slowness, like a Victorian actor registering stunned astonishment. Jaw muscles slackened, his mouth opened. The voice which emerged had a quaver in it.

"How?"

"A razor blade on her wrists. It seems she couldn't face up to reporting failure. The party she belonged to isn't understanding in these circumstances."

"But . . . a dead woman? The police?"

"Only you and I know."

"You've concealed the body?"

"Yes."

He was staring.

"Why?"

"To buy time. I need it. There's a busy night ahead for me. Would you like to stay close during it?"

I got no response to this invitation. I was only given that over-fleshed profile again while he stared through the windshield.

"Teng, you haven't by any chance been in communication with your father's cousin over in Penang?"

It positively hurt him to squeeze out the truth, but this came after a time.

"Yes."

152

"Was my adoptive father greatly concerned about the attempt on my life? Or hadn't he heard?"

"He'd heard."

"I thought he would have, somehow. Did he tell you about the train as well?"

"What train?"

"They made a second bid to get me on it. Death in a sleeping car. And do you know who I think 'they' are, Teng? Lum Ping's boys. Someone has tipped off the Red leader that I'm still active. They want to stop this. Because they're highly jumpy just now. They don't want any premature leak of their plans in southern Thailand. That would spoil the surprise element, which is such a great psychological factor."

Teng's small hands were tight on the wheel.

"I wonder who tipped Lum Ping off?" I said.

His breathing suddenly became audible.

"Paul, you listen to me. Give this up now. All of it. Stop whatever you're trying to do."

"Is this a recollection of old friendship just tearing you apart? Or am I getting warmer than any of you thought I would?"

"I'm not involved in any of this!"

"That sounds like a press handout. I never believe them."

He had to look at me then. I don't think my expression was open and warm; it wasn't meant to be.

"I just don't know what you're driving at?"

"Very well, it's this. You didn't come tearing down here to warn me about Mrs. Hasmah. No one knew what was happening up at my house. You were sent to find out."

"No! Mrs. Hasmah—"

"Let's forget about the nurse. She failed. There was every expectation that she would succeed. And that absolute dead silence from my fortress was beginning to get on everyone's nerves."

"You suggest I'm working for the Reds?"

"Teng, it could be that you're just sitting on the fence, with a foot scuffing the dirt on each side. I pointed out to you before that a lot of your big people are playing it that way and it isn't healthy. Maybe you're down here just as a message boy. Well, whatever the message, it's not accepted."

It got so quiet in the car I almost wanted to switch on the radio. Teng was sweating.

"All right," he said finally, and with a kind of bitterness. "I'm a message boy. I don't expect you to understand. What do you know about the pressures Chinese like me are under?"

"Quite a lot. I just wish that more of them were resisting those pressures. I can take it you haven't?"

"You can . . . think any damn thing you like! I got a message, yes. But not because I work for them."

"What was it?"

"A phone call last night. A voice I didn't know. Chinese. I was told I was known to be associating with you. The man said he thought I had a better chance of seeing you than anyone else. And if I took you the message, it would be remembered."

"Blackmail."

"All right, call it that. But I was thinking of you!"

"Sure. What were you told?"

"If you give up what you're doing now things will be made easy for you."

He got that out in a rush and then stared at travel dust on the engine hood of his beautiful car.

"How will they be made easier?"

"Your business troubles will be ended."

"I see. All my crews will be ordered to renounce their Communist party allegiance and serve me faithfully as good little capitalists? What else?"

"There will be finance if you need it."

I was really flattered.

"From mother China?"

"Paul, stop making a joke of this!"

"I know it's no joke. And if I don't play?"

"The man didn't say."

"It's tremendous news they're unhappy enough to try and buy me off. Foreign currency doesn't come easy to them. I'm beginning to feel important."

"You won't be . . . dead."

I could have given Teng a little lecture on the ethical principles behind Harris and Company's operations, but it wouldn't have done any good; no one seems to understand them but me.

"What am I going to say?" he asked.

"You've got a number to call? How about letting me have it?"

"There is no number! I'm to get a call."

"When you do, tell them I made a rude noise."

Teng's voice was harsh when he said:

"This could be the last time we meet."

"And in some ways the thought is quite a relief to you. But it's a bit too soon to order the wreath."

The car moved off the moment I was clear of it, and much faster than the park speed limit. But the drives are scenic, which means a devious twisting in and out among all those masses of labeled flora. The pedestrian paths are straighter and I strolled along one of them until I got to the cover of a vast, groomed clump of bamboo which looked like a setting for stuffed tigers. Then I ran fast, passing from the bamboo into a patch of artifically preserved jungle with a mock trail through it which had been sprayed with weed killer. If there are any snakes in this nature reserve they all have their poison fangs removed before being granted visas into it. I can recommend the Botanics in Kuala Lumpur to the tourist who wants his tropics packaged and sterilized. You can see it all here as safely as you could from a moviehouse seat, and with smells added, together with more tree orchids visible in half an hour than you would come on in a week's ramble through the natural rough stuff.

I was in sight of the main gates when the nose of a Cadillac came poking down toward them. The car braked. A man came out of shrubbery, ran to the door flanking the driver's, and got in. A moment later he got out again with a purpose, which was me. I knew this from the way the man was traveling through a park grown silent over the lunch hour. He was coming at the double toward the spot where I had last been seen.

Cover about me was flimsy. I went under the big hardwoods, hoping to merge with their shadow, but not too happy about the way secondary growth had been kept thinned. I could feel the faint stirring of a breeze, which was wrong for jungle; the air should have been still and drained of oxygen.

There wasn't a long wait for Teng's assistant and probable postman. He came jogging down the path I had left at an easy lope which somehow seemed to put his feet weightless on packed earth. And then he stopped.

I had seen stops like this quite recently during my border expedition. It was the trained tracker's halt for frozen listening, something provoked by an extra instinct and apparently quite beyond the rational. It is as though anything abnormal to a particular place sends out some kind of psychic tremor which can be picked up on the invisible antennae of those who are equipped with these. Only one of my guides along the frontier had appeared to be in possession of this extrasensory perception, the other man being not a great deal more perceptive than I had been, and slightly in awe of his companion.

I had been slightly in awe myself, and felt this again as a head turned slowly in my direction. Teng's helper was no stranger. The man out there on the path had kept me company for two weeks in Thailand.

Shock did unpleasant things to my pulse rate, though I tried to keep this from my breathing. I remembered, not happily, that dogs are supposed to be able to pick up the scent of fear at some considerable distance, and anything a dog could do Ho Tai could do better.

I had never liked his eyes much, probably because you rarely saw them; he preferred even in shadow to shelter his intelligence behind slits that would have left a European blind. I couldn't see his eyes now, just the hollows in his skull which held them. He was massively strong, able to lift a rotting hardwood tree trunk and send it sloshing down into a sluggish jungle stream to make a bridge for our passing. I had seen him break branches for a fire with two bare hands, solid pieces of timber I would have needed to work on for some time with my little hatchet. It had been quite obvious early in our journey that any matching of physical strengths was to be avoided at all costs. The matter hadn't arisen. It looked as though it might now.

He was at a slight disadvantage out there in leaf-filtered sunlight, but I didn't see how this was likely to serve me. Ho Tai knew I was in my shade and almost exactly where. My identity meant something to him; there had been plenty of time for it to become established as part of his receptive patterns, and a radiation beyond my control, very much more potent than any smell of sweat, had stopped this man dead in an automatic recognition.

I have no explanation of this thing. It happens, and it is pretty horrible to witness it happening to you. I knew then what a fool I had been to let curiosity about Teng's assistant make me wait to see the man. The Botanic Gardens are a big park, too far out from the city center to be much used by lunchtime sandwich eaters, and probably Ho Tai and I had at least some well-wooded acres to be alone in. A body would be found in due course by the disinfectant squad or someone's imported dalmatian, but that was no comfort. I could shout, but with small hope of help.

I remembered the man's hands. These had no hint of deli-

156

cate Oriental boning, but were swollen from hard use. I was going to have to shoot Ho Tai before those hands got near enough to touch me, and the time to shoot him was while he was still exposed.

More of my life than I like to remember has seen a gun in my pocket available for use, but that use has almost always been as a threat of extra power in my possession. I didn't think this threat would serve with Ho Tai. He had an arrogance that would bring him on where another would be held. A bullet smacking near him would be likely to send the man lunging into shelter, and under these trees he could make a highly skilled use of cover I wouldn't be able to match. The stalker's total silence wouldn't be easy to match, either.

I had the feeling he would know when I reached for the Colt, that the lifting of my arm would flick him into action. My rigidity was acting as a kind of partial baffle to his complete perception of my presence, and he was now waiting for fear to betray me into movement.

The city intruded, a sudden, screeching violence, brakes jammed on, tires skidding, then the explosive clang of metal being shattered by impact. It was as though a distant, practically unnoticed hum of town traffic had suddenly been turned up for catastrophe, and the hysterical shouting which followed a car crash reached us magnified, tearing away an illusion of jungle stillness under park trees. Ho Tai's weirdly held spell dissolved around him, and he stood there looking almost physically diminished, unnerved and spent, like a medium emerging from the trance state. His head turned toward that din from a boulevard and his hands lifted slowly. He wiped the sweat off the palms of his hands on his trousers.

Ho Tai didn't look back toward the shadow which held me. The cutting off of that reserve power had left him little better than a servant with specific instructions. He had been told that I was probably hurrying to get out of the park by the gate I had used to come in. Suddenly the man began to run. I let myself have the deep breath for which my lungs had been petitioning.

TEN

Ohashi's mother had continued to live on in her little house at Kamakura, declining politely over the years all invitations to come down to Malaysia for a long visit or to stay. It seemed rather as though she had given up the usual Japanese parental claims on an offspring until one day a letter arrived, quite a short one, in which the lady announced that she had found Seki a suitable wife in Yokosuka through the good offices of a well-known and highly reputable go-between. Son was expected to fly home the following week for the formal engagement party. Ohashi had translated the letter for me and been somewhat sheepish about the whole thing.

"It is necessary that I obey my mother's wish, Mr. Harris."

"Even though you've never seen the girl?"

He bowed.

"Truly. My mother certainly most careful in choice."

And Mrs. Ohashi senior had been. The bride arrived in Malaysia after only one meeting with my codirector, and that over ceremonial tea cakes, wearing the polite, gently smiling expression of someone who has been taught to take life as it comes and never to indulge in extravagant hopes or romantic fantasies. Mitsuoko was representative of a new generation which seems to have taken to conservatism as a reaction against a postwar over-Westernization of Japan, and if any contemporary influences had been brought to bear on her twenty-year experience of living, none of these showed. She came down the plane steps wearing kimono and thick flapping sandals, carrying an airline bag as though still slightly suspicious of this, and bowing with precisely the same degree of politeness, first to me as Ohashi's boss, then to her future husband.

The girl was pretty enough in an unemphatic way, but the thought that her entrance into a room could cause a stir of male interest would have shocked her to the core. That sort of effectiveness was left to geishas and whores, the respectable building their futures on totally unexhibitionist virtues. I had arranged a small party for the occasion, which Mitsuoko's reserve rather kept from being a riotous success, and though both Ohashi and I had sore heads the next morning, it was from alcohol resorted to in desperation and not the result of any really festive intemperance.

I must admit that I feel the Japanese approach to marriage has a lot to be said for it. In the first place, the parties contracted to each other for a lifetime under the same roof enter into the relationship with the massive advantage of having no personal responsibility at all for their situation, and if things don't work out can blame mum and dad and the go-between, not their own youthful folly. The psychological boost here from the start is obvious. And since true love is regarded by most Orientals as slightly comic, if not downright indecent as an idea, its gradual erosion under wear and tear never becomes a depressive factor, because you can't lose what you never expected or even contemplated as a byproduct of the married state. Also, the go-between takes his responsible job very seriously indeed, and does his best to balance temperaments, match social backgrounds, religious environments, and financial reserves, as well as doing a careful check of health records on both sides as far back as three generations. If there is anything at all to be said against this well worked out tradition, it is perhaps that marriage by arrangement doesn't seem, on the whole, to produce a high degree of gaiety in the home. Everyone is just a shade too resigned to the inevitable from round one onward and this naturally cuts down on the fun content.

It seemed to me that Ohashi was happy enough with his Mitsuoko, but that she hadn't done a great deal to increase his capacity for laughter, which had always been fenced around anyway by a certain nervousness about what was permitted as risible matter. Then, too, insofar as I was concerned, I remained a shade uncomfortable about whether or not my colleague's wife liked me at all, which was of course just a hangover from the silly Occidental desire to be loved for myself alone and not just smiled at because I was boss.

Mitsuoko always smiled, and twenty-five minutes after I had left the Botanic Gardens she opened a door to the apartment over the downtown offices of Harris and Company, the smile at once there, an instant ceremony of it. Mitsuoko's smile was just about as meaningful as the one that Japanese

159

airline hostess is continually being shown offering to the world at large.

"Ah. Good day to you, Mr. Harris. You will please come into this house?"

That had been the idea which had brought me sneaking in from a back courtyard and up the service stairs—temporary sanctuary in these rooms which I had so expensively provided for my assistant.

Mitsuoko closed the door and continued smiling. If she had been washing up the lunch dishes or getting on with some cleaning, this didn't show. Not one of her oiled black hairs had drifted out of place. Her day kimono was bright without being frivolous. Her hands, folded together at navel level, suggested infinite leisure available in which to play gracious hostess.

"The weather is still very hot," she essayed in her provincial school English. Since the weather in Malaysia always is, this didn't provide much of a talking point, but it had probably been one of the basic phrases in her textbook.

"Please enter sitting room, Mr. Harris."

What Ohashi's wife had done to that apartment had acutely depressed me the first time I saw it after they moved in. It was a gracious room, converted from the offices of moribund palm-oil brokers, and at startling cost to me, long and low, with three windows onto a cool balcony which I had envisaged as a kind of terrace. Mitsuoko, an exile from the only reasonable civilization the world has produced, had decided to furnish the place as a continual reminder to her husband that he was in an alien land and sojourning among glossy savages. She had packed in a vast amount of the kind of chain-store furniture likely to produce a moan of pain from anyone with even moderate good taste: experimental chairs with chromium supports, sectional bookcases but with no books, a vast radio console of shining mixed veneers, a bright upright pianola, two cocktail cabinets which lit when opened, and fifteen or sixteen large and lurid oil paintings of the Malaysian scene done by a local artist for the station waiting room trade. Under all this was a vast, hot jute carpet which fought for its share of attention with huge purple roses. Mitsuoko had been grimly determined that not even the faintest hint of traditional Japanese restraint should be allowed to mar her achievement and there was no *ikebana* flower arrangement, just pots of shiny leaved exotics scattered about, these climbing as high as seven feet and giving out a faintly repulsive smell which even whirring fans couldn't dissipate. On my first viewing the girl had used the air-hostess smile, producing along with it a gentle impertinence:

"You like, Mr. Harris?"

That might have been the moment to state flatly that I saw through a plot to undermine her husband's easy content in South Asia and get him back to a paper-walled house in Kamakura as quickly as possible. Mrs. Ohashi senior had done a subtle job of wife-picking which almost certainly meant that son would be resident in Nippon again by the time it would be necessary for proper rituals to be observed, with him as high priest, to Mama's departed spirit. Mitsuoko would get the boy home even if this involved a steady but nonfatal dietary poisoning. And through it all she would wear that smile of sweet docility.

Once again I walked into a room offering a slow death of the spirit and with all my attention seized by its clutter. It was perhaps half a minute before I noticed that a chair in a corner by a terrace door was occupied. Inspector Kang was sitting in it.

"Hello, Paul," he said with the politeness which never deserted him.

I was near enough to the man to see now a patch of flesh-colored bandage worn in the middle of his forehead. He was smoking and had been sipping beer. The Japanese hostess nips off at once when there are two men in a room likely to produce some rough male talk which it is better for her not to hear, but before she left Mitsuoko gave me a lager, a bow, and that smile. I watched her bouncing sash to a door, with the thought coming to me that the girl could easily have given a gentle warning that alien forces were in occupation of her house. I didn't believe for one moment that she had been too frightened to do it. I turned to Kang.

"Very smart," I said.

He shook his head.

"Not particularly. All I had to do was follow some baking, not too close. Though I made the mistake of deciding to follow you on foot in the park. Which meant that when your friend Teng decided he didn't like children I got left behind. It's a big park."

"You know Teng?"

"I know nearly everyone in this country and in Singapore

161

who has in one way or another made himself prominent." Then he added, as though he paid the taxes on the place, "Do sit down."

I chose a contour model in his area and was glad of the support it gave my tired body.

"Your assistant had an early lunch," Kang told me. "He's gone back to work."

"By arrangement?"

"Well, yes."

"What hold have you got over him? I thought it was the Americans."

"We used persuasion."

"We?"

"I'm not alone. It seemed time to refer to higher authority. Send for it, in fact. So I called in my chief from Singapore. He flew up. He's out on the veranda."

This sent a twinge along my nerves. The Inspector was not referring to his superior in the police force, but to the controller of his moonlighting. Down in the big city on an island I had sat in the Cricket Club over my drink and played a guessing game about which of the many prominent businessmen coming in for lunch was, in fact, also the branch manager for British Intelligence Southeast Asia. It seemed obvious that he would be a businessman, someone well rooted in commercial respectability and probably a pillar of the chamber of commerce. The game is an interesting one, and I'd felt I was getting warm once or twice but in actual fact had never really come up with a clear lead. My private sources of information had also let me down on this issue.

The fact that this man with two lives was now hidden out there beyond masonry, but within earshot, was somehow acutely disturbing. His quick flight north seemed to give me a personal importance of the kind I didn't want at all.

"Is your boss going to stay faceless, Kang?"

"That's up to him."

"I could dash out there and have a look."

"I wouldn't," the Inspector said.

There was now a little revolver out on the arm on Kang's overstuffed chair; mine was still in a trouser pocket. All I did was lean forward, while Kang's finger closed over a butt, to peer through the French doors. I saw the tip of one shoe, from the Bata cheap range. The fragrance of the cigar smoke, however, said Havana leaf, which these days, certainly in the Far East, means the smoker is in the real money.

162

Kang was watching me, his face suddenly rather stern, as though a twinge from that bump on his head had reminded him once again that I sometimes played by ungentlemanly rules. But his voice stayed cool.

"All we want from you, Paul, is a straightforward account, as honest as you can make it, of what you've been up to since you signed on with the Americans. Don't skip anything. We have a remarkable number of cross-checks."

My loyalty to Washington was pretty new and had been subject to undermining stress. Besides, I had resigned, whether this had been accepted or not. So I talked.

Kang didn't ask many questions and somehow, put into words, my career as a spy seemed not only brief but starred with ineptitude. I might have been convincing myself that this wasn't a field for which I had been cut out at all, that the secrets I uncovered best, and knew how to use when I had, were commercial ones.

There was a short postlude of total silence when I had finished, during which I drank lager.

"Want me to work for *you* now?" I asked.

"No," Kang said, without hesitation.

"You aren't startled to learn that the Reds have a major supply line through this country?"

"We knew they did."

"Do you know more about it than Clem's lot?"

"It wouldn't be policy to answer that."

"Then if I'm no use to you, how about letting me go home? I haven't had any lunch."

"I think we might do that. And you can take a message from us to Mr. Winburgh."

"Delighted."

"Just tell him that he can have a private escort out of Malaysia and Singapore any time he asks for it. Or even a British Navy helicopter flight if he would prefer that. Perhaps to some U. S. hospital ship?"

"I think he'd prefer to travel by commercial airline if you'd lend him the fare?"

"That could be arranged."

"I can scarcely wait to get home with the good news. You get tired of having your house turned into a hospital. And if you send an ambulance for a body it will be allowed through my gates. After a search, of course. You would like to have a look at that body?"

"Yes."

"Make the collection in about an hour. With no more than one man besides the driver. And call off the local police watch on my place."

"Paul, you're scarcely in a position to start laying down terms."

I smiled at him.

"I don't think my position is too bad. You can't touch me. The real problem now is getting my business back on its feet."

"And that's going to be one helluva job," said a voice from the veranda, a voice I have known well ever since I was a laddie in short trousers.

I don't think my jaw dropped, but it could have. The figure blocking light was huge to the point of indecent obesity. He was a man who moved rarely, and then usually only to the source of his beer supply. He had lived in Malaysia for thirty years, been interned by the Japanese in Changi jail, survived to rebuild his interests to a point which at times threatened mine. He was my lawyer, and one of the three directors of Harris and Company, Russell Menzies.

I simply hadn't looked under my own nose for the man with two faces. But he had been sitting there in an office chair all the time, the perfect candidate, a practicing lawyer and businessman, with fingers in every conceivable pie from Mindanao to Christmas Island, unmarried, with no one in this world he cared enough about for his enemies to kidnap and use against him. Almost an untouchable, in fact, humanly speaking, who had plenty of Scotch sentiment but no heart. Anyone in Singapore, or indeed Southeast Asia, from blackmailed *towkays* to adulterous British wives caught in the act, could and did come to that office, sometimes dozens of them in one day. No visitors there, no matter how weird, would cause any comment among other tenants of the building. It looked as though London still knew how to pick its man on location.

"Doesn't this put an end to your security?" I asked after about a minute. "Or do I have to swear another oath of secrecy?"

"A lot of use your oath would be, my boy." He trundled to one of the many chairs available. "As it happens I'm leaving the service. Handing over to my successor next month. And you won't find out who he is until he's also ready to retire."

"I hope you're getting a knighthood out of all this?"

Russell put his feet on a small table. They had a tendency

to swell up when they had to bear his weight for more than five minutes.

"Only the OBE. The thing they hand out to guitar players and designers of miniskirts since we ran out of empire. In my case for services to Anglo-Malaysian friendship. It's more than I expected from the present government and they've been remarkably considerate. On account of my phlebitis I don't have to travel to London to collect, which is just as well, since I wouldn't have gone anyway. Too busy here."

"Doing what, if you're retiring?"

"Saving Harris and Company from the ruin you've devised. It's the only active interest I'm retaining. And I'm doing it for the sake of your father and your brother. I was fond of them."

I was suddenly conscious then of the years during which I had been under close observation from this man, most of what I was up to known to him, or at least guessed at, and never once in all that time had he contemplated using me as part of his network. It wasn't highly complimentary.

"How did you recruit Kang?" I asked.

"That's one of the few good things I owe to you. He was on your trail for something or other when we made contact. And a most satisfactory relationship it has turned out to be, eh, Inspector?"

"Better for you," Kang said, which endeared him to me. Russell ignored the comment.

"I'm moving up to this town, dear boy. To live with you, actually. It's vital that you have me available day and night during this delicate phase in your affairs. I don't like the climate here in Kuala Lumpur particularly, but I'll endure it. I'd even become a Malaysian if that would help, though it seems rather a surly thing to do just after receiving that high British honor. And I belong to a generation which doesn't switch nationality easily, just passports when this is called for."

I stood up.

"Before you commit yourself too deeply to my affairs, Russell, there is one thing you ought to know. The company junk fleet is about to be mothballed."

"Oh, I heard all about that from poor Ohashi. He was most distracted. And, of course, it's a bit of emotional extravagance on your part. Certainly find the ringleaders and sack a few. Disciplinary action, that sort of thing. But, my dear boy, you can't purge a whole fleet."

"I can."

"I'd be interested to hear how?"

"I'm hiring Dyaks."

Russell's feet crashed to the floor.

"What? Those Borneo pirates!"

"Ex-pirates. There hasn't been a conviction against them for years. Further, they're totally untainted by Marxism. Out here Marxism comes from China and they hate everything Chinese. And they know these seas like the tines on their hands."

"You're being quixotic."

"You've said that about some of my other plans. But they paid off in the end. Russell, I intend to have crews I can rely on as working for me alone."

"You've tried Dyaks before."

"I've tried mixing them with Chinese and that didn't work."

"And you think you can train those fellows in your kind of trading?"

"Yes. It may take a year, even longer."

"Who's going to finance you during that time? From all I hear, you won't get credit from a bank or any of your Chinese associates."

I smiled at him.

"You're coming up here to devote yourself entirely to my business in your retirement. Under these circumstances I should think you'd want to make that personal investment in Harris and Company which you've always avoided so far. Say a round hundred thousand pounds?"

Russell's eyes have always suggested an acute thyroid condition. Now they threatened to leave their sockets. It was rather pleasing to have rendered the head of British Intelligence Southeast Asia totally speechless. When he did make a sound it wasn't much more than a croak.

"Kang. Get me a beer."

I waited until my codirector had a glass in his hand, then said:

"If Clem decides to accept your assistance out of the country, how do I get in touch with you?"

"Through my office in Singapore, of course. I'm going back there on the three-o'clock plane."

"And the code word?" I asked politely.

He glared.

"There isn't one, damn you! Get out!"

The patient had suffered a slight relapse, probably brought on by overexertion. He lay looking pale and back into that deceptive innocence again. He opened his eyes with reluctance.

"What was all that row in the passage?"

"Ambulance men carrying out Mrs. Hasmah."

His eyebrows lifted.

"What's happened to her?"

"She became unconscious in the bathroom."

Clem stared.

"Ambulance? You mean the police?"

"Yes."

"And you let them in?"

"I had to."

"They just took her away and no questions asked?"

"The questions may come later. But I hope not."

He had no comment on that. I was quite certain that Clem knew his former nurse was dead. His surprise wasn't a very good act, probably because he really was feeling feeble. I believed he had been active. To a man with his training, forcing back a simple mortise lock with a piece of plastic wouldn't be a very formidable task, even with one hand and shaky knees. He would have had the house to himself during Chow's lunch hour.

"Have you been exercising today?" I asked.

He looked at me, suspicious.

"I had a walk in the garden. Must have overdone it. Got back into bed with my heart thumping and thankful for the pillows."

"I think you need better medical attention than you're getting here. And you can leave any time you want to now."

"How come?"

I told him, in some detail. He didn't like any of it.

"So you were caught?"

"In a way."

"One is either caught or one isn't."

"All right, I was caught."

"And by the British."

"You make that sound as if the British were public enemy number one."

"There have been a number of times in our history when they were."

"Long ago."

167

"Oh, sure."

My news had soured him. I went out and took Taro for a circular walk around the grounds and then we both went back and lay on our beds. I stared at the ceiling and thought that though Russell had probably returned to Singapore on the three-o'clock flight, Kang certainly hadn't. They had both been a little too ready to let me walk out of the Ohashi sitting room as though I were a totally free agent again, when both of them knew perfectly well I wasn't. The only relief to the pressures on me was the fact that the local police had been called off.

It is difficult for us to put our associates of long standing into a role totally outside anything we expect from them. I could see Russell as the perfect candidate for his undercover job, but still couldn't really picture him functioning in it. And I was almost grateful that he had retired so I didn't have to try. It wouldn't be easy getting that money out of a close-fisted Scotsman, but I was going to do it. As a replacement for my slowly vanishing Japanese assistant, the lawyer would be less mobile, but with his contacts a positive magnet for any further financing we might need. And if I could get him onto the board of the shipping company as well, for something like a third of my interest in it, there was a fair chance that before too long I would be able to take that long holiday in Scotland I had been promising myself for years.

The idea of sharing my house with the old beer tank wasn't exciting, but this, too, would offer positive advantages. Russell got on with dogs and I could safely leave Taro with him when I was in Europe. It would also mean someone for Chow to fuss over in my absence.

There was yet another point. Malaysia being what it is, no one in the country was going to believe that Russell had been given the OBE just for making money, and he hadn't apparently done much else. There was no record of his public beneficence to Singapore or, insofar as I knew, even small contributions to charity. This all meant that the moment the honor was announced, there would be much speculation about it, something that a grateful British government had apparently overlooked. In the end the truth, or an approximation of it, would leak, something which wouldn't do Harris and Company one little bit of harm. In fact, the news that such a man had now switched his complete attention to my company would scare the pants off some of my rivals. Spying at the top executive levels still retains a suggestion of slightly supernatural concealed talents. It might be sound policy for me to leak that news about my partner's past.

This sudden upsurge of kindliness toward an old party who, for all his years, still had a commercial potential was sedative, and I slept almost content, waking to find Chow's tea tray by my bedside with the pot on it stone cold. I ate a slice of cook's special marble cake, had a shower, and then began to dress for a party.

When I take time to do this carefully I can achieve a fair approximation of the conservative type who has always gone to the tailor his grandfather patronized and has never had to worry about the rent even under a left-wing government. There was a special incentive to do this, for cocktails at Betty's meant fellow guests from pretty sharply contrasting worlds—her professional associates on the one hand, and her husband's on the other. It was as well to walk into that living room uniformed for the group of your choice, and I much preferred the medicals to middle-aged beatniks who had come to bring their light to an Asia which didn't want it.

Clem noted my suddenly acquired glossiness with an eye that held all the venom of a recently caged puma.

"Fun time now, is it?"

"That's right."

"Choke on the caviar."

"There is no need to be bitter. I warned you I was getting out of the spying business and I have. Just a civilian again. Tomorrow we'll make our plans for you."

"Will we?"

He wanted to tell me that he made his own plans, but thought better of it. When I was at the door he called out:

"You won't be back for dinner?"

"I thought I'd have it at the club. You don't mind?"

"Why should I? Got your gun?"

That was slipped out to see if there would be an involuntary tightening of my upper arm against a chest holster, but all I did was grin at him.

"Just a social evening. To mark my retirement."

"Settled your debts yet?"

"What do you mean?"

"All those bribes to get me to sanctuary. And especially that ham character with the plane. He gave the impression of being a man who likes prompt payment for services rendered."

"As a matter of fact, I have a check to him in my pocket,

169

just in case we meet up at the club. Ohashi is taking care of the others. That relieve your mind?"

Clem was pale again. All the cerebration he was forcing on himself wasn't good for a convalescent, who should lie still and let the world flow on without him. His act of being the happy prisoner had worn thin, as though a tension he was now under didn't leave him the reserves to play it.

I went thoughtfully out to the garage and stared at the huge car which at one time had come near to being the big love of my life. I didn't feel this anymore, having been partially seduced from an earlier enthusiasm by that smashed Audi, but there was a strong residual affection and I walked around the brute thinking that the Germans do turn out a nice piece of machinery. There was, too, this evening the added satisfaction of the feeling that maybe, after all, the Mercedes mightn't have to end up in the hands of my receivers. And from that quiet inspection of a great hunk of my property I switched to another check, which had rather become one of my routines.

In our time it is so easy to attach a little gadget full of plastic explosive to the steering or ignition of a man's personal transport that I had cultivated the habit, when I felt that my car just might have been exposed to people who didn't really like me, of not jumping in casually and starting to drive off. A check doesn't take long and can be a life saver. I wasn't, therefore, totally astonished to find a small bakelite box attached to the fuel tank by suction clamps, but I was considerably shocked. For one thing, that box meant that my perimeter fence was just about the folly which Clem rated it. The Mercedes had not, to my knowledge, been out since well before I went north to walk in jungle. The device had been stuck on it right here.

I read *Popular Mechanics* to keep up with the changing world and in a lay manner have a fair idea of what goes on in contemporary gadgetry. That box didn't look like a bomb. Further, in a car as big as a Mercedes a charge on the fuel tank is so far from the driver there's a fair chance he will escape the blast. This suggested strongly an electronic device which had rated an article to itself in my near-technical reading, a piece of current sophistication which sends out radio bleeps enabling a portable monitoring set to keep a reasonably accurate check on the car to which the sending device is attached. This cuts out an actual shadowing of the car you want to follow, with all the risk of being seen which that entails, but lets the pursuer keep out of sight, even quite a long way behind. Those bleeps are your guide, giving a sound picture of the quarry's direction and even speed. You follow as you like.

The gadget may not be as sharply useful on land as radar is at sea, but it was particularly suited to Malaysia, where, once you clear the main cities, there aren't too many feeder side roads. And I could see that the moment I left town the monitor would give a pretty fair indication of where I was going.

In my mind there was suddenly a list of people who had access to this garage. It was quite a long list. I left the box where it was and drove down to the fence, trying not to look with suspicion at the Sikh who let me out, and conscious all the time of a gadget sending out its steady flow of electronic messages. When I stopped at traffic lights somebody knew. The direction I was taking when I turned right beyond them somebody knew, too. It was no way to get into the party mood.

The Hill homestead was in the flattish southern suburbs of the city, a rather unfashionable area. It was a large, two-story wooden house fringed with verandas upstairs and down, which rented cheap because it had been the setting for two suicides and was reputed to be haunted by both these deceased. The one had been a public-works contractor threatened with a bribery exposure, the other a discontented wife who was remembered at the club for her favorite remark that she would die if she had to stay in the country for another year. No one, including her husband, had really believed she meant it.

The place had large grounds, these well wooded and somewhat ill kept. Betty had no time for gardening and Tom no interest in it, and the Tamil they employed mowed some grass but mostly left it at that. It had always seemed to me highly depressive in general effect, the huge trees continuing to drip long after tropic showers had passed, with the ground underneath perpetually damp and highly productive of anemic weeds. The drive twisted about in two acres as though trying to make the approach to the house as impressive as possible but only managing to increase a visitor's sudden sinking of spirits.

However, tonight there was a note of bustle, even a bid for gaiety, many lights, and at least a dozen parked cars, including Betty's Ford tucked slightly clear of the rest as if ready for a sudden getaway when the hospital called. There was no one around in the arrival area though the hum of people growing loud over drinks reached me. I didn't hurry toward the porch steps, suddenly uncertain of my welcome and rather caught by the feeling which hits the solitary from time to time that he is going to be the odd man out at a party entirely composed of couples, half envied and half distrusted because of his state. Further, whatever confidence Betty might have had in our security arrangements, there was unlikely to be anyone in the room, including her husband, who didn't know all about those lunches at Yung Ching Wa's.

Penny met me in the hall, or rather she was posted there like a guard for family heirlooms, dressed in blue jeans and checked silk shirt as though the word about teen-age dominance had reached her five years too soon and in that house the takeover had already started. I got no greeting, but it was quite probable that no one else had, either. She continued to sit on a teak chair with her legs crossed, only removing her lips from the straw into a Coke bottle for long enough to shout, "Daddy!" then returning to her own interests.

Tom Hill was dressed for his side of the party, in white shorts suspended from the kind of waist which looks as though there had been a recent slide of flesh from an earlier chest development. His shirt was red and open necked, with long red stockings to match, and on his feet were Indian sandals. Twenty years earlier he had certainly had the sort of carved classic head which caught everyone's eye when he came into a room, but the carving had slipped here, too, and only his hair, now prematurely snow white, remained perfect, so shaped and tended it looked like a wig.

A decline from great beauty must be a hard thing to adjust to over the years and I have often felt sorry for those who have to do it. Very few of these unfortunates manage the job gracefully and Tom's whole living was now somehow a reminiscence of youth, with his talk an almost continual reminder of the period—just after World War Two—when he had been one of London's literary stars, with just enough talent to sustain that role. Within twenty-four hours of our first meeting he had given me the seventy-two-page book of verse on which his then reputation had been based and the talent was evident enough in most of the pieces, though already flawed by a basic flimsiness of personality. His poems suggested the thin English tenor voice, charming in youth, but which is never going to be beefed up by solid feeding, soon to fade and be lost. Tom had not yet, to my knowledge, taken to drugs as a method of providing dubious fuel for the dying flicker of his gift, but a number of his colleagues out from home to similar Eastern roles had gone in for the cheap opium and an output of gibberish, and the temptation could well be just in front of him.

He smiled at me. His teeth, along with his hair, were well preserved and as white.

"Well, if it isn't our tycoon. Are you relaxing tonight from a takeover bid?"

"No. Just from fighting one against me."

"You chaps never achieve any security, do you? No matter how much money you make?"

"You have a point there, Tom."

"I watch you, dear boy, with a kind of wonder. At your motivations."

"Power," I said, clenching my fists.

He laughed.

"Come and have a drink. I think you'll know everyone. At least in Betty's section. Mine may offer one or two interesting new faces."

It depended on what you call interesting. I was given a gin and a woman from Hampstead Heath in iridescent beads who was on the way to Java to make a definitive study of gamelan music, financed by an American foundation in Poughkeepsie. She had spent the last two years, also under its auspices, writing a definitive work on the Japanese *shakohachi*, and was obviously highly trained in the art of getting dollars for worthy causes, in this case herself. She spoke of the United States with infinite toleration, as well she might, and once again I took a small vow to myself that if I ended up in a state in which it looked as though I would die rich, I'd leave a will in which no trust, foundation, or any other organization for fostering the arts would have a chance to get their hands on one cent of my money.

The lady told me that the great charm of Americans was their utter naïveté, which was unquenchable, to which I said it would be a bad day for all of us if anything quenched it. Her face at once went blank with dislike and she swung around to get another drink. I drifted over toward the men in suits and ties, with their women, and was allowed in, if without any cries of joy. Down the middle of the room was a river of emptiness that might have been a frontier between two hostile states.

The other section was much the loudest. Strident cries

came across to overpower our gossip. They were solving the problems of Asia and had all come to separate, definitive conclusions. One of the things I find disturbing about the large numbers of people these days who have skillfully avoided anything like real work is that they are invariably the most vocal. They are also, by sad default on the part of the workers, the creators of what passes for public opinion. We are in an age when noise counts for so much more than tiresome solid achievement. Anything which moves modestly toward its goal can't be with it, and gets kicked downstairs.

"You look hot, Paul," said a gynecologist.

And at that point our hostess came up with a jug of martini to which ice had been added and allowed to melt. She poured carefully before lifting her head. In her eyes was comment on my presence at the party. There was something else, too, a pain I had seen before, as though at times something drew Betty up to a sharp halt, forcing an introspection of the kind she usually avoided and which left her frightened.

"Can I see you alone?" I asked softly.

"No."

"It's important."

"Not to me."

"What's happened to you?"

"Nothing I want to discuss." She made her voice louder. "So glad you could get *out* tonight."

Betty went off with her jug, a dutiful hostess if not quite able to be a gay one on the fruit juice which was all she allowed herself. I had always had the feeling that her temperance was from heritage rather than a professional need to keep her fingers steady, and she seemed now to move among us not unlike one of the consciously godly surrounded by proclaimed sinners. She certainly gave an impression of having lost her own party, which was thundering on its ginned course. She served it as best she could, with her jug, with Malaysian small eats, and cigarettes, making deliberate intrusions on set pieces of screaming guests, but appearing defeated each time, glad of a little chore which permitted escape.

For the occasion Betty had her hair done in a new way, somehow lacquered straight up from her face. This seemed to me only to accentuate a boned firmness of jaw and put unnecessary emphasis on ears that weren't particularly shell-like. At times she came near to an individual beauty, but this wasn't one of them. Even her dress had fuss points on it which somehow mocked an athletic but still very good figure.

There are only two things which give me a headache—a blow on the skull and a cocktail party. I wasn't drinking much, not from piety, but because these are not the conditions under which I like to do it. And after about an hour I went out for some air, totally unnoticed, I thought, because for the previous five minutes I had been standing alone by open French doors without anyone trying to rid me of solitude.

There were board steps down from the veranda into a section of garden now illumined from the house. This looked remarkably like a cemetery in which no one has been interred for a couple of centuries. Mosquitoes, wiped out in most of Kuala Lumpur by scientific oiling, had persisted here, though their whining was inaudible above that din from a vibrating building.

"Well, what is it?" Betty said from behind me.

Without the jug she looked oddly lost.

"Good news. The patient is leaving my house tomorrow. You don't have to come anymore."

"Oh. All I do now is send my bill?"

"Yes."

"Did you make an expedition here tonight just to tell me this?"

I didn't answer. She watched me light a cigarette, then said:

"I've something to tell *you*. Tom knows."

If I was supposed to reel with shock, I didn't.

"You mean he has told you he knows?"

"Yes. Last night."

"Do we have to feel guilty over lunch once a week?"

"In a place like Yung Ching Wa's, yes. It's a call house for whores."

"It's also the best restaurant in town."

"Don't quibble, Paul. We went there so that our meetings wouldn't be known. And you suggested it that first time because you thought we were going to become lovers."

"I did not! I would never try to seduce a woman on one of those benches. I took you there for the duck and mushrooms."

"All right. We went there just to eat, once a week. But who is going to believe that?"

"I don't suppose Tom does?"

"No, he doesn't. And I didn't try to explain. It was his scene. High drama. When my husband starts to throw his soul around I have to watch him; there is nothing else you can do. And this was quite a remarkable performance. It started with humility. There's nothing really more embarrassing than humility."

"Have a cigarette," I said, opening my case. Betty rationed herself to six a day. She took one now.

"Thank you." Her fingers trembled. "Tom said he knew he hadn't been any use to me. But he wanted to know if we hadn't made something. He believed we had. It came down to Penny. It all hung on Penny, really, the thing we had made. And then I knew that . . . he was on to me there, too. And probably always had been. Right in the middle of his big scene I had the feeling he could name Penny's father any time he wanted to. But he didn't. That would have weakened his position. Penny was the trump card. He talked about the details of life."

"The what?"

"The little things, Paul. The good . . . small things. God in heaven!"

"Betty, don't cry."

"I'm not going to. I know where I stand."

"By Tom and against lunches?"

"Yes."

"Betty, you told me that you had thought of leaving Tom after you'd been married for a couple of years."

"That was when I met Penny's father."

"But he wasn't a long-term possibility?"

"Not with a wife and three children. Anyway, Tom needed me. He always has."

But that wasn't why she had married him, and perhaps it wasn't even true. I couldn't see Tom, in his heyday, needing anyone. He had the whole of his own particular world. Betty had married a golden boy, stunned by beauty. It can be quite blinding when you have been brought up economically in a parsonage and more than slightly starved of it. They had met while the beauty still held and people still turned to look at that head—beauty with its attendant medical mouse.

"He tells me that I'm the chief source of his poetry," Betty said. "That he needs the pain I give him. How is that for an argument?"

"Lousy."

"That's what I said, too. It made him cry."

"All right, you can't stand seeing your husband's tears. What's for us? Occasional meetings in friends' houses?"

"Yes. You won't be troubled for long."

"I wanted to marry you, Betty."

"You had the idea at times," she said.

In the house phone bells rang, from the hall and from a bedroom upstairs. Her head came up.

"I've never yet been able to play hostess without an emergency call from the hospital. The duty surgeon is operating already. What do you bet?"

I walked around toward the parked cars. In ten minutes Betty came out of the house by the front way, half running. She had changed. The party still roared behind her. She went to the Ford, got in, switched on the ignition. Nothing happened. I stopped her yanking at the starter button.

"Damn all cars," she said. "I hate the things."

"Take mine. It's over there."

She stared. Her face was pale, party makeup wiped off. There was only a faint smudge of mascara under one eye.

"What will you do?"

"Someone will give me a lift or I'll get a taxi."

"Oh . . . all right. I'll get it back to you tonight somehow."

"Tomorrow will do."

She got into the driver's seat of the Mercedes and smiled.

"You'll hate it if I nick this."

"Yes. Don't. The car drives itself almost. Let it. You don't have gears to fight."

She laughed.

"Good-bye, Paul."

The move off was gentle. I waited until red lights were extinguished by a turn and then went over to where I had put the Ford's distributor cap under a stump. I lifted the hood, refitted the cap, and got in behind the wheel. It was only when I was in second gear that I had the impression of a face peering at me from bushes, white in the light from the house and against an almost jungle blackness. Penny's face. I braked, then accelerated hard again.

Before the main gates I switched out lights and stopped, getting out to check the main road. It was empty. If anyone was following a bleeping Mercedes they would have a short journey. I had a long one.

ELEVEN

❀ ❀ ❀

The Linguin mine is seventy miles north of Kuala Lumpur, part of the way by the main route north to Perak, then on a branch off it which climbs three thousand feet to a pass over the main range. Just beyond the pass is a side track barred by a lift gate, and a Tamil is in attendance there day and night, controlling single-line traffic over a private road. This pushes up for another two thousand feet, on a gradient starting at one in four and getting worse almost immediately. The track, carved from canyon walls, was designed originally for horse carts, and even though those horses climbed back up it without loads, they couldn't have had long working lives. A medium-power car on this now tarmacked route soon starts sliding back in ratios, settling for a groaning low before the top.

Linguin has been in operation for nearly sixty years, one of the few deep mines for tin in a country which mostly dredges this mineral from low-lying surface workings. But particularly rich loadstone seams up in those peaks have kept the whole elaborate operation highly economic, justifying the expense of continually deepening shafts. The labor is entirely Tamil, which is unusual in mining, mostly third and fourth generation on the job, workers who live under the kind of openhanded paternalism which reconciles them to an isolated life. Linguin was started with European capital, and even after the Japanese occupation, when Chinese money moved into most things, it didn't move in here, and the concern is still entirely in the hands of a Franco-British commercial combine.

Those moonlit views, sharpened by swinging headlights, would have been tremendous if I had been able to look at them, but about all I got was a sense of increasing coolness and the occasional roar of a mountain stream spilling down over sheer drops. Up here even the flora changed: there were pine trees and heaths, and the gardens on top held English

178

flowers, not coaxed into sickly life, but growing happily, enjoying an occasional hint of frost.

Betty's abused car took the climb well enough, though its engine announced my arrival some time in advance and I reached the second gate to find the bar already lifted. The Tamil on duty here gave me a polite little salute of the kind which has rather gone out of fashion in recent years, suggesting that this particular Shangri-la still contrived to operate on rather antique patterns.

The mine wasn't in a high valley, but on a ledge beneath peaks, the shelf perhaps three miles long and about a third of a mile wide from steep final slopes to cliffs which spilled away for nearly a thousand feet. The area had long been cleared of any jungle and was set out with an almost Prussian neatness, the great spin wheels of the shaft lifts to the back, along with storage sheds and tin-processing areas, while in front of these were the Tamil "lines," tidy houses all whitewashed, and with their own gardens. Practically edging the chasm, only separated from it by groomed lawns, were the manager's bungalow and three others for technical assistants, these recently built in concrete and looking remarkably like transplants from European suburbia. Even those gardens seemed to deny the tropics, the shrubs in them under control and kept small, as though lush growth were against company policy.

I moved slowly along now level but twisting drives, not quite sure whether that passage through control points meant an automatic announcement of a visitor's arrival, but no one came out of Mickey Davenport's verandaless house to meet me, even when I slammed the car door. A dog barked somewhere, but that was all. I looked at the view.

It was screened by moon-whitened night mist, but I remembered what it was like from visits here with my father, range upon range of jungle-upholstered hills beneath. On a clear day the plain was visible in map detail, the Straits of Malacca beyond it steel blue, the far horizon as much as sixty or seventy miles distant. The windows of this villa offered quite a panorama, but they faced it with a kind of lace-curtained smugness. I walked up steps to rap on something you don't often see in Malaysia, a solid front door. This even had a brass knocker from some Devon cottage industry, a molded dolphin yawning at the world.

Nothing happened, though I began to hear a distant booming inside the house, punctuated by what sounded like rifle shots. It was Western hour on Malaysian television, the dialogue dubbed but the action Hollywood. My second rap wasn't gentle and produced first a glow from a fanlight, then the door opening cautiously as if this were a desirable residential area which had recently been hit by a wave of armed burglaries. That door wasn't actually on a chain but Mickey gave the impression through a crack of being ready to slam it shut again quick and fast. It took quite some time for one eye to identify me, then he said:

"Good God!"

"Sorry to drag you away from 'Stagecoach' and it's a horrible hour to call. But I had something on my conscience."

He looked as though he had something on his. Though perhaps Mickey, for all his good cheer at a bar when someone else was paying the rounds, wasn't the sort of man to let bygones be bygones too easily.

"Where the hell have you come from?"

"Kuala Lumpur. I checked the club but it wasn't one of your nights to fly in. So I drove up to see you. I thought a personal delivery of this check would be more gracious. Especially since you feel I nearly killed you at one point."

"You damn well nearly did," Mickey said, staring at the check.

"I've had warmer welcomes but have learned to control touchiness and accept any. We went down a passage which bisected the building, toward an opening from which came the television noises. The sitting room had been placed at the back, away from the view, apparently with the idea that the manager could sit there and check that all his wheels were revolving properly. Though I had known Marjorie and Mickey even before I came to live in Kuala Lumpur, it had been something of a club relationship, intimate after the third gin Collins, but somehow grown cold again the next morning. I had been asked to the rare parties they gave, but somehow had never managed to make it.

Now, looking around that contemporary sitting room, I couldn't but remember the old bungalow which this precast box had replaced. There had been a mongoose imported from India who lived under elevated teak flooring and frequently put on a snake-killing act at sunset when it could be sure of a drinks-hour audience. I must have been about ten when I witnessed that, and it suddenly seemed long ago.

Mickey switched off the television with all the obvious reluctance of a host who has been interrupted just when he has settled in for a solid evening's viewing with his feet up and a bottle of whiskey handy.

"I must say that was a long drive just to deliver a check."

I smiled at him.

"But a fine night. I decided to break with routine."

"I suppose you'd like a drink?"

"Thanks."

While he poured he glanced down at the check I had placed on his chairside table, as though to see whether I had met promised liberality. I had, and this seemed to force him further into the role of host.

"You've eaten, of course?"

"Actually not. Except some anchovies at a party. I rather thought you might be there. It was the Hills'. Their big annual."

"I don't know them well. She's almost never in the club, and Tom's so blasted arty. You've read those poems of his?"

"Everybody has out here."

"They gave me the creeps."

He glanced up at an electric wall clock which said eight fifty-three.

"Look here, my boy's gone, but I could make you a sandwich or something?"

And suddenly he welcomed the idea of getting away on his own for a time. I sat by myself in the living room wondering if the phone here gave a little tinkle when an extension handset was lifted. After a few minutes I checked rather cautiously to see if the manager's line out of Linguin was in use. It wasn't.

Mickey was gone for nearly half an hour, returning with something more than a sandwich—hamburgers tucked into rolls which were so fresh they must have been plucked from deep freeze and popped into a quick oven. He was having one himself. With Marjorie in Majorca supervising the building of that house, her husband had got into bachelor habits of being handy about preparing odd snacks and this was just beginning to tell on his waistline. He needed wifely disciplines about him again, not being the type who could establish many of these for himself. I wondered then how much of his relatively successful career had been Marjorie pushing.

"That do you, old boy?"

Something near to clubhouse joviality had returned.

"Marvelous. Mickey, I want you to know that when I

asked for your help I thought it was a situation which just involved transport. Things got complex again while you were coming to us, and there was nothing I could do about it. I'm sorry you were put to risk."

"Good Lord, is this Paul Harris apologizing?" He grinned. "I'm positively touched, old boy. I don't mind admitting I was livid at the time. And after. But, well . . ." He picked up the check, folded it, and put it in a trouser pocket. "This makes quite a difference. And you being decent about it. Sorry if I was stuffy and all that."

"The police have made no inquiries about your plane?"

"None. I was in a bit of flap that they would. But they can't have seen our markings."

The plane had been identified, all right, and no visit up here suggested the hand of Kang.

I was given another whiskey. Mickey seemed to have forgotten about "Stagecoach." He was now a man able to believe what he wanted to—that my longish journey had been taken on a casual impulse and as a bid to reestablish good relations. I had arrived at a time when the sharpness of his perception was more than slightly blurred by the drinks he had enjoyed before dinner and after. That stab of panic felt when he saw me on the doorstep had been sedated away by more doses from the dimpled bottle.

We talked about the house in Majorca. Marjorie was having some trouble with the local builders, who claimed that the special jungle hardwood imported from Malaysia was blunting their chisels. Plumbers, too, were being difficult and had been caught trying to use Italian plastic drainage pipes not yet trial tested and likely to prove tasty to rats.

"It must all be costing you a packet," I said.

"Don't mention it, old boy. But it's the one house we've built ourselves. We're determined to have it right."

"When do you go to it for good?"

"In a couple of years."

"A bit early for retirement, isn't it?"

"Well, I don't know. I'll be fifty."

He waited for my surprise, which I gave him.

"Quite a number of companies out here are going along with this idea of early retirement at managerial level. The tropics use you up, old boy. Especially if you have to live with my kind of responsibility. Best to get out while you're still ticking over properly."

"And if you've made your pile."

He laughed.

"I won't say that. But the company's being quite generous. I get a big enough golden handshake to make me think they'll be glad to see the last of me. And a pension, of course. That's small, but . . . well . . . Majorca, where the brandy's cheap and all that. And we'll have a little orchard, you know the sort of thing. Start a new life before the old arteries begin to harden. I might open a small shop, or something. I'm told a lot of our people do. Sell postcards to German tourists, what?"

He was suddenly too comfortable in a pink haze of contemplating future bliss, the simple life which, when reached, might last for seven or eight years before he got the bored man's nearly inevitable massive coronary. I let in some cold air.

"Your job's to oversee mine modernization before you go?"

That reached him through the whiskey. Major developments up at Linguin were something he had never chattered about at the club. It seemed a shade strange that a great talker like Mickey had carefully refrained from any moan at a bar rail about a great deal of extra work put on him.

"It's a new pumping system and complete reventilation, isn't it?" I asked. "That'll be tearing your mine apart."

He stared at me.

"So you know one of our Singapore directors?"

"Not well enough to discuss Linguin. No; actually, I heard about it the other day over in Penang. As a kind of byproduct of some investigations of my own. In the line of business."

"Oh?"

His hand went out for the dimpled bottle but dropped before his fingers touched it.

"I was interested to hear about a major refit up here because it just could be an opportunity for Harris and Company."

"How?"

"Well . . . when a company is going in for massive modernization you can sell them more equipment than they had originally planned for. I find this all the time. They get in the mood for spending money."

Mickey had control again.

"This company doesn't. It's as mean as hell with capital expenditure. It's only doing now what should have been done

183

twenty years ago. We're deep enough to have a real water problem and the equipment we had to deal with it was installed in the early thirties. I've been at them for years."

"And finally got your way?"

"That's right. What are you trying to sell?"

"A new engine for your gallery bogies. Dolphin job. We haven't actually started to make it yet, but it's off the drawing boards and in prototype. An order from Linguin for thirty or so would be a nice little production start. I could demonstrate any time you like."

He smiled.

"I see. So this wasn't just a social call?"

He lit a cigarette. His hand was steady.

"Look, Paul, I couldn't even initiate this without consulting the directors. They make the decisions. I'm just a kind of overseer of the modernization. Wimpole and Cleghorn are doing the new pumps and ventilation."

I knew this and had been slightly puzzled. Wimpole and Cleghorn are a British firm who have suddenly, after a long period of rather solemn conservatism, got off their chairs and actually started selling. Some bright new boys in the concern have gone out into the world and in our part of it have managed to put enough contracts into the bag at one time to make their prices competitive. They have done this by deliberate rationalization, sending out British personnel to work on a number of projects consecutively, moving sharply from one to the other. It all makes the kind of hard economic sense which gives the feeling that the old country, with enough Wimpoles and Cleghorns, may still stay solvent.

"When do they move in here?" I asked.

"In a couple of months. The moment they've finished a Thailand contract."

"Which they won against American competition?"

He nodded.

"They did, yes. Keen prices, old boy. Surprisingly."

"I know. They've learned how to cut corners. And shipping in Polish freighters helps. That Gydansk company is undercutting our bottoms. And the Germans' and the Danes'. By as much as twenty percent sometimes."

"So what?"

"It's just smart of Wimpole and Cleghorn not to be patriotic about shipments, that's all. Just as it's smart of them to manufacture so much of their raw material under license in Italy, where production costs are a lot smaller."

184

"You seem very interested in the firm?"

"All businessmen watch each other."

"Well, you won't get much on them from me. I'm just the manager up here. I don't know the first thing about Cleghorn and Wimpole's affairs. My job is trying to keep the mine producing through all the mess they're going to make. When only half our old pumps and generators will be working and the new ones aren't in operation."

"Trying time."

"You can say that again. I'll be earning my money."

In Penang the fact that the *Bialystok* had anchored a month before with two holds full of material for Linguin, and the *Poznan* with a similar cargo a month earlier, hadn't really rung any bells in my mind. The almost scared name of Wimpole and Cleghorn had kept them from ringing, together with the fact that Linguin itself was so immaculately free of any Chinese directorial influence. And questions had really only begun to bite as a result of that sleepless night sitting up with a gun in my lap in a railway carriage. Further, those queries hadn't coalesced into anything more than one of the Harris hunches which I prefer to keep to myself until I can shape the facts to fit, because so often the facts won't oblige. I was beginning to feel that this time they had, and that both Clem and the service Kang represented had been put off by the basic mistake of searching for a strong local Chinese scent when it might turn out that there wasn't even a whiff of China in phase one of the Red supply line through Malaysia.

All that was really needed was one man in the know at the reception center and it made sense that this man wouldn't be Chinese, either. Mickey was retiring early to life in the temperate sun with a golden handshake from the Linguin directors—and who else? All the material the British company was going to need for the modernization was scheduled to have arrived and be in storage here at Linguin before even an advance party from Wimpole and Cleghorn arrived on the scene.

I looked at my host. For all the effective disguises undercover Reds can wear, and successfully for many years, I didn't believe for one moment that Mickey was a big man with them, or even a secret party-liner. He fitted nicely into Category D., intelligent but with a potentially gelatinous backbone, sound to buy for one use and then allow to retire quietly. The East, and for all I know the West, too, is dotted with these characters, men who have provided for agreeable declining years by one big gamble and one big risk, and have got away with it, maintaining before and after a splendidly established and orthodox respectability. There is plenty of Red money available, even with balance-of-payment difficulties, for this kind of temporary hiring of souls. The chances were that Marjorie hadn't a clue as to what her husband was up to, and she might have been pushed off just at this time so there would be no chance of her tripping over one. Her function was to go ahead, to prepare that final nest, with only feelings of gratitude for Mickey's providence, which would allow them a Spanish cook as well as the maid for housework, to say nothing of Pedro in the garden. Marjorie was a staunch Tory with political theories based on the old-fashioned adage of a fair wage for a fair day's work. She had avowed in my hearing that she would never set foot in Britain again because it had now become a land for gamblers and wide boys, with no room in it at all for the honest citizen. And Mickey, over that Majorca brandy, would approve her sentiments.

He was uneasy now, watching me as though a silence fallen between us had given him time to assess my reasons for showing up at Linguin at this hour, and these seemed flimsy. I wanted him uneasy. If he was the Reds' local man, and this mine was their supply point for that line to Thailand and to the sea, then Mickey would be under very close supervision indeed from center control. Almost certainly he would have orders that anything even slightly out of the ordinary happening at this sensitive point on their undercover route was to be reported back at once. It was highly unlikely that Mickey knew anything about two Red attempts to kill me, or even now why I had been in Kelantan. He was a temporary, down for dismissal after use, in no one's confidence, just a watchdog who would be well fed after a hungry spell of duty. But his half-innocent report back to control would explode like a bomb at the other end of the line.

Or so I hoped and planned. It was a shaky plan, as so many of mine have been, a gamble in which I was putting myself in the most exposed position I have ever deliberately chosen.

"How about giving me a bed for the night, Mickey?"

He frowned.

"What's the idea? The drive back too lonely?"

"That, and the fact that I'd like to have a look in the morning at those ore cars of your underground. I need to see what my engines would have to do. You have some pretty steep gradients?"

"Yes. But I can't just show you the mine like that. With the directors knowing nothing about it."

"Why not? Say I came as a tourist, that you had no idea I was trying to sell anything. How about going down now? You've got a night shift working, haven't you?"

"No! I mean, yes, we have a night shift. But it's no time to take people round. Daylight would be better. And I suppose there's no harm in this. But for heaven's sake don't let the directors get even the hint of an impression I'm behind this. They're quite capable of thinking I was trying for a cut of the sale price."

I smiled at him.

"I'll keep you covered, Mickey. But . . . ah . . . between ourselves let me say that I'd be most willing to remember afterward any effort you put in toward fixing the deal. You know . . . a few timely complaints about the engines you've got. Liable to be a hitch up in the production belt if you have to go on patching them up. That kind of thing."

He stared.

"God! No wonder you make money. Palm oil all over the place."

"Not all over. But you have to be flexible these days. Can you lend me a razor in the morning?"

"I haven't got a bed made up in the guest room."

"A blanket's all I need for your cool air. And I wouldn't complain about being asked to turn in now. Oh . . . how about some Seconal? I'm off natural sleep."

"The executive's complaint?"

"Well, I'm having some strain in one or two areas. A couple of tablets will do."

He gave me three and a nightcap. The bedroom was completely square, and sealed for air-conditioning in a manner likely to keep me in a half-claustrophobic wakefulness. Up here, where night temperatures dropped steeply, that gadget built into a window, and gently whining, was as unnecessary as it would have been in Tibet, but it went with the standardized building and king-size deep-freeze boxes.

Mickey closed me in and as he did it I noticed there was no key in the lock on my side. I was beginning to feel like a minor court official in the Egypt of the pharaohs who had blotted his copybook and as punishment been prematurely sealed up in his economy-model family vault. The Seconal tempted for a moment but I flushed the tablets away into the drain of the washbasin and lay down in the dark with my thoughts.

These revolved around death, and the feeling that I wasn't ready for it yet, not having had enough living time to get my philosophies sorted out. Probably even the very old are continually asking for another postponement on these grounds and, if they get it, continue to waste the reprieve just living.

If my plan worked, Red control would be coming up to Linguin in person. The job of dealing with me wasn't just something to be left to specialized killers, not now when I had reached home base. There were questions to be asked and I wanted a good look at my inquisitor, preferably before the session started.

The Colt was under my pillow. It's a potent weapon but having it close to me was less comforting than usual. I knew that Mickey would be phoning; it had been in his eyes when he left me, his uncertainty again, his doubt. There had been silence in the house for perhaps twenty minutes, then doors opened, the bathroom cistern flushed, and finally the crack of light under my door went out. After about half an hour he came creeping down the dark corridor, standing beyond panels listening for a sleeper's breathing, which he got. A key mated with its lock, and turned.

My situation now had something in common with Mrs. Hasmah's terminal one, and I remembered her laugh for nearly everything. But as something to sustain you in a real crisis, humor has its sharp edges. Men who have had particularly individual and dangerous roles in wars have told me how under stress there is no escape from overpowering loneliness, with comrades somewhere in support no comfort, and the thought of wife and waiting little ones at home not really assistance factors, either. Ego is left facing itself and wanting to scream. If you are properly trained you don't scream. Right then my training felt very decidedly an X quantity, and untested.

We all tell lies about our insomnia, about nights spent tossing without a closed eyelid. Sleep was the last thing that should have come to me after hours of stretched-out strain, but it did. And not just a doze. I went to sleep good and proper somewhere around one in the morning, fortunately waking, as I do quite often, in a motionless reserve which is a kind of testing of environment. A light on my face had certainly done the waking this time, and it was now probing my body, pencil thin, a tiny, selective ray. The ray steadied on my

188

thrown-out arm and into its beam came something else, a glittering needle descending.

I hit up with that arm, hard into something which felt soft. Breath sucked in above me, a moan just controlled. I groped for the Colt.

A ceiling bulb glowed. In the doorway stood Mickey, like a drunken ghost carrying a Smith & Wesson.

"He's awake!" Betty shouted. "With a gun! Shoot him! Shoot him, you fool!"

Mickey's mouth opened. He lifted the revolver just slightly while I stared. He pulled the trigger. I saw a great deal of very white light.

Above me were stars, nothing artificial, but the big, low-hanging stars of tropics, which can sometimes seem menacing. There was one with a red tone. I felt no pain, just an intense heat.

"Mickey! Pick him up again! We're halfway."

"It's the blood . . ." Mickey said, in a childish whine.

"Oh! come around here and take his feet then."

"You can't carry . . . ?"

"Yes I can."

"Betty, wait! When they find him . . . how can you be sure they won't find a bullet wound?"

"After he's dropped three hundred feet, hit rocks, then dropped another few hundred? Don't be an idiot! If you've never seen what's left after that kind of fall, I have."

The stars came a little closer, like an eager audience. I was without feeling, but also without control. I knew that I couldn't move any part of my body. My voice might have worked, but I didn't experiment.

"It's all right for you! I've got to face the police. I've got to produce the explanations."

"Keep your voice down! There will be no explanations. Because you don't have any. The last time you saw him was when he shut his bedroom door."

"They might still find the bullet . . . ?"

"The bullet's not in his head. It's in the bedpost. We've got to get rid of that damn bed some way. That's the problem. Not this."

"You can say it. I've still got to face the police. I never thought—"

Her voice cut through his.

"Well, what do you suggest? We leave him here? With the

189

gun artistically laid alongside. He'd recover. I don't think his skull is even splintered. He'd talk."

"Oh, God!"

"God isn't around to give us a hand. We have to rely on our own planning. If you haven't learned that yet, it's time you did. Now listen to me: I'll cover you every step of the way. You won't be alone. I'll do the thinking. But I can't drag him over the grass by myself. There'd be marks. Get him under the arms again and lift."

In my head there was now sensation, not pain yet, but the feeling of something being slowly inflated above one ear, a great bladder that could suddenly explode. My fingers and toes held a tingling, like a recovery from cramp, and my lips felt bloated from a dozen bee stings. But I parted them, getting out audible words.

"She'll kill you."

The lift didn't start. Mickey screamed. Betty came around and hit him hard on one cheek, emergency therapy for hysteria.

"You gutless pimp!"

Then she stood motionless, legs near my head, listening. The scream could have come from the jungle, not even probing through the surface consciousness of early-morning sleepers. The night stayed still, no sound from those other bungalows near the manager's. Mickey wept.

"Where's the gun?" Betty asked. "Didn't you bring it?"

"I don't know. I mean . . . yes, I left it. In the bedroom . . ."

"Stay by him. If he starts to crawl a kick will stop that."

"Betty, what are you—?"

The bladder by my ear exploded. I rolled over on dew-wet grass. Mickey was saying something, but it was meaningless. I was making my own pain noises into the ground.

I don't know how long that went on, perhaps a minute. Then I was obsessed, against pulsing sickness, with the idea of pushing myself up. There was no reason in this, just a need. I braced my arms and shoved. Mickey didn't try to stop me. I sat, slumped over, dizziness blinding, then it eased slightly.

My Mercedes was parked behind Betty's Ford, the long shape of it unmistakable in star sheen. A figure came round the hood, running toward us. Then it was circled by white, hard light. Betty stopped dead.

A voice shouted:

"Drop that gun!"

Betty lifted her arm and fired up the beam. She dropped flat. The beam lowered to cover her. From behind it came three heavy Luger coughs, bullets furrowing turf. Betty brought her arms over her head, as padding.

Light swung to us. Mickey yelled:

"Don't shoot! We surrender! Don't shoot!"

The bullet which came our way wasn't from the Luger. Light swung back, groping, finding a place on the grass now empty. It caught Betty running.

"Stop! I drop you!"

The voice was Ohashi's.

Betty didn't stop. She swerved out of light, which lost her for seconds. When it caught her again the Luger range was dubious, though the gun sounded twice more.

Betty ran on, no longer trying to escape light. At a three-strand wire fence she jumped, clearing it, steadying on the few feet of solid ground beyond. Others were running across grass now, the light jerking. Mickey made blubbering noises beside me. I didn't close my eyes, I saw her go, over the drop. There was no cry at all, and the jungle slopes beyond didn't record that fall with any protest from startled birds. All we heard was a distant rattle of small stones, and this curiously delayed.

Mickey began to talk, as though Betty's disappearance released his tongue. He had a lot to say. This nightmare was no part of his real life at all, just an intrusion into it. His real life stretched for long years behind him, with an impeccable norm as its core. The intrusion couldn't really mean anything. He seemed to want confirmation of this from me, but didn't get it.

The light came toward us again, slowly. When it arrived it was beamed down on me. A voice rasped:

"Is there a doctor up here? You! A doctor?"

"What? Oh, no. He just visits. Clinics, that's all. Though we have a little emergency hospital. And there's a Tamil dresser. I think Paul could perhaps be taken there. . . ."

"Where's the doctor?"

"Kampar."

"Number?"

"Let me think." Mickey now sounded rather like an old lady forced to deal with an emergency in the middle of her tea party. "Oh, I know it quite well. Two something. Yes, two, two, four."

"Put through the call, Ohashi. Ask for an ambulance." To me Clem added: "Lie down flat and don't move around."

I was given a nice private room in Betty's hospital, with a view from the window over the tops of those jungle trees for which the city is celebrated. It was air-conditioned but when I asked to have a window open to allow in the sound of traffic and the smell of spiced cooking mixed with exhaust fumes, this was permitted. For twenty hours I had to lie flat as Clem had instructed, even though I no longer felt sick and the pain had been doped away. I wasn't allowed any visitors, but the house surgeon, a plump Bengali, came in frequently to bring cheer.

"We have been rather ingenious with you, Mr. Harris. Because we didn't think you were a gentleman who would like a permanent parting of one quarter inch wide. Also, it was somewhat too low on the side of the head."

He laughed.

"I take it you mean scarring?"

"Quite. But this will not now occur. There has been a slight realignment of tissue to allow for renewed hair growth. Also, the top of your ear has been repaired."

"Splendid. I fuss over my looks. What about headaches?"

"Unlikely. Your skull was merely chipped. Death only seared you in passing."

The doctor had a positively literary turn of phrase. I suspected he had taken his B.A. first.

"When can I see the papers and get back into the world?"

"You are having no trouble with sight focus?"

"None."

"Then perhaps this evening. Though there is to be no excitement, you understand? This is most important."

When the papers arrived they were for two days, as requested, and I took them chronologically, stopped on page one of the first by a second banner headline.

TRAGIC DEATH OF KUALA LUMPUR SURGEON

Dr. Elizabeth Hill, well known in the capital, and to a wide circle of colleagues in Malaysia, met her death by a drowning accident at Morib beach, apparently during the early hours of yesterday morning. Her body was found by a local fisherman and had been in the water for some time. It is learned that Dr. Hill visited the Central Hospital after seven the previous evening, and direct from a party in her house at which she was hostess. She was not, however, called upon to operate and left again within minutes, after which she was not seen until her body was recovered. Her car was found in the public parking at Morib. Her husband, Dr. Thomas Hill, the special Reader in English Literature at the University in this city, did not raise any alarm until the morning, since his wife was often detained at the hospital overnight.

It is thought that Dr. Hill had decided to drive down to the resort of which she was very fond for a moonlight bath and, though she was a strong swimmer, the sea was heavy as the aftermath of a recent gale in the Straits of Malacca, which increased the undertow at Morib. It is believed that she must have got into difficulties at a time when there was no one about to answer her cries for assistance.

Dr. Hill's tragic death will be felt keenly by her friends in medical circles both here and at Gemas, where she was a consultant. During her years of service in Malaysia she has impressed all who worked with her as a brilliant surgeon whose presence was a great asset to our country, and the professional loss sustained by our medical services will not be easy to replace. Dr. Hill is survived by her husband and one daughter.

Our local paper has never been celebrated for the candor of its reporting, but that item read like some handout from the office of medical PRO's, and as a piece of stilted whitewash was startling. I reached out for a bell and pressed it hard.

The nurse came in. She was Chinese and pretty, as I had been pleased to note when I first saw her.

"There's a plug down there for a telephone," I said. "And I want the instrument."

She shook her head.

"Oh, no, Mr. Harris, that's strictly forbidden. You're to have quiet and rest."

"If I don't get that phone I'll walk out of here in pajamas."

"I'll call the house surgeon," she said, and fled.

Dr. Verisammy arrived with a syringe already topped up with sedation peeping out from the breast pocket of his white coverall.

"Now, Mr. Harris, I am going to be quite candid with you."

"Please do."

"Conditions such as yours are very similar to concussion. Any excitement can have serious consequences."

"If you don't want me excited let me use the phone. That's the only way to slow my present pulse rate."

"But this is not allowable procedure!" That was almost a wail. Then he backed himself up. "I am the doctor. You are the patient. I give the orders."

After that there shouldn't have been any debate, but there was. It went on for some minutes, and at one stage Verisammy's hand fumbled up toward that syringe, but he decided against extreme measures when I started to get out of bed.

"Back, back! You must not try to stand! All right, two minutes only." He waved both hands. "And I accept no responsibility for the consequences."

Though it was after seven, Ohashi might have been sitting by the instrument in his office waiting for my call; the bell rang only once. We established personal contact again after the gap there had been in this, but with a certain crispness on both sides. His inquiries after the state of my health had the formal note of Japanese ceremonial, and from them I rather got the feeling that if I passed on from the sudden clot to my brain which Verisammy was expecting, my assistant would attend the funeral as a matter of professional duty. I probably owed my life to his off-target shooting, but I saw no need to make a point of this. The young man was slipping away from the Harris orbit, in fact had already slipped.

"Is Mr. Winburgh back in my house?"

"No. It seems he has disappeared."

I took a moment to digest that.

"And you have no knowledge of where he is?"

"That is correct," Ohashi said.

He was lying.

"Is Inspector Kang still in town?"

"Yes. He has been wishing most urgently to see you but was not permitted."

Things must have looked darker for me than the doctors would now admit if they had been able to keep that policeman from getting into his victim.

"Kang has been in touch with you, Ohashi?"

"Indeed, yes. There has been much coming and going."

It was a nice phrase which could cover a lot of activity, much of it not reputable.

194

"Can you get a message from me to the Inspector?"

"Most easily. He is now in my office. He greatly rejoices that you are fit for visitors."

Verisammy's authority must have been totally undermined, for twenty minutes later Kang insinuated himself into my room with the gentle tread reserved for the mortally ill and perhaps dying. He took one look at me and relaxed. From the change in his expression, the bandages I was wearing almost amused him.

"Do sit down," I said politely. "And you may smoke. The window is open."

"Thank you."

"Now what the hell is this?" I shouted, pointed at the paper spread out on my knees.

"I'll be ejected, Paul, if you are heard bellowing. I've been given five minutes."

"We'll take as long as I need!"

"Very well. So that item surprises you? What did you expect to see, the truth?"

"Why not?"

"Naïve," Kang said, delicately choosing the word. "You, of course, haven't had time to think. I'm told that the bullet probably jarred your brain inside its protective pan."

He remained bland under my eyes.

"All right, I'm punch drunk. But I'm still asking you why all this guff about Betty? And how did her body get from the bottom of a canyon in the mountains to a stretch of coast a hundred miles away?"

"It was transported. Together with her car."

After nearly a minute, during which I tried to use my scrambled brain, I said:

"I don't remember the journey down here in the ambulance. I think I must have passed out there on the grass. Would you mind giving me the whole story from the moment I did?"

He obliged in simple words, rather like a man trying to make a bedtime story for kiddies out of something a shade more complex than these usually are. And the quick-thinking ogre in the piece appeared to be Clement P. Winburgh, who also seemed to have taken a lot on himself for an alien in a country which hadn't granted him a visa. Round one had been to bring Mickey, still babbling, under control. This had been achieved by telling him that if he followed instructions he would be all right, which wasn't a policy line I would have adopted. Next had been the need to quieten down alarm aroused among immediate neighbors by the sound of shooting out on a lawn. This had been managed simply enough, by a whacking great lie involving me, to the effect that Mickey had been disturbed by the sounds of someone trying to break into his house. He had picked up his revolver and gone to investigate and when he opened the front door a figure had gone bolting away into the dark. He fired at it a few times.

I stared, speechless.

"Now don't get excited, Paul. You'll understand in a minute."

This seemed improbable.

"Mr. Winburgh's service and mine may have seemed to be at cross purposes recently. But we're not basically. Far from it. We both wanted to find out how that Red supply line was operating and stop it. We also wanted no publicity about the whole business when it was uncovered. No leak at all, in fact. I suggest you use your imagination, if you can make it work. Just think of the real story in that paper: a major Red supply line through Malaysia, controlled by a Red supervisor neatly planted at the heart of life in this city. It would result in the biggest internal flare-up since the country became independent. There would be a political crisis of the first order, just when a very real stability looks like it's being achieved. All hell let loose, in fact."

"The truth is usually healthy in the end," I said.

He looked at me, then fitted a new cigarette into his holder. The smoke from the last one was beginning to make me feel slightly sick.

"That's a nineteenth-century concept, Paul, as you ought to know. This particular truth could have been turned to Red propaganda and most certainly would have been. Look at this carefully. Certainly we have uncovered the route they were using, but not until after it had been functioning for almost a year. They have sent enough small arms and ammo through this line to supply a small army up in Thailand, and that's what Lum Ping has got. The estimate is something in the region of fifteen thousand guerrillas waiting for their signal. The number may be a slight exaggeration, but may not. All this is bad enough, but not half as bad as the free publicity the Reds would get from the truth about their feed line. If the facts were made public, people on the fence all over Southeast Asia would say that if the Reds could get away with this in a country like Malaysia, they could certainly do it anywhere else in southern Asia. And probably were. It could be a most unpleasant and dangerous chill to anti-Red morale. Can't you see this?"

I could, but wouldn't quite admit it. "The tide's running against Red China at the moment with all their Red Guard atrocities. Their stock's low."

"True. Let's keep it that way. The Linguin affair, made public, would send it up points."

I changed tack.

"When did you catch up with Clem?"

"We followed him out of Kuala Lumpur. We were watching your Japanese. Mr. Ohashi collected his car and took evasive action around the city in it. Then he went to your fortress, was allowed in, and came out again, presumably with a passenger. It was too dark to see who the passenger was, but we didn't need many guesses. My driver was a little awkward and they saw they were being followed. There was quite a chase up the Kampar road. It looked as though they had won when we became mixed with some heavy trucks on a succession of bends. And we made the mistake of going on toward Kampar for about five miles beyond the fork. Then we backtracked and made for the hills. The gateman at the Linguin road confirmed that we were on the right trail."

It made a clear picture, Clem and Ohashi following the bleeps from a Mercedes driven by Betty, and Kang bringing up the rear of the procession.

"Your two services joined forces at Linguin over my inert body?"

Kang smiled.

"You could put it like that."

"And how did you account for your combined activity to the people who live up there?"

"We said we were following up a rumor that the mine was to be sabotaged. This tied in rather nicely with the prowler their manager had shot. And no one was allowed close enough to identify you. The sabotage story also gave us an excuse for a thorough search."

I controlled my reaction.

"You found what?"

"Nothing. The arms which had come in had gone out again. There is absolutely no evidence of the use Linguin was being put to. But Davenport has sung like a caged canary. The arms arrived concealed up in the middle of angled ten-

197

inch pipes, held there by plastic sealing. The job of packing them in there was done at sea on board the Polish freighters, and they had the whole voyage in which to make things very neat indeed. The angled pipes were a good touch, too. You wouldn't expect to see through them in unloading and there were a great many of these. We have a feeling that the ship which is due next month at Penang will get orders to go somewhere else fast."

"And are you now following up Red trails from Linguin north and east to the sea?"

Kang shook his head.

"No. The trails are of no importance now that the source of supply is eliminated. Let the jungle take them again. A follow-up would mean using large numbers of police and regular Army, which isn't possible if we are to maintain security on this matter."

It wouldn't be possible even if they abandoned security. More than half of Malaya is made a no man's land by jungle, too vast to patrol even when you're fighting a war, and at the moment there was a technical peace in the country to which everyone was clinging as hard as he could, even the Reds for the time being. Lum Ping was being swept back into his cupboard under the stairs and the door shut tight.

I poured myself a glass of ice water, sipping it to bring down the temperature I'd developed.

"How about my friend Mickey?"

Kang didn't rush into his reply.

"I don't think you are going to like this, Paul. But in view of what I've said you must see that we can scarcely charge the man with assault on you."

"Assault? Deliberate, attempted murder!"

"All right, any label you want. But the plain fact is we can't prosecute. The local police have cooperated with me up to a point but they haven't been brought into things officially at all. As far as they're concerned, Dr. Hill's body—"

"Cut all that! What happens?"

"It's . . . ah . . . actually happened. Davenport was put on board an Air France plane in Singapore this afternoon. Bound for Europe. Now before you start making a noise, *think!*"

So I thought, about Marjorie and the villa in Majorca, and about hubby coming to it, the retirement a year or two earlier than had been anticipated, without quite as much money available to them as Mickey had hoped, which would prob-

198

ably mean they would have to do without that cook. Mickey would get his nerve back in time, to become the life and soul of expatriate parties of Britishers on the run from a socialist Chancellor of the Exchequer.

"This is what you call a compromise peace, isn't it?" I said. "Nobody wins."

"Something like that, perhaps."

"The trouble with our bloody age is expediency, do you know that? Everybody lives by it. It's the slogan done in red wool hanging on the walls of policy-making rooms all over the world."

"You're shouting again, Paul."

"Sorry. I expect it's bad for your nerves."

He smiled.

"You are actually taking it better than I had expected. Tell me one thing. When did you first get onto Dr. Hill? That was your exclusive line. No one else had it."

I looked at him.

"I got onto her when it became obvious that she had murdered Mrs. Hasmah in cold blood in my bathroom."

TWELVE

❀ ❀ ❀

It was Kang who needed the ice water then. He came around to help himself from the table by my bed, but before he drank he asked:

"You have proof?"

"Not a scrap."

"Then why do you say it?"

"Because everything I was up to afterward stemmed from a few minutes alone in that bathroom with a corpse in a tub. Mrs. Hasmah was a dope peddler. Most of these are addicts themselves. As long as she had access to her drug the woman was unshakable. But in that cooler of mine she might have reached the breaking point, the addict's hysteria."

"You put the woman in there to bring her to that point?"

"Yes."

"And Dr. Hill guessed what you were up to?"

"Yes. Mrs. Hasmah was her plant, through Teng. Carefully chosen at that. There was plenty of time to go into the question of choice between my phone call to Betty from the north and our arrival in K.L. She had already used Teng to have me tracked to the north, and she used him again. She treated Clem's arm and then told me I had to have a nurse, that I wouldn't get one of the kind I needed in this town. It was Betty who suggested that I contact my Chinese friend Teng, and believe me, that came back into my mind later. The object of all that was to get the assassin over the wire to kill Clem. Finishing off a job that had been muffed up north. Clem was right up top on the Reds' seek-and-destroy list. He had been making too many private trips into this country. We'll never know who the assassin was, but I can have a good guess. My guide up in Thailand. Also supplied by Teng."

"How did Dr. Hill know you were going to Thailand?"

"I had to tell her at one of our lunches that these would be interrupted for a time. I was off on a business trip. I wasn't on the Reds' seek-and-destroy list then, but I was down to be watched. And I was watched, all right, practically led by the hand for two weeks by one of their murder squad."

"Paul, how would Dr. Hill have access to that bathroom?"

"The key was on the outside of the door. A doctor washes hands after seeing a patient. Clem had said something about the nurse having gone and Betty hadn't seemed very interested. But she was interested, all right. She knew that Mrs. Hasmah was in trouble simply because her patient was lying there getting better. So she turned that key and went into the bathroom with a hypodermic in her hands, to be received with relief by Mrs. Hasmah, who right then wanted nothing more than a shot in the arm. She got it. An overdose. I don't know much about medicine but I know you can easily kill a junky that way. And Betty didn't need the woman dead, only right out. She then put Mrs. Hasmah in the tub and slashed her wrists. They were cut in the right places, neatly. It was all done in minutes."

"This is all surmise," Kang said.

"The packet of razor blades isn't. Why would a woman like Mrs. Hasmah need a whole packet of Wilkinson stainless in that leather trunk of hers? Betty slipped up bringing in those blades. It would have been better to use a pair of scissors I found in Mrs. Hasmah's sewing box. But the surgeon liked neatness, planned for it. Kang, I'm not pretending that all this hit me when I was in that bathroom with the door locked. Far from it. It was a kind of seepage for a long time, one thing after another coming through, until I had to admit a possibility. The last thing I wanted to do was admit it, but I simply couldn't get away from the feeling that the nurse was no candidate for suicide."

"A drug addict?"

"All right, I know. But she still wasn't the kind who would kill herself, even in semihysteric depression. That stuck, I couldn't shake it off. I kept coming back to it."

The Inspector put another cigarette into that holder, not so neatly this time; it was a shade bent.

"I find it difficult, even with what we know, to understand Dr. Hill's motivations."

"Because she was a Western woman?"

"Perhaps that's it. I can understand a British Communist doing undercover work out here; we've had that before. Even carefully planted like Dr. Hill was. But it seems to me that she was the wrong candidate for what she became. It's not idle to say that a doctor has a whole life, and a creative life, too."

"She had two lives, Kang, and she saw both of them as creative. Betty had also lost one faith and found another."

He shook his head.

"I'm not quite with you."

"I don't know whether she got to know me well as part of her job, or as something separate from it. Probably a mixture of both. She may have talked to me to bring me out, to fill in the blanks in her file. At any rate I learned quite a lot about her past. She wouldn't see any risk in this, but the past does provide a key of sorts, sometimes. Betty's father was a preacher who took most of his texts from the Old Testament. It was a big family—he took that from the Old Testament, too. They lived by rules, under a stern God who was likely to punish you if you forgot your nightly prayers before you jumped into bed. Or sneaked off to the pictures instead of going to Sunday school. That was sin. So was dancing. It's hard for a Chinese to imagine the basic joylessness of a life like that. I mean a worldly Chinese like you, and living out of China."

He didn't smile.

"There are still these sects in England?"

"There's even one where you can't sit down to a meal with people who aren't in your clump of the anointed. Betty's situation wasn't an extreme of that kind, but it was still that solemn paternalism over everything. She broke from it, she lost faith. But the point is it had once been complete, dominant. The rules were life, to break them was death. Her mind wouldn't let her believe anymore. She was cut off from the family completely because of this, out on her own. She had to make a totally new life and she did this through medicine. Afterward she filled up the personal with Tom and a child as well as a lover or two when the marriage turned out badly. But there was still a vacuum from that earlier conditioning. Vaccums tend to get filled, in this case by a new religion which she thought she could accept with her mind as well as feeling."

"Feeling?"

"Yes, and near to the sentimental. I was kicked around up north just a few days ago by a guerrilla from your world. Better than your world—I suspect a lot of money. He was very far from being any kind of fool. But it wouldn't surprise me if

202

certain selected passages from Mao could bring tears to his eyes. Betty and he had the same religion."

"Chinese Communism for Dr. Hill?"

"Why not? It was pure, it was absolute. Kang, I think Betty probably joined the British Communist party some time when she was studying medicine. But like so many new candidates, she was told to stay under cover. There are many more of these than the ones who appear on protest marches. But even in her undercover role she would still be subjected to party bickerings over policy. This is a line as wavering as one on the drum of a seismograph. One week Yugoslavia is in, the next it's out. There is internal fragmentation over East Germany and Romania, and all the time the Muscovites seem to be becoming more and more absorbed in bourgeois preoccupations. You mayn't need a dinner jacket yet for a night out in the Russian capital, but you wouldn't be mobbed these days if you wore one. All this lack of coherence would be almost unbearable for Betty. She had joined for a faith and she was in danger of losing a second one. That could have driven her to the Chinese line while she was still in Britain. They take on their recruits, too. No sign with them of the stern rules being relaxed."

"A doctor, Paul, is no fool!"

"The man who kicked me around at the edge of the jungle wasn't a fool, either. He was leading a hard and dangerous life for his belief. There couldn't have been any other motive. I don't believe he was on the run from anything."

"But a doctor's position! The emphasis on the humanitarian."

"Is it always these days? Betty was a specialist. She was a long way from the GP with the black bag. Much more a trained technician. She told me once that she sometimes saw a patient twice before operating, more often once, and in emergencies not at all. There was a certain amount of after-care in the surgical wards, but that was mostly left to an assistant. She could save a life or fail to save it, but was immunized from any real personal involvement, whichever happened. She had another immunization as well, a secret personal philosophy which lays down that the necessary goal to aim for is the greatest good for the greatest possible number. That's humanism sterilized by a statistical approach. It's happening in quite a number of areas."

"So logic enabled her to kill? Personally kill, even though she was a woman?"

"It would have made her very angry to hear you say 'even though she was a woman.' Yes, Betty could kill personally. She was in control in this area. When you have worked yourself to that eminence you have rationalized away the unpleasantness."

"You're guessing, Paul!"

"I'm not guessing. I heard her shout to Mickey, 'Shoot him.' It was an order strong enough to make that poor fool obey, against every instinct he had. Betty was trained for command, all right. She had earned it."

Kang stared at the floor. I looked again at the newspaper on my knees, rereading that amalgam of bogus news item and obituary.

"Betty must have gone home when she left the hospital," I said. "She was there to get a phone call from Mickey. Where was Tom?"

"He had gone on to another party from his own. Paul, do you think that man's a Communist, too?"

"Probably. But not the kind you have to worry about. His variety is poster carrying and velvet jackets in Moscow. We've rather avoided talking about my friend Teng. How is he?"

"Quite well, I believe. In Macao."

"I see. I wasn't sure for a long time, even after Penang, whether my fence-sitting friend had come down on the wrong side. Still, Macao's a nice place to sit in your hotel with access to your Western bank accounts while you watch streams of refugees coming by from the thing you have been helping to build up."

"We may get him yet. Even in Macao."

"I think I'm sorry for Teng. He was just frightened."

"And your feelings for Dr. Hill?"

"As you would say, no statement."

He got up.

"It's a wonder they haven't thrown me out. It seems very quiet on this floor."

"Mostly terminal cases," I said. "Put out that main light, will you?"

When Kang had gone I looked about for a switch for the remaining shaded bulb but couldn't find it. Perhaps there is always one they leave burning to keep the patient from any consciousness of being nearer to that total dark than most of the people walking around outside. Noises from the city had stilled down, like an agitated heart quietening.

The nurse came in to settle me for the night, tight with reserve from that terrible violation of the rules. She took my temperature but made no comment, just marked it up on the chart. I was asked if I would like some cocoa, but said no. When I was alone again I felt sick, but not to the point of ringing for a basin.

The figure standing by my bed was carrying an armful of American Beauty roses sent from Australia in cold storage and costing a fortune in Malaysia. In the dim light he looked like a man paying a first visit to a wife who has safely delivered twins. He wasn't quite sure whether to be madly gay, or weep.

"I hope I didn't wake you," Clem said.

"No."

"Can't sleep?"

"I've been lying here like a survivor from a war wondering why he fought in it."

"Oh. Well, I brought you these."

"Nurse will be delighted. They're my first flowers. What time is it?"

"Shortly after three A.M."

"Scarcely visiting hours."

"I came up in the service elevator."

"An old CIA dodge. Why?"

"Well, I didn't like the look of the gorgon at reception."

"You'd better sit near the bed and keep your voice low. And put those flowers in the basin."

"There's a bottle of whiskey in the middle of them."

I warmed to him, just slightly.

"What are all these tokens? To atone? To say you always knew I was pure in heart even though you had your suspicions?"

"Something like that."

"Is Kang still looking for you?"

"Ohashi thinks so."

"You've been hiding out with my Japanese boy?"

"No. Just in a place he recommended. Your favorite restaurant. Yung Ching Wa's. Those benches may be all right for love, but they're hell to sleep on. Still, they got these flowers for me. Waitress' choice. And the whiskey."

"They can get anything."

"I hear Kang's been here. Did he mention me?"

"No."

205

"He didn't even tell you I'd put the Mercedes back in your garage?"

"He didn't even tell me you'd pinched it. Was that at Linguin?"

"I ended our collaboration rather suddenly. I still want to get back to Vietnam my own way."

"It's a long walk up the peninsula and around by Thailand and Cambodia. Who's financing you? Ohashi?"

"Uh-huh."

"I've got a feeling that boy is slipping right out of my service."

"You might be right."

"Your firm offer better pensions?"

"Paul, you don't really mind."

"No, no. You try to kidnap me for trial on trumped-up charges, you wreck my business, and pinch my newest director. I don't mind."

"I practically saved your life up at Linguin. At least, I held the flashlight."

"Badly. The score is still three to one-half, my favor. And I hate you, man."

"If you knew how hard it is to carry roses and a bottle of whiskey with only one good arm, you wouldn't say that."

He sat down, looking tired and pathetic.

"Clem, who was your man inside my perimeter defense?"

"Ranji Singh," he said at once.

"How long have you had him?"

"Ever since you hired a guard."

"Through Ohashi?"

"That's right."

"So your Japanese boy could walk in and out when he liked, too?"

"That's right."

"What did you think when you found Mrs. Hasmah dead in that tub?"

"My first thought was that you'd done it."

"And your second?"

"That another party had bought another of the guards. You really must scrap that fence. Or at least the current."

"I'm going to. You never suspected Betty?"

"No. She was kind to me. Paul, would you mind if I borrowed one of those junks which have been assembled in Kuantan waiting for the boss to descend in Jovian anger?"

"Yes, I would."

"Well, I'm going to do it, anyway. Ohashi's downstairs waiting to drive me there. It's all fixed up."

"You're going to travel home with a Red crew?"

"Ohashi says they aren't all Red. That you got carried away. He's picked the purest."

"He's sacked."

"He knows that. His wife is packing. How about letting me have a nip of your whiskey, eh? One for the road. And they tell me the South China Sea is rough to travel on at this time of year. Steady north wind blowing."

"From Vietnam," I said.

He stopped pouring to look at me, puzzled.

"I never asked how you were feeling, Paul?"

"Weary."

"Sure. Well, you can get plenty of rest in here. And there's Chow waiting for you up at the house."

"Do me a favor, will you? You've had your drink. Drift. Quietly, like a ghost."

"If that's the way you want it."

"That's the way."

I didn't hear the door shut, but I heard it open again. The nurse stood by my bed, her mouth and even slant eyes round with outrage.

"I saw a man come out of your door. Just now!"

"Oh, well . . ."

"Mr. Harris! There are rules. We have to keep to them. You can't just do what you want in a hospital. You can't!"

"The last of my visitors. Your rules from now on."

Ohashi had still to come, but formally, during the set hours, and probably bringing me a carefully chosen jigsaw to counteract boredom. We wouldn't have a lot to say to each other.

"Those roses are for you," I said, seeing she was staring at them.

She stared at the whiskey.

"You can take that for your boyfriend. I haven't got a taste for the good things back yet."

"Mr. Harris, I'll have to report this. . . ."

"It would save a lot of trouble if you didn't. And I'm feeling weak again."

"No wonder!"

She went over and looked at the roses, then turned with a crackle of starch. She had been trained by a Scotch matron and had picked up that terrible professional third person.

"Well, then," she said, tightening my one blanket. "All we need now is to get comfortable, isn't it?"

"That's all we need, nurse. Make us cozy."

It sounded like a prayer, a kid's prayer by the bed before he dives into safety under a quilt.